PRAISE

"*Grace and Serenity* is a dark, gripping novel that kept me reading late into the night. Set in Plymouth, a city I know well, this book shines a light on the reality of domestic abuse. It tells the story of a desperate young woman who finds herself on a difficult path, and hurtles towards a thrilling conclusion. A tense and compelling read."
VIKKI PATIS, AUTHOR OF *THE GIRL ACROSS THE STREET*

"Heart-breaking and poignant, this beautifully written novel will draw you in and wring you out. I was gripped from the first page."
LEAH MERCER, AUTHOR OF *THE PUZZLE OF YOU*

ABOUT THE AUTHOR

Annalisa Crawford lives in Cornwall, UK, with a good supply of moorland and beaches to keep her inspired. She lives with her husband, two sons, and canine writing partner, Artoo. She is the author of several short story collections, and this is her first novel.

www.annalisacrawford.com

ANNALISA
CRAWFORD

Vine Leaves Press
Melbourne, Vic, Australia

A catalogue record for this book is available from the National Library of Australia

To my parents, for their love and support

12:Ø1 A.M.

How did I get here?

Stock-still in the middle of my room, hypnotized by faint blue flashes of light and a sporadic siren weaving through slumbering streets and housing estates toward the hospital. An eerie sound, resonating on the crisp January air like a cat fight.

A moment ago I was fifteen, lying on my bed watching Rihanna and Katy Perry on YouTube, my legs swinging in time with the music.

A moment ago I was meeting Neil for the first time, at some stupid party.

Run, run away.

Mum said I shouldn't wear such a skimpy dress—a flimsy red thing I had to keep pulling down my thighs, and which hugged my 34Bs into a deep cleavage. She made me change into jeans, but I hid the dress in my bag and slipped it on before I got to the party.

Should've listened, you stupid girl.

He watched me from the moment I stepped through the door, this guy who looked like Robert Pattinson and had brooding, bottomless eyes like Daniel Radcliffe. Janie and I were separated in the squash; sixth-form girls with perfect makeup and sky-high stilettos sneered at me, while I fussed with the hem of a dress I didn't belong in.

If I could stop time, I'd stop it here.

A moment ago I was sixteen and invincible, the way only sixteen-year-olds can be.

Run, run away.

But it was already too late.

A moment ago I was seventeen and telling him I was pregnant.

Gracie-Lou

1.

You remember the little things, don't you, when big things happen.

The first flurries of snow settling on the window ledge. The kitchen tap drip-dripping into the sink. The Christmas lights, looped around the banister, making our faces green and blue and red as Neil backs away from my outstretched hand and calls me a liar.

"You stupid bitch." He glowers at the blue line of the pregnancy test. His lip curls; his eyes dart from me to it.

We're frozen, statuesque. I hold my breath.

A smirk creeps across his face and he shrugs. "It ain't mine."

It's almost a whisper; I lean forward to hear him. This close, I smell his reassuring woody aftershave and see the tiny hairs on his neck raised. I wait for him to kiss me, one hand on the base of my skull like he usually does, but he straightens up and takes another backward step.

"It. Ain't. Mine."

"Of course it is."

"You can't prove it."

"Prove it? What do you mean? You're the only man I've ever been with."

"Yeah, right. You're a fucking whore, and that kid ain't mine."

Still edging backwards, almost at the front door. He stumbles and bounces off the wall.

"No, I promise. There's no one else. It's your baby." I grab his hand, clinging to him, but he snatches away as though I'm toxic. Tears trickle down my cheeks, burning. "We're having a baby."

I didn't expect him to be happy; I'm not. Last night I cried myself to sleep and woke far too early. But I'd hoped he would hug me and comfort me, sit in a devastated stupor with me. Face my parents with me, promise them he'd look after me. Not this. I wrap my arms around my stomach to protect the child inside.

"You're trying to trap me. You've done this on purpose."

"Trap you? No. It was an accident."

I'm supposed to be going to university. I'm supposed to be revising for my A-Levels.

"You've been sneaking off—I've seen you." He thrusts his finger into my face, stopping short of gouging into my cheek. I flinch.

"No! Please." *Please love me. Please love our baby.*

"We're done. Finished. Slut!"

His hand raised, I push against the banister, bracing myself. Then, nothing. He's gone. Kicking walls, slamming the door so hard it ricochets off its frame.

I sink to the floor, numb, unable to hold myself up.

Drip, drip, drip.

My hands green and red and blue.

I lean over and vomit on Mum's brand new rug.

2.

That party where I met Neil? It was the first time I'd done anything rebellious, and even then, it wasn't really. My brother was the one who snuck out to meet girls, who came home late, who bunked off school sometimes. Me, I was Miss Goody-Two-Shoes in comparison. I was dragged along by Janie, who had a huge crush on one of the sixth formers; I don't remember what happened with him.

I hated that red dress. *Do something wild*, Janie said. So I bought it, and immediately regretted it. I should have stuck to my jeans.

Squashed in the corner, wishing I was anywhere but there, Neil saved me. He sauntered over and draped his arm around me, and the sneering sixth-formers walked off with disdain. I thought myself so grown up when he handed me his can of cider to swig from and we left together.

He wasn't like the boys at school, they were just *kids*. Neil was nineteen, enigmatic, and didn't give a shit what anyone thought of him. And *I* was special when I was with him; other girls scoffed with envy, but I didn't care. I meant something now. He hung his jacket around my shoulders and fought boys who looked at me disrespectfully. He hated being away from me, he wanted me all to himself.

We were immediately inseparable. Like Danny and Sandy. We'd go to see his friends play gigs in small, dark bars or sit in his house drinking beer while he played on his PlayStation with them. As the days slid toward the evenings, someone would pass me a joint, but Neil always tenderly took it from me and shook his head.

He didn't like my friends. He called them babies. I hung around the mall with Janie or went to the cinema when Neil was busy. Sometimes, there'd be lots of us, but when Neil realized the group included boys, he'd ask why I wanted to spend time with them instead of with him, so I stopped going. When we were on our own, we'd spend all day in bed. In that manner, the whole summer melted away.

Neil came with me to get my GCSE results. I shrieked in delight at the flurry of As and Bs.

"Didn't have you down for a swot." He leaned against the wall, blowing cigarette smoke into the air with a frown.

I shrugged. "Just worked hard." I wasn't sure what else to say—wasn't he supposed to be happy for me?

"You'll be off to college then?"

"No, I'm staying here for A-Levels."

"What's the point? You'll end up in a shop or summat—everyone does."

My dream of going to university, of traveling flashed before my eyes. "I'm going to be a journalist."

"Yeah?" He checked his watch dismissively. "Said I'd meet the lads. You coming?"

I waved the results slip in the air. "Got to phone Mum and Dad."

"Can't keep mummy and daddy waiting." And he sauntered away.

He's always walking away, it seems. I open the front door in case he's waiting for me to run after him and beg him to come back, but the garden's empty. Icy air swoops around me; snow settling on walls and flowerbeds, on car bonnets and rooftops. I hold my hand out to catch flakes, gazing in wonder before they melt in my palm and run along my wrist.

My stomach trembles. It's been doing that recently; the baby moving around, I guess. I've looked at pictures online to imagine what it looks like. It could be a tiny bean, or already have hair and fingers and toes. It could already be smiling and hiccupping.

It's getting harder to hide the bump. I should have told them months ago, but I thought it would go away. I didn't think I'd *actually* be pregnant.

I text Neil, but don't send it. My words swim through a flood of tears. I'm afraid without him; I can't do this alone. I thought he loved me. He *said* he did. Last week he promised we'd always be together.

I phone him, but it goes straight to voicemail.

3.

They come home together. Twice a week their hours coincide, and they meet at the garden gate. Mum shakes out her coat and sits on the bottom step to take off her shoes. Dad hangs his keys on the hook and rifles through the post I left on the side. He's concluding a story about a colleague—I don't catch the name—and Mum laughs. "Oh dear, I bet they'll think twice next time."

I listen wistfully to these reliable, homely sounds before I go down to wreck everything.

"Gracie, we're home. Do you want a cuppa?"

Mum, I'm pregnant.

I don't know what to do, Dad.

I stand in front of them in the kitchen. "Mum..."

Her eyes flicker to my stomach straight away.

We sit at the table while Mum pours the tea.

"I'm sorry," I say because no one else is speaking.

The silence folds on top of us. If we don't break it, it'll grow larger and impenetrable.

"Oh, Gracie, I just..." She shakes her head. "You don't have to make any decisions right now, but there are options. This doesn't have to—" She cuts herself off. *Doesn't have to ruin your life*, I think she was going to say.

I push my mug away. The milk tastes funny.

"Does Neil know?" she asks.

My face crumples. "He—he... doesn't..."

She squeezes my arm. "It's okay. We'll forget about him for the moment."

Dad snorts and Mum shoots him a hard warning glare.

"What do you want to do?" she asks.

My finger traces the pattern on my mug. "I don't know."

"How far gone are you?"

My clothes are tight; I've stopped wearing my jeans altogether. I don't even know why I bought the test; when I look in the mirror, sideways, the solid shape is obvious. Yes, I do—to show Neil, to make it real. I feared what he would say. And yet I still love him, and I still wish he was here.

"I don't know." I sink down into my chair, shamefaced, letting the adults take over and make all the decisions.

Mum blows through pursed lips. "Well, that'll be the first job."

This isn't how today was supposed to go. I was going to post my university application and revise for my English mock. This evening, Neil and I were going out for his mate's birthday. He'll be there already, I expect, getting wasted and not giving the baby a second thought.

"For how long, exactly, are we forgetting about Neil?" Dad asks, spitting out his name as though it's something hideous.

"Mike. Not now."

"Then, when?" They glare at each other, with Mum making comically pointed head-nod gestures toward me.

"It's okay. I know you've never liked him."

"That's not true," Mum says.

And I know it's not. Because he was clever—he brought Mum flowers or chocolates when he came for tea. He watched football with Dad occasionally. Later, we'd laugh at how far he could push his charm.

I rest my hand on my stomach. Already it feels so much bigger than it did this morning.

4.

Mum takes me to the midwife. In the waiting room, there are women of all sizes. Some alone, reading battered copies of *Woman's Weekly* and *National Geographic*; some sitting with partners who hold their hands proudly. A couple is besieged by toddlers, and the ones without children look horrified at the bedlam. I'm the youngest by far. I slouch and avoid anyone's eye.

The midwife says the baby's due in May, only four months away.

"Oh God," Mum says in shock. "Are you sure?"

The midwife smiles grimly, sympathetically. The options Mum was talking about dribble away. She runs her hands through her hair, and I watch a robin land on the fence outside the window, flitting about for a few seconds before dashing away.

The midwife presses the monitor firmly into my stomach and the heart beats around the room, rapid and insistent.

Mum wipes a tear away, a soppy smile plastered to her face. "That's my grandchild," she says redundantly.

I'm hypnotized and terrified. It's real. Not a mistake or a fantasy. Not a dream.

The midwife talks cheerfully as she makes an appointment for the ultrasound I should have had weeks ago.

"I'll see the baby?"

"Yes, love. And you can find out if it's a boy or girl, if you want to." She wraps the blood pressure cuff around my arm, and types notes onto her computer. "Perfect. Is there anything you'd like to ask? Anything you're worried about or not sure about?"

I shake my head and shrink back into the chair. Why me, I want to ask? Why not Janie or Ali, or anyone else but me? Why weren't we more careful? Why does Neil get to walk away?

Mum asks questions in a bright, clear voice to indicate I should be listening. But I'm not. I let her voice fade away while my world, my plans, disintegrate.

"My exams are in May," I whisper, although loud enough to interrupt their conversation.

They look away clumsily. Of course, I won't be taking them, I know that. My place at uni will go to someone who didn't get pregnant and I'll be home changing nappies and sterilizing bottles. Neil thought university was a ridiculous idea; he'll laugh when he realizes what he's done.

"You can re-take your A-Levels next year, when the baby's a bit older and you're more settled," Mum says on the way home, reading my mind. "We'll make it work. I can rearrange my hours at work to fit your classes."

Her words are a blur. I watch the pavement disappearing beneath my feet. Everyone's staring. Everyone knows. I hunch forward to cover my bump.

"I can't do this."

She squeezes my arm. "Okay..." She sucks in air. "Have you considered, thought about, giving the baby up for adoption?" She doesn't look at me when she says this. I have no reply.

The baby flutters inside me. I shudder. It feels like someone's dragging their finger across my skin.

5.

I leave school unexceptionally, simply by not going in one day. I don't say goodbye. My so-called friends watch me in wordless discomfort—judging me, laughing at me. They know Neil' finished with me; they're all thinking the same thing. Murmurs and gossip follow me.

I'll be the girl parents use as an example. *You don't want to end up like Grace Newman, do you?*

I'll be the girl who walks down the road to a chorus of censure.

My bump will grow, and people will point and gawk, or yell obscenities from the safety of the busy road between us.

The house has a different feel during the day—a secret life. It's cold and stagnant, apart from creaking radiators and the hum from the fridge. I coast with an ominous sense of being watched, as though the house is rejecting me. I have the urge to keep doubling back to check. Even the road that's so busy during the school run is forsaken.

I make tea and eat leftover Christmas cake. Mum's written a list of chores for me. Not fair; I deserve a couple of days' respite. My life is utterly screwed up, and she wants me to dust? I push the note under the toaster and pretend I haven't seen it.

I stand at the window. Harassed mums push heavy prams; gray-haired men plod with their newspaper tucked under their arm. Sometimes they bump into each other and say a few words. Miss Price has that thing where she's terrified of leaving her house—she lives right opposite, and she's looking out of her window at me looking at her. I don't know if I should wave or not. She gawps impassively then slides back into the gloominess of her front room.

The TV's on for the noise, to hide the humming and creaking and lack of sound from outside. I lie on the settee, feet up to stop them swelling, and stare at the ceiling. There's a cobweb in the corner of the room, stretching from the curtain pole right across to the framed family portrait we had taken a couple of years back. I watch it wafting as the heat rises from the radiator.

Janie texts. I try to chat for longer, but she stops replying—it's two o'clock, she'll be back in class. I insert myself into the long resonant corridors, sit at my desk in the history room, imagine the drone of Mr. Solomon's voice.

I fetch the duster and attack the cobweb.

Janie kicks off her shoes at the front door and calls out, "Hey, I'm here. I'll put the kettle on, shall I?"

"I've opened a packet of Custard Creams. They're in the barrel."

"I'm on it."

Five minutes later, she's handing me a mug and a plate of biscuits. I heave myself into a sitting position. The baby objects and seemingly burrows her head into my pelvis. Janie presses her palm against my belly.

"It's just so fascinating. I love the way they move around." She sits back. "You're glowing, by the way."

"Yeah? I don't feel it. I'm itching all over and my legs ache all the time. No one tells you that stuff—they really should." I twist myself around, trying to get comfy. "How's school?" God, I'm turning into my mother already.

She shrugs. "I still can't get used to you not being there."

"Have people stopped talking about me yet?"

"Um…" She glances at her phone and smiles, setting it back down on the floor.

"Great."

"It's not like that. They're concerned. They ask about you."

"I bet they do. And then laugh for good measure." I know I'm being grumpy and horrible. I blame my hormones.

She checks her phone again.

"Everything okay?"

"I've just got… I'm meeting someone later, he was just—"

"He? A boyfriend? You kept that quiet."

She blushes. "No, not really. It's only been a couple of weeks. I would have told you, but you're busy being…" She gestures my whale-sized body.

"Being pregnant isn't a job. Who is he?"

"Andrew Lakey."

"No way, he's gorgeous. Lucky cow."

"You'll have to come out with us, he's got a mate—" Her sentence skids to a halt. "Ahh." Her eyes brim with tears. "It's never going to be the same again, is it?"

"It never would have been. We applied to different uni courses—we'd have drifted apart."

"How are you so calm about it?"

Calm? That's funny. On the inside, I'm screaming, but people have stopped listening. My parents are so busy making plans and pretending they're cool with this sudden about turn in our lives they've forgotten to ask how I'm doing. It's all about the baby; the girl who stares at me every morning in the mirror, looking exhausted and puffy-faced and bewildered, is just bumbling along wishing this was all a dream.

I shrug in reply, and Janie's already forgotten her question.

6.

Mum's taken to looking at me. Sitting across the table, across the room, passing me in the hall when I go to pee *again*. She glances sideways when we walk down the road together, and I realize I can't remember when I spent so much time with her. She's swapped shifts at work to come home earlier, as though I'm incapable of being left alone.

When I am alone, in the mornings and over lunch, when the hours drag and the walls play with boredom, I imagine any number of ways to escape—from here, from the baby, from the future which doesn't include Neil.

I text him, watching the words fuse into permanence on the screen, without response. I keep my phone close, checking, re-checking.

"I spoke to your head of year today," Mum says before *hello*.

"Why?" I continue to scroll—Facebook then Twitter, back and forth so I don't miss anything.

"She says you can take your A-Levels next year instead. That's good, isn't it?"

"What's the point? I won't be able to do anything with them." I gaze into that bleak spot in my future which is entirely empty. The baby squirms— no, not empty, ballooning.

"Of course you will. We'll make it work. Maybe not Brighton, but Plymouth... Falmouth maybe? It's all possible."

"No." I rub my hand across the bump and wince as although I've been pricked with a needle. "*This* is my life now. When the baby's older, I'll get a job, a flat for us. Her and me."

"This isn't what I wanted for you. You had plans, dreams—you were going to change the world."

"It was a stupid dream. Journalism doesn't change the world anymore. I should have been born decades ago."

"Don't be like this."

"Like what? Practical, realistic? Perhaps you should try it. It might not be what you wanted, but it's what I've got."

Dad, in contrast, is reserved and contemplative. We absorb each other's thoughts. He frowns a lot, but everything is tightly bunched up. I catch him gazing at the corkboard in the kitchen where Mum pins photos—all the way back to their wedding and our childhood; her favorite memories on show for everyone to see—as though it's a magical portal into our misty, perfect past. The photos hardly register with me; they've become part of the décor, nothing to linger over.

"I can't make it better," I overhear him saying to Mum—not just once, several times, a gnawing regret. "I've always been able to make it better."

"A hug won't work this time."

How I wish she was wrong.

7.

I slip into being eighteen like putting on an old shirt. It's just another day.

The baby shifts uncooperatively, pushing a foot against my spine and forcing me out of bed to gyrate her into a better position. So, I'm dancing around my bedroom at two-thirty in the morning on my eighteenth birthday, while Mum and Dad sleep. I stroke my stomach to soothe her; she pushes against my hand, my darling daughter.

Dawn advances across the city. Leaves are appearing on the trees again, birds are singing. There's a warm hue in the air which contrasts with the bleak metal-blue tinge of winter.

"Gracie?" Dad taps softly on my door.

"Come in." I prop myself up on my elbow. He's got his coat on already, his work bag slung over his shoulder.

"Happy birthday. Did I wake you?" He hugs me tightly.

"No, it wasn't a good night."

"Eighteen, eh? I remember the day you were born, so tiny I thought I'd squash you." He pulls back to look at me. "Have a lovely day. See you tonight." He kisses the top of my head. "You've become an amazing woman, Gracie-Lou."

On Facebook, there are *Happy Birthday* messages, a few grinning and cake emojis. All of them from friends I haven't seen since I left school. Further down there are posts about trips to the cinema and parties I wasn't invited to. Janie's timeline is plastered with pictures of her and her boyfriend, beer bottles and shot glasses in hand.

If I was at school, I'd be wearing badges, fancy dress perhaps. My locker would have been filled with streamers and balloons. Tonight, I'd be going to the pub and buying drinks for Mum and Dad, the way Darren did on his eighteenth.

On Twitter, I tell six hundred and sixty-two strangers it's my birthday. #adulting #eighteen #allgrownup.

I force myself out of the house. Thick cloud dawdles like a large duvet thrown across the streets. I smile politely at my nosy neighbors and keep my head low, so they won't cajole me into conversation. I walk, hobble, along the road heading toward the village. It's not a village; it used to be, before Plymouth swallowed it up. Now it's a small street of shops catering for the basics.

In the middle of Co-op, I remember it's my birthday and wonder if I should buy myself a cake. Mum's probably got it covered. I wonder if I could buy one anyway and eat it before anyone gets home. I pick up a caterpillar cake.

Suddenly, a little further along, Neil stands with two loaves of bread in his hands.

The baby kicks. I catch my breath, and my heart plummets to my stomach.

I take a step backwards, and crash into a trolley.

"Grace."

I don't trust myself to speak. I'm stunned, panicky.

"How are you?"

"Okay."

His eyes dart to the box in my hand. "It's your birthday."

I nod.

"Eighteen, wow." He smiles, and I revert to the kid who met him at a party, awestruck and meek. "Happy birthday."

"Thank you. I'd better—" I wave my hand toward the till.

"So you're keeping it then?"

I pivot on my heel to face him. "What? Of course I am."

"Sorry, I didn't… Is it weird, having a baby inside you?"

"You get used to it."

"I never thought about having kids before."

"Well, don't worry about it. You made your decision."

He frowns, remorseful perhaps, wavering.

I wonder how many of these elderly shoppers would be willing to intervene if needed, if his temper rose like last time.

"Mum and Dad have been great. We've got everything pretty much sorted."

He strokes his chin with his thumb and forefinger, pulling on a beard which doesn't exist. "You're not going to uni then?"

"No. It's all about the baby now." *Just tell me what you want.* "It's a girl, by the way... if you're interested."

"A girl." This smile is genuine, reaching the creases of his eyes. He drifts off into some kind of reverie.

"I should be getting home," I say abruptly.

He readjusts his gaze and nods. "Enjoy the cake."

8.

After school, Janie brings party-poppers which make the baby jump. She's sheepish when she hands me a chocolate-and-bubble-bath gift box.

"I wanted to buy you a bottle of Champagne or something, but…" She gestures toward my stomach, as though I've forgotten it's there. "We'll go out in the summer, though, yeah?" She nods eagerly, and I wonder how easy it is to leave a three-month-old baby to go drinking.

She doesn't stay. She's got an essay due, she says; she has to work. But she'll be back, she says. When she's finished it, she'll bring films and pizza.

Dad wants to take us out to eat, but I'm exhausted, and Mum suggests a takeaway instead. The doorbell rings while Dad's fetching the Chinese and Mum's putting the kettle on. I waddle to answer it.

Neil.

In front of me for the second time today.

Nervous and anxious, hands thrust into his pockets.

I can't deal with him right now; I move to slam the door on him, but he catches it.

"Please?"

"What?"

"I've been thinking." He pauses. He's not his usual cocky, confident self. He's small and diffident. "It should be me, shouldn't it? If it's my kid and all."

"Should be you, what?"

"Taking care of things. Of you."

"Yeah. But you're not. You left."

He says nothing, tangled up in whatever ruminations have brought him to my house.

I want to kiss him. Just like I did the first time I saw him. And I want to slam the door in his face, because he's scaring me. I want Dad to come back and chase him off. I want him to kiss me. I want him to tell me he's going to live in Wales, so I'll never have to worry about bumping into him again.

So many conflicting wishes, I don't know which would be best. None of them. The best thing would have been him sticking by me in the first place.

"I thought maybe we could give it another go, you and me." He waits with puppy-dog optimism, kicking the wall with the back of his heel, drumming softly.

I gawp, dubious, hand covering my mouth. The pain and tears and wretchedness haven't left me. I still wake up crying, some nights. And he's standing here, as if none of it matters.

He's chewing his lip, half-smiling, hopeful. I think he may be blushing, or it could be the streetlight causing a shadow.

"You're supposed to say something."

I open my mouth, but there are no words. I've imagined this very conversation, run every possible reply over and over in my head. It all seemed so easy, then.

"You're not serious. You said all those horrible things about me."

"And I was wrong. I miss you." He runs his finger along my forearm and my skin tingles. He smirks. "You've missed me too."

"But..."

"You still love me."

"Yes," I whisper with reluctance. "But I don't think it's what you want. I'm afraid you'll leave again."

Our heads are close; his aftershave filling my nostrils. Neil's lips hover over my forehead and his breath is soft on my face. This isn't happening; it's not real. I'll wake up soon, alone and cold in the middle of the night. I want to kiss him. I want his arms around me.

The kitchen door opens. "Neil," Mum says, startled.

We pull apart abruptly, our moment ruined.

"Hello, Mrs. Newman, it's nice to see you. I came to wish Grace happy birthday."

"Gracie?"

"It's fine, Mum."

"Don't be too long. Dad'll be back in a minute."

She pauses, trying to ascertain the situation, wordlessly demanding to know what's going on. I stare at the patterned rug on the floor, at the stain in the corner, and she retreats.

Neil leans against the wall and exhales. "She hates me, doesn't she?"

"What did you expect?"

"I get it. I messed up." He steps to the door. "I should probably go."

Don't. But I stop myself. I don't want to be the awestruck teenager anymore. I'm going to be a mum soon; everything I do should be for the baby. He left me; he rejected our baby. But he's so docile and faltering. All his usual brazenness has receded. Even his hair is a limp imitation of how it normally is, making him look younger. I reach for his hand and squeeze. He strokes each of my fingers in turn, lingering on my ring finger.

"We could get married," he murmurs.

I pull away. Did he really just say that? Am I putting words into his mouth neither of us has a right to say or expect?

"What?"

"I said, we could get married."

"No. No. Why would you...?"

"We could be happy. We could be a family."

He's using my life against me, my happy family. His parents split up when he was seven. He lost contact with his father. He's always said it didn't bother him; he'd shrug it off like it was no big deal. But what if it is? What if he sees his daughter disappearing from his life?

How simple to just say yes and have this nightmare finished with.

"You're scared I'll leave you again, and I understand that. So, I'm asking you to marry me, so you'll know I won't."

The baby kicks, turning somersaults, it seems. So many reasons to say no. But he's her daddy. And I love him. And he's proving he loves me too. It's enough. It's all I need.

I'm suddenly a soggy, snotty mess. "Yes," I blurt out, and Dad, walking through the front door right then, is the first to know.

9.

Mum browses through the lists I've made, scattered across the table, and chews on her lip. We have a tight budget. Mum and Dad have offered some money, but Neil's mum has stayed quiet. We got a cancellation at the registry office, so some of the things—like a cake and photographer—aren't available with only five weeks' notice.

"So soon," Mum said when we told her the date. In truth, I'd expected a much longer wait. Next year, after the baby was born. But this is so much better.

Over cups of tea and chocolate cookies, we write out invitations. The pile is small. The registry office is small, and the reception afterward can only hold about forty people.

My dream wedding evaporates. I won't have a luxurious hotel venue with sea views and a showstopping staircase to glide down into the ceremony. I won't have a stunning white dress and five bridesmaids in lilac. I won't spend the morning being pampered by a hairdresser and makeup artist.

At times I wonder if I shouldn't just move in with Neil and spend the money on the baby instead.

"Are you sure this is what you want?" Mum asks as if reading my mind. "You could wait a year or so and plan it all properly. This seems so rushed."

The same words from her lips are duplicitous and cunning.

"Of course it's what I want. The wedding doesn't matter, not really. It's just a day." When Neil said the same thing a few days ago, I shuddered. Now they slide naturally from my lips. "I want to be married before the baby comes. It's important to me."

She frowns. "Are you sure about Neil?"

"The father of my baby? Yes. Who else would I marry?"

"You don't have to marry *anyone*."

"But especially not Neil. That's what you're saying."

"I'm afraid he'll let you down. He's proven himself to be selfish and unreliable and immature."

"You liked him enough before."

She smiles wearily. "I have a feeling I didn't know the real Neil before."

I blush involuntarily.

"I think it's a mistake," she says, gathering the stack of envelopes into a neat pile. When she looks up at me, tears are snaking down her cheek, dripping from her chin.

I laugh. I run her words around my head a few times and they still say the same thing. I push the chair from the table and stand.

"Gracie . . ."

"Everything I know, I learned from you. From you and Dad. How to be in love, how to be married, how to bring up children. When friends' parents were splitting up, I'd come home and you'd be sitting together, holding hands on the settee watching TV or something." My voice shudders. "I always wanted that for myself, for my baby."

"I didn't mean—"

"We're going to get married. If you can't support me…" I falter. "Perhaps it would be better if you don't come."

Our shock is mirrored on each other. I want to hug her, but I remain where I am with the table between us. Mum still has the bundle of invitations in her hands; she runs her finger along the sharp edges.

Where is Dad in all this, while my mother takes aim at my dreams and beats them into a pulp? At work. She chooses her timing carefully. Perhaps they talk privately while I'm out shopping, deciding on the best way to wear me down and highlight my error in trusting Neil, and its Mum's job to disseminate their opinions. Or perhaps Dad's warned her off speaking to me in such a way—whether agreeing or disagreeing—trying to find peace between us. He's a calm, thoughtful man—a trait neither his wife nor either of his offspring share.

"Of course we'll be coming to your wedding," he says at teatime.

We're sitting around the table, Mum and I focused intently on our plates.

"We love you," he continues, glancing at Mum for her agreement, "and we wouldn't miss it. Your mum just wants what's best for you."

"I'm eighteen now, I can—"

"I know. *We* know."

12:33 A.M.

The neighbors' lights prickle through the orange glow of streetlights. They'll be watching the closing credits of a film on Netflix or trying to placate a fractious baby. Traffic on the main road is a steady hum.

There's a scuffle below my window—just lads on their way home, pushing each other so they fall into parked cars and privet hedges. Their raucous conversation carries on the still air. They kick a can between them, and the tin grinding against the tarmac sets me on edge. Their jollity in the middle of the night is aggressive and alarming.

I close my eyes and imagine the sound of the sea rolling gently on a frozen winter day. I feel the ice crack across my skin. Memories of a life I don't even think of as mine anymore. I wrap my duvet around my shoulders, folding TuTu—my recently discovered childhood teddy —into my arms, trying to suppress my persistent anxiety. He's battered and threadbare after years squashed into a box in the attic, but warm and familiar.

I track the silhouettes staggering along the road, voices diminishing, until they're tiny dots disappearing out of my eyeline.

The can stops rolling. For a second, there's absolute silence.

Mrs. Gibson

1.

There's a hubbub of chatter around the registry office. Guests stand as the music starts. Neil is ashen and somber at the front of the room. His best man, Angus, is trying to crack a joke, but he's staring straight ahead, glancing back just once and catching my eye with a wink.

Janie fusses with my hair. I want to run down the aisle, but Dad holds me back and takes a breath.

"Ready?" he asks, but I know he means a lot more.

It's been a difficult few weeks. We've co-existed politely, but all those unspoken concerns and threats have lodged heavily. Mum put a bout of unexpected morning sickness down to panic and viewed it as confirmation she was right in her doubts. But what bride doesn't have jitters just before the big day?

Whenever Neil's come over, Mum has found something unimportant to busy herself with, while Dad's been awkward and muted.

We found a house to rent and friends donated furniture to get us started. Neil moved in last week, so he could get the place ready before I join him tonight. Dad helped to take my stuff over yesterday while I was having my nails done with Mum.

Standing beside Neil, I know this is the right thing to do. Neil and I, together, bringing up our daughter. Having more children, spending our lives together.

Mum's in the front row, proud and distraught in equal measure. When I glance around, Dad is holding her hand. He smiles when I catch his eye, but it fades rapidly.

On the opposite side of the aisle, Neil's mum has her arms folded tightly and an irritated expression on her face. Mum and I tried to include her in the preparations, but she rejected us at every offer. I'm trapping her son apparently; he could do better than me. I'm a flash in the pan, she tells anyone who'll listen in muted, clandestine confidence.

Further back, there are sparse groups, couples, some empty chairs. I try to forget about the people who aren't here—my wider family, my grand-parents. A lot of people. Mum said, in the circumstances, we should keep it small. Money, she said, and I pretended to believe her.

The baby kicks. In years to come, I'll tell her about today, how she brought her parents back together. I'll keep the bouquet of carnations I'm holding and show it to her; I'll let her wear my silver tiara.

Our voices echo; our vows coast into the air and around the room and into the laps of the congregation. Neil concentrates on the wall in front of us, brow furrowed. He runs his finger around his collar, trying to loosen his tie.

When directed, he takes my hand and slides the ring onto my finger.

"Neil and Grace, it gives me great pleasure to declare that you are now legally married."

2.

With crumbs of confetti floating around the car park, guests take pictures on their phones. We pose and smile with fixed grins as people ask us to turn this way and the other. I watch our warped reflections in the car windscreen. We look like petrified kids. When we're gray and wrinkled, we'll look back at these pictures and laugh at how young we were.

While most of the guests are making their way to the reception, we go up onto the Hoe, moments away. We pose in front of the red-and-white stripes of Smeaton's Tower and we sit on the bronze plates that denote where the Beatles sat when they visited Plymouth in 1967. We mimic the picture that was taken—Mum arranging our postures in accordance with the photo on the plaque. It was a struggle to get me onto the floor, more so to get me back up again.

I don't want this part of the day to end. I do my utmost to memorize every detail.

In a whirl of white taffeta and pink silk, we're at the reception—in the function room of Neil's local, dressed by Mum and Janie with burgundy and pink balloons, and ribbons tied to the backs of chairs. A large *CONGRATULATIONS* banner hangs over the bar.

The fusty air is nauseating. I detour to the beer garden and sit on the far side of the small courtyard to avoid the smokers who've already flanked the entrance. The mild March sun is shrouded now by leaden clouds. Dad passes me his coat and shivers beside me, refusing to leave me alone to go inside.

Mum calls us in to cut the cake—another surprise. Simple, one-tier, shop-bought; Mum has iced our names on it and pressed Mr. and Mrs. figurines into the top.

"Thank you," I say, and she kisses my cheek.

"Anything for you."

Neil is reluctant to join in these traditions and walks toward me through a chorus of jeers from his mates. I place his hand on the knife and gently restrain him until Mum has taken photos.

Dad's speech is brief, succinct. He welcomes Neil to the family and wishes us every happiness. Neil quickly nestles back into his group, and I'm left holding the knife as everyone turns away.

I rest my head on his shoulder. "Thank you."

He hugs me toward him. "I hope you'll be happy, Gracie. I've only ever wanted you to be happy." He pauses, his gaze drifting toward Neil, then rallies with a bright smile. "May I dance with the bride?"

I drop in and out, as my nausea allows, circling the edges of the room. Everyone's having fun. There are more people now—Neil invited his mates who shunned the formal ceremony but appeared for the booze and free food. I don't have many friends now, but Janie got a few people from school to come and she's sitting with them in the corner. She keeps waving me across, but I don't want to go.

Mum and Dad are commanding the dance floor, laughing as they misstep. I watch them enviously. They've had a happy marriage. Their wedding was smaller than this one, on a non-existent budget; their parents didn't approve either, they practically eloped. Mum wanted better for me, which is why she made sure there was a cake even when I said it didn't matter.

Occasionally, Neil remembers me and lurches across the floor to find me. He drunkenly falls into me and I prop him against the wall. He wraps his arm around my shoulder and calls me his wife.

"Oh God, that makes you sound so frumpy." And he giggles heartily while I feel every inch frumpy.

We dance. The DJ plays *The Way You Look Tonight* and we sway, more from necessity than design. I feel his heartbeat through my cheek, and he mumbles the lyrics into my hair. The rest of the room vanishes as the song continues.

We have the room until six. After that, the regulars swarm in and chomp on the left-overs —the pub gave Neil a discount on the understanding this would happen. I grab a warm ham sandwich before they disappear.

Our guests disperse, gifts are stacked in the corner. The main lights are switched on and the room is left austere and functional. I assumed we'd be going home ourselves, but Neil's tie and jacket have been flung to the floor and he's buying another round.

"Ah, Mrs. Gibson, this is where you're hiding." Janie slumps into the seat beside me and flicks off her shoes.

"Hey. You were a wonderful bridesmaid. Thank you for everything."

"Anytime. Well…" She laughs nervously. "Just this once, I hope." She nods toward the dancefloor. "I see Neil's enjoying himself."

He's cavorting with a group of women, short-skirted and overly made up, just his type.

I rest my hand on my bump and play with my wedding ring, all shiny and new.

"You okay?"

"Sure," I say, and watch her face contort into disapproval. "He's my husband now."

"I know, I wasn't…" She sighs and fumbles for her shoes. "Your parents are packing up the presents and going. They wanted to know if you needed a lift."

I try to attract Neil's attention. "I guess so. He doesn't look like he'll be leaving any time soon, and I'm knackered." I hold my hands out so Janie can pull me from the chair. "Come back to mine, I'll put the kettle on. I've got Custard Creams."

"Perfect."

The sun sets, and the crescent moon pushes in and out of the clouds. Disco lights diffuse through the frosted glass and cast green and red and orange streaks across the road.

3.

I wake up alone; Neil hasn't made it back from the wedding yet. I wander around my new home aimlessly. I don't like it; I don't belong. I'm a visitor, a stranger.

It's a peculiar little house. The front door is on the side, the kitchen-diner is at the front, and the roof slopes from the ground floor as though its greatest wish to be a bungalow was thwarted at the last moment.

The furniture is scant and unmatched. The fabric of the settee and armchair is stained with someone else's use. I lean against the magnolia-colored wall and note the ominous stains on the carpet and the hideous curtains with irritation.

All new wives must feel like this, mustn't they? Isolated, unprepared? The focus on the wedding is so intense and exciting we forget the estab-lished life we're leaving behind. We're flung into something different and daunting; the future stretches ahead of us. Six months ago, I was a school-girl. Now I'm a wife and mother-to-be, without anything in between.

It's cold but I don't know how to alter the thermostat—I consider it for a moment, wary of breaking it, then search Neil's wardrobe and find a scratchy, woolen jumper I've never seen him wear. It's huge on me, falling over my bump and hanging half-way down my thighs. The sleeves bury my hands. But it's warm and smells of Neil. I wrap my arms around myself and pretend he's hugging me.

The floors need hoovering; the bathroom needs cleaning. Dirty dishes from Neil's hurried pre-wedding breakfast are on the side. I look for the cleaning things, but there aren't any. Of course, he's only been here a week himself, he probably hasn't thought about it.

"Where've you been?" Neil says gruffly, emerging from the kitchen. He's clammy and disheveled. He hasn't changed out of the suit he wore yesterday.

At the very most, he's only been home the hour it's taken me to walk to the supermarket and back. Yet he's asking where *I've* been? I draw a breath and count to three.

"I asked you a question."

"We needed some stuff." I hold up the bag of spray bottles and squeezy bottles and soap. "You weren't here so—"

"You don't get to tell me when I should come home."

"I wasn't." I take a step back, the smell of cigarettes and stale lager making me queasy. "I was waiting for you, though. It was our wedding night—I bought something sexy."

He scoffs, glancing at my bulging stomach. "I'm hungry."

"Perhaps we could have our wedding night now." I smile seductively and hold my hand out to him. This time six months ago he'd have chased me upstairs.

"I *said* I'm hungry. What's for dinner?"

"A sandwich?" I chuckle and step into the kitchen. "How did you manage without me?"

He grabs my forearm and restrains me.

"I don't expect you to question me like that, right?"

I twist inside the scratchy, oversized sleeve and the friction burns my skin. I yelp and he lets go. I hold my arm out and watch the graze deepen.

"I was just messing," Neil says, gazing at my arm.

"It's okay. It was an accident."

"Yeah." His eyes are fixed on my arm. "Put the kettle on too, eh?"

Last week, yesterday, two minutes ago, I'd have asked if he could make it himself since I was doing his sandwich. Now I simply squeeze past him and put the kettle on. The mark on my wrist stings. I pull the sleeve back down and grab the bread from the cupboard and cheese from the fridge.

He goes to bed after he's eaten, closing the curtains against the mid-afternoon sun, and I'm alone again. I gather the lunch dishes and fill the sink with sudsy water. I wipe the sides, put on a load of laundry, peel potatoes for tea. The stillness is distracting, but I don't dare put the radio on in case I wake Neil. I hum to myself but feel daft and stop. I consider phoning Mum, but she'd ask barbed questions, so I don't do that either. I make myself a cuppa and stand in the middle of the kitchen to drink it.

4.

Neil buys me daffodils.

"What are these for?"

"Because of your arm." He shrugs awkwardly and glances away.

I immediately touch my wrist. The skin is still raised and flaky, there are small bruises flecked around the bone. When my sleeve catches on it, it stings.

"You didn't have to do that. I know you didn't mean it."

"Yeah, well."

I arrange them in a jug because we don't have a vase. I mentally add it to the list I'm creating: things to make the house a home. There's already a physical list of baby things—Mum keeps jotting items down, then scrawling *I'll buy this* after it. So far, she's buying most of it.

The flowers are pretty, but I avoid looking at them—they make me uneasy, reminding me of something I want to forget.

For our one-week anniversary, I make a special dinner—steak with a mushroom sauce I found on the internet. I borrow a candlestick from Mum, and some fancy wine glasses. One glass won't hurt. I spend all afternoon cooking, sitting when my ankles start to swell, and finding inventive ways to bend down to the oven.

The table's set and I'm wearing the only dress which fits. I even put on a bit of makeup.

"Happy anniversary," I say, when Neil walks in.

He's grubby from his hard day of laboring, red brick dust and sweat smeared across his forehead. He hesitates at the door.

"What?"

"We've been married a week. I cooked you steak."

He scans the table, flicks his eyes at me. "You're wearing makeup."

"I wanted it to be special. Sit down, it's almost ready."

I dish out the meat and potatoes while he washes his hands in the kitchen sink. I put the vegetables in a dish so he can serve himself—I've already given up trying to make him eat broccoli. He peers at his plate.

"What have you done to the spuds?"

"I saw it on the internet." They called them hassleback on the website—I think I did it right. "Do you like them?"

"Yeah, not bad." He pushes them around his plate. "I was going to pop down to the pub tonight."

"Oh."

"It's not like you do much at the moment. Thought I'd get out from under your feet. You don't mind, do you? You'll be able to relax."

"But I've been on my own all day."

"Your mum didn't stop by? Unusual."

"I thought we could watch a film or something."

He shovels the steak into his mouth and chews animatedly. He reaches for his wine glass. "Haven't we got any lager?"

He's oblivious to me, to what I was hoping for tonight—recapturing the passion and romance. He'll go out whatever I say. If I complain, he'll get angry. I fetch a can from the fridge and set it down in front of him a little too firmly.

.

5.

The days grow longer; I slow down. I don't walk as fast; I don't sleep so well. The baby presses on my bladder so I spend half my time waddling to the bathroom. My clothes groan at the seams, but I can't afford to replace them—I'm on the loosest button of my adjustable jeans and the elastic of my skirts have no more stretch.

Mum's been doing some of my housework because I can barely bend to vacuum or reach the washing powder in the cupboard under the sink. Neil won't help—he says he's exhausted from working all day, the least I can do is cook and clean and pack his lunch. He says he has to work even more now, to earn enough money for the both of us.

"Even so," Mum says in a tight voice, and I ignore her.

I flick through the magazine she bought me, at the bright, smiling, wide-eyed babies on every page, while Mum cleans the microwave and writes her own list of groceries to bring with her next time.

"You don't have to," I say quietly, trailing off because it's nice to feel taken care of.

"If we stock the freezer and cupboards now, there'll be less to do when the baby comes."

I inhale sharply. *When the baby comes.* She says it so casually, as if my discomfort and fatigue will give way to something better. And I'm terrified. I've only ever held one baby in my entire life. The models in the magazine are beautiful and slim and fresh. I wonder how relieved they were after the photoshoot was done and they could hand the babies off to their real mothers.

"It's probably time to get your bag ready for the hospital, too." She scribbles it down on a different list.

"But I've got ages yet."

"Four weeks is not ages. Any time now, Gracie-Lou." She laughs at my horror, then sits beside me and holds my hand. "It'll be okay. No one's ever ready. It's life-changing. But, it's also incredible and exciting and rewarding, and I wouldn't be without you and Darren for a moment. You'll feel the same way, I promise."

Four weeks. How did it become four weeks so quickly? I want it to stop.

Day after day, closer and closer. My anxiety is occasionally traded with the anticipation of meeting my new baby, this tiny person inside me who'll be brand new to the world.

When I imagine her, the miracle of a new life overwhelms me. My GCSE Science lessons flood back, but the idea of two random cells joining together, then doubling and doubling and continuing to do so, to create us all, seems impossible.

Inside me, she's smiling and pouting and frowning. Her hair and finger-nails are growing. She's listening to every word I say. I stroke my stomach and she curls toward my hand. I sing to her.

As she gets bigger, her sudden kicks catch me off-guard. Neil, sprawled across the floor playing video games, glances over.

"She's not *that* strong. Is she?"

"Apparently she is." I lift my shirt and watch her tumbles with fascination. My stomach lurches from left to right. "Look, I think that's her hand pushing out."

Neil pauses his game and kneels beside me. I press the bump and the baby pushes back. I press twice, and the baby pushes twice.

"No way! She's counting."

I smile. "No, it's instinctive."

He reaches out, tentatively. I take his hand and place it on the side of my stomach.

"Push down."

He does. His hand is warm, gentle. My stomach pitches toward him, snuggling against him. My heart melts at the softness and awe on his face. He moves his hand a little and the baby follows. He places his palm flat, so it almost encompasses the whole of the dome shape. I feel her spread out, her arms and legs stretching to the edges of my body. I hold my breath, not wanting to break the spell.

Neil moves closer, not quite resting his head on my stomach, but nearly. I run my fingers lightly through his hair.

6.

Janie's school bag strains with notes and folders, with textbooks and note-books. And I'm jealous. I want to have those books open on *my* desk while I scrawl notes in the margins and highlight chunks of text in dazzling yellow. I want to chart the minute details of Kristallnacht and debate the use of Hardy's imagery in *Tess of the d'Urbervilles*. I want to glue myself to the whiteboard in the psychology classroom so I can't be dragged away.

"It's probably not as fun as you remember, and the exams start next week."

And a week after that, the baby's due.

"You're bigger every time I see you."

"I think I'm going to explode. I don't even want to eat anymore, there's no room for the food."

Janie chuckles, but I'm not joking. The recent hot spell has made my body swell, none of my clothes are comfortable, and all I want to do is sit in a dark room or a cold bath.

"I can't wait to cuddle her," she says. Unlike me, Janie has cousins and a nephew she looks after all the time. I've never even changed a nappy before.

I smile weakly.

"What's wrong? Aren't you excited?"

"Sometimes." I gasp as the baby twists into my diaphragm. "And then sometimes I get so scared. What if I'm a bad mother? What if the baby hates me? What if—"

"What if none of those things happen?"

She reaches for my hand, and I look at my puffy fingers. Everyone's holding my hands, at the moment, apart from Neil. Everyone thinks I need support and help and comforting, while Neil goes to the pub several nights a week and rolls in when I'm pretending to be asleep.

"I think you're going to be amazing. And your baby will be lucky to have you." She pulls back a little and holds my gaze. "Okay? And I'll be here."

"Not for long." Tears start to well, and my nose tingles. I take several deep breaths, sit up straight and brush away my melancholy. "Sorry, that's not fair. But I'm going to miss you so much when you're gone."

The front door slams and Neil appears in front of us. A frown passes across his face, but he catches himself before Janie notices.

"So this is what you do all day while I'm at work." With a smile, it doesn't sound sinister. He sits on the arm of the settee and rests his hand on my shoulder, pushing down.

He's home early. "Janie just popped round to see how I'm doing."

"Well, wasn't that nice of Janie." He tilts his head toward her and sighs. "But I'm afraid Grace has busy grown-up things to do now. It was nice to see you, but…" He smiles with an apologetic shrug. "Time to go."

"Thanks for coming," I say.

"O-kay…" She stands and looks around for her bag. "I'll see you soon, yeah?" She tries to hug me, but Neil is adamantly between us. She looks confused but remains quiet.

Neil sees her out, and his face is puce when he returns.

"She wasn't here for long—"

"I don't care. I don't like her. She's a bad influence on you."

"She's my best friend."

"You don't need friends, you've got me. And soon you'll have our baby to look after. You won't have time for anything else." He draws me into a suffocating hug. "Wives look after their husbands."

"I do."

"I don't smell my tea cooking."

"You're back early. You never said." I stop. "I'll start it now."

My face is still flattened against his chest. I breath in a mix of new buildings and sweat and aftershave.

7.

My midwife appointment runs late, and I hurry along the road, uphill, to get home before Neil.

No matter how vigorously I swing my arms, the momentum doesn't pull me forward any quicker, and I have to keep stopping to catch my breath. I should have put a casserole in the oven. I shouldn't have accepted an appointment after three o'clock.

I check my phone. He hasn't called. Which means he isn't home yet. I have just enough time to get something in the oven and be settled before he walks through the door. I turn onto my flat road with relief.

The car's in the drive as I approach the house. The curtains are closed in the dining room. It's a warning. Dark house, dark mood.

My hand lingers on the handle. I don't want to go inside.

The door's thrown open. "Where've you been?"

"Seeing the midwife."

I wait for him to let me into the house, but he expands and fills the doorway. His lips curl into a snarl and the furrow between his eyebrows deepens. "I don't believe you."

"I had an appointment. She was running late. There was an emergency or something."

"Who were you with, really?"

"I was at the surgery," I say slowly and deliberately, "with the midwife."

I regret my tone immediately, before he's had chance to process it. Our neighbor pauses on the shared driveway and searches her bag. I think she's pretending—nosing in. I catch her eye and she bustles into her house.

"Get inside," Neil hisses, grabbing my arm. "Don't ever speak to me like that."

He drags me into the house and throws me against the wall. I bump my forehead.

"I have a right to know where you are, you're my wife."

"I told you this morning—"

He grips my neck, just below my jaw. My teeth grind as I try to move away. He watches his hand with fascination, as though it's a detached manifestation he has no control over.

Any tighter and I won't be able to breath.

"You didn't say anything this morning."

"I—" *I did, I told you exactly where I was going.* "I'm sorry." My voice trickles out of the tiny gap he's allowing me. "Must have forgot."

"Or you're lying." Slowly, he relaxes his grip, tenderly stroking my cheek—the past few seconds already disregarded. "You will learn to respect me."

"I need to put the oven on, for tea," I say, trying to keep my voice calm and neutral. My hands are trembling. I want to push him away, but I don't want to reoffend.

I flee to the kitchen and breathe painfully, leaning across the worktop to compose myself. We eat without conversation and I go to bed early. I can't sleep. I replay it over and over, each time his face is darker and more contorted with rage.

Neil brings flowers the next day—tulips, my favorite, although I'm not sure it was on purpose. He pulls me into his arms and waits for me to say thank you. Which I do. I empty the jug of the last ones, curled and drying but not yet dead.

8.

I sit in the nursery. The brand-new cot is at odds with the exuberant flowery wallpaper of the previous inhabitant. Neil says there's no point decorating a rented house, it's wasted money. To disguise the walls, I've put up framed posters of Disney princesses, ones which depict them as badass heroes rather than fragile damsels. I don't want my little girl waiting her whole life to be rescued.

I'm going to call her Serenity.

She's going to be strong and spirited. She'll be honest and thoughtful and kind. She'll have a laugh so infectious I'll always laugh alongside her.

She'll never be alone; she'll have many friends who'll all look out for her, and a mother who'll do anything for her.

She'll follow her dreams, and never be trapped or tethered. She'll soar into the world with fervor and the sun will always shine.

And she'll be nothing like me. This is my greatest wish of all.

1:Ø5 A.M.

The lights from the cooker clock and the microwave are bright enough I don't need the big light on. I sit at the table while the kettle boils. I wanted hot chocolate, but we've only got the stuff you add boiling water to—it's not the same. It's the warm milk in proper cocoa which helps you sleep. This will just give a vague approximation. A placebo.

I trace the marks in the wood with my finger and remember childhood breakfasts at this table—hurried ones when I was late for school, Saturday morning ones in front of the TV, summer holiday ones which were so late and lazy they merged into lunch.

My finger brushes over the candle wax burn Darren caused the Christmas before I found out I was having Ren. Just a week separating that happy family day and the one when I told Mum and Dad I was pregnant. It's surreal, the way time passes.

I pour water over the chocolate powder and stir vigorously, smearing inadvertent lumps against the side of my mug with a spoon. I add milk to make it creamier, but it's still nothing like the real thing.

Dad stands at the door, leaning against the frame, yawning. "Everything okay?"

I gaze at him for a moment and wonder how to answer. "Sorry, I didn't mean to wake you."

He shakes his head. "You didn't. Mum's snoring."

"Do you want one?" I hold up my drink and indicate the kettle.

"No thanks. I heard you moving around and wanted to make sure you were all right." He crosses the room and hovers in the middle.

I shrug, hopeless. There are so many things I want to say, have wanted to say over the past couple of years, *need* to say tonight. I don't know how to start. I bash a few more lumps.

Dad shuffles around the kitchen, randomly stacking the few discarded dishes beside the sink and folding the dish cloth over the tap. I look away, avoiding his eye, and my hair falls across my face.

"What happened to your neck? It's bruised."

Shit. I hold my hand up to hide it. "It's nothing."

"Looks like…" He tries to pull my fingers away.

"It's nothing."

He's still and thoughtful, and just as I think he's going to press for more, he bends to kiss the top of my head. "I'll buy some proper cocoa tomorrow, and those tiny marshmallows you used to like too. Try to get some sleep."

I watch him vanish back into the blackness of the hall, hear his footsteps creak up the stairs, and his bedroom door close gently so not to disturb Mum. The light from the cooker and microwave illuminate the room; the hum of the fridge saves me from silence.

The Good Wife

1.

Neil's out when I go into labor. No surprise. At first, it's not so bad—maybe it's one of those Braxton Hicks things I read about. So I pace around the house, pausing and panting and groaning when the vice-like ache pulses through me. But the contractions get steadily worse.

This is it. It's really happening.

I lie down on the settee, curling around a pillow, trying to rest. *Rest,* says my book, is very important in the early stages because labor can last for many hours.

The pain intensifies, rippling across my stomach, up and down my spine. The book says I should have a bath to help relieve it, but I can't lean over to reach the taps. I guess the book is aimed at people who have supportive partners at home with them.

Neil's phone goes straight to voicemail and he's not replying to texts, so eventually I call Mum.

By the time she arrives, I'm on my hands and knees in the dining room, howling, half-laughing hysterically, picturing how ridiculous I must look. Mum helps me to my feet so I can lean across the table and feel a semblance of comfort at last.

"Where's Neil?"

"Not now, Mum."

"I just thought I could send Dad to fetch him."

"I don't know!" I gasp through another gripping contraction, clenching my teeth. I cry out as it hits its peak. I won't cope with *many hours* of this.

"Time to go to the hospital, I think."

"It hurts."

"We've all been there," she mutters as she heaves me up and grabs my bag on the way.

At the maternity unit, the midwife takes charge. With the benefit of gas-and-air and her quiet proficiency, everything slows to a relaxed hum. The throbbing of the contractions ebbs away; the baby loses her urgency.

I lie back into the soft pillow and close my eyes. Mum makes small-talk with the midwife and helps me sip from a glass of ice cold water. She rubs my legs when they're restless and wedges extra pillows behind me when I need to alter position. Neil wouldn't be half as useful or attentive.

Even so, I wish he was here. I need him here with me.

And he doesn't come.

The contractions amplify. Each squeezing my body to exhaustion, attacking me until I'm almost unable to gather strength for the next. But it builds again, growling like thunder. Over and over and over…

"Push," says the midwife, but I want to sleep. I want to close my eyes and erase the pain. I can't do this. It's too much, too arduous.

"Push," she calls again and again.

Sometimes Mum's voice overlaps hers. They're both urging me, but my body is on the verge of breaking.

"Push, come on now. You can do it… Good girl, keep going. There you go, that's it. I can see the head. I can see your baby's head. One more push. Just one more."

Suddenly, the pressure diminishes. I'm empty and limp. I'm a burst balloon. And Serenity is screaming. Serenity is here!

She's purple and scrunched up. I'd been expecting a rosy-cheeked cherub, a cute pouting bundle, like in the magazines. But this one, handed to me naked and slippery, is unsettled and inconsolable.

I hold her close, skin to skin, and smooth her wrinkled cheek. I did it. My miracle.

Her tiny heart beats rapidly against my chest; her breath is soft on my skin as she nuzzles into my breast. Her cry makes my body ache.

I play with the small amount of black hair plastered to her scalp. I'm vaguely aware of my mother taking photos, of the midwife writing her notes and her remedial tidy up. It's just my daughter and me. When she takes Serenity to weigh her, I am desolate and lonely, and her cry fills the room.

Gradually she's appeased by the warmth of my body and begins to suckle. She opens her eyes briefly and gazes at me. I dip my head toward hers and whisper, secret words between the two of us. I can't remember a time when she wasn't lying in my arms.

2.

"Serenity?!" Neil sneers, and I'm thankful Mum and Dad have left, basking in the joy of cuddles with their first grandchild and furnished with enough photos to wallpaper their front room.

"You said you didn't care what I called her," I say in the quietest of voices.

Several people peer across from their own happy unions, but swiftly avert their gaze when I catch them. I slump down, red-faced, trying to be as miniscule as possible. I want to close the curtains around my cubicle, but Neil's standing in my way.

"Like fuck is any kid of mine gonna be called *Serenity*!"

He peers at her lying in the crib beside my bed, roused to crying by his aggression. I lift her, rocking her, hushing her, my lips pressed to her temple. But she can't be pacified—the world is a scary, noisy place after the peace and sanctuary of the past nine months. Her father is a scary, noisy man.

"She's…" He grapples for a name. "Sarah. And if you don't like it, you can fuck off."

"What about Bethany? Chloe?" Both of those names were on my list. "Poppy?"

I fall silent under his glare.

Her little fists are clenched, her arms beat against the air, her face is screwed up. I'm in anguish listening to her. I turn her so Neil can see her and allow his heart to melt as well.

"Do you want to hold her?"

"I…"

Around him, fathers are holding their newborns, bending over cribs, sitting beside their partners in impenetrable groups of three.

"I don't know how."

"Sit down." I pat the bed beside me, and he does as asked. I hand my precious baby to her father, and he holds her tentatively, awkwardly. "Hold her closer, so she can feel your heart beating. It comforts her."

"She wants you," he says as soon as she starts to fuss and gives her back.

Later, when we're alone, we lie together. She's so beautiful, with tufts of hair and intense eyes watching my every move. I allow my eyes to close. I feel a midwife take Serenity from my arms and put her in the crib, but I'm too tired to protest. We sleep, completely exhausted.

3.

Serenity, Sarah, whatever I'm supposed to call her now, is not an easy baby. She fusses in my arms; she doesn't settle to sleep; she wails pitifully, and I am useless. She doesn't feed as much as she should—she doesn't latch on well and gives up too quickly.

"She's hungry, the poor mite," Mum says.

"I'm trying."

I sit with her in my arms, my breasts aching and engorged. I can't remember the last time I slept for more than an hour. I want to put her in her cot and leave the house. I want to stand at the end of the garden and pretend it's someone else's baby I can hear.

Neil refuses to let me try the bottle. "It's better for the baby," he says with conviction. He means I should be a *proper mother*—I can see it on his face.

Another time, he says, "My mother breastfed all of us. You're too good to feed your own baby, is that it?"

I sit on the bathroom floor, in tears. I wander the house when Neil's out and Serenity will only sleep in my arms, in tears.

I practice the name Sarah, but it's not right. It catches on my tongue, sticks to the roof of my mouth like peanut butter. For weeks, in my head and in my dreams of our lives together, she's been Serenity. My Serenity, my tranquility, my comfort. I don't know this child with another name— she's willful and stubborn.

This isn't what I thought motherhood would be. We should be spending these early days in bed with our gurgling little girl between us; we should be sharing our sleeplessness and our delight. We should be an unstoppable force, the three of us together.

Instead, Neil's still out at all hours, disturbing us both when he stumbles home, expecting his breakfast and tea on the table as though nothing has changed.

He watches me failing. While Serenity fights against me, screaming fractiously, Neil stands at our bedroom door and slaps the wall loudly. "Make her shut up. You're her bloody mother."

"I'm trying," I say, my overused refrain falling out of my mouth again.

He's hungover, with his tell-tale grayness and heavy sunken eyes. I savor his suffering. I've been up all night while he's snored and grizzled beside me; I've had less sleep than him. I abandon the idea of feeding her and stand to rock her. I press my lips against her cheek and murmur.

Serenity, my little Renity... my Ren-Ren-Renity.

Her bawling reduces to a soft simper as she feels my words tickling her face. I've done it. I catch Neil's eye for approval. Then she starts again, forcing herself louder than before.

4.

A motorbike growls along the main road and Ren, in her cot beside my bed, stirs. Her face scrunches up and her mouth opens as if to scream. I rest my hand on the mattress beside her—she senses my warmth and settles. It seems I only parent well when she doesn't realize it's me. I could be anyone right now, and she wouldn't care. It's the pressure on the mattress that's important.

On the other side of me, Neil stretches out—a heavy, immobile log of a man. I fold into the curve of his body. I should be sleeping; Ren will wake soon, with her shrill demands and incessant wailing. But this peacefulness, with a soft wind buffeting my window and birds tweeting the earliest hint of dawn, is perfection.

Too soon, Ren shrieks herself awake and I swipe her from her cot and out of the room. Neil flails but remains asleep. I wish I could do that, just ignore everything going on around me. I sit in my favorite armchair to feed Ren. With every suck she gnaws on my enflamed nipple and the pain sears through me. She wails, still hungry, when Neil stands at the door.

"Where's my breakfast?"

"I haven't had time." My stomach rumbles at the mention of food. I should have grabbed some toast and a mug of tea before I sat down—that's what the book says. I didn't even turn on the TV to relieve the boredom.

"You didn't wake me up. I'm going to be late."

"I had to feed the baby. I'm sorry. Just grab yourself something on the way." *Or switch on the kettle and offer me a drink.*

He swoops down on me. I flinch and pull Ren toward me. She fidgets against my body, trying to push herself away. Neil runs his fingers down my cheek, digging in and pushing my head to one side.

"That's not the point. *You* should be doing it." He drops his hand and kneels beside me. "Why do you think you're any different than any other mother? They cope. Is there something wrong with you? Do we have to give Sarah away to a better mother?"

"No." I cling to Ren as though he might wrench her from me.

"Tomorrow. I want my breakfast ready. Got it?"

I nod, feebly. Caving in. I kiss the top of Ren's head to remind Neil she's between us. He bunches his fist, hovering over us, and leaves.

When he comes home from work, he brings me roses.

5.

Ren battles against sleep, against me, against being soothed. She settles only when I hold her upright into my shoulder and pace around the house. I'm a zombie, barely functioning.

Mum gives me a sling, the fabric kind which swaddles Ren to me, and finally she yawns and curls into me. But now I'm chained to her instead. Her weight hangs from me.

"Give Sarah to me," Mum says. "I'll take her for a walk. You need a break."

"No. She'll need feeding soon."

"Then let me hold her while you lie down for a bit."

"Neil says—"

"I don't care what Neil says, I care about you. He's not an expert in childcare. You need a break—you don't have to do it all by yourself."

A tear skims my cheek. So tired, so depleted. I surrender and guiltily liberate myself from the sling. Mum takes Ren from me and makes funny noises and silly faces. Ren watches with fascination; her little hand reaches out.

My body is light without her in my arms, as though I could drift to the ceiling. I step backwards. Ren doesn't notice. I step further away, almost out of the door. Run, run away. I grip the door handle to ground myself, to stop myself fleeing.

"Here's her teddy." It's a hideous pink thing Neil's mum brought round, but for some reason Ren likes to hold it while she sleeps.

My sleeve rises as I pass Mum the toy. The small bruise circling my forearm is revealed. I pull my hand back swiftly.

"Gracie, is everything okay? With Neil, I mean. Are *you* okay?" Her voice is so tender, so concerned.

I swallow. "This? Oh, I just banged it on a door this morning, it's nothing." I laugh it off, hiding it away.

No, it's not okay, I almost say. I'm confused and scared. I'm trying my best but it's never good enough. He's not the man I thought he was. This was all a big mistake.

Words poised, I swallow them back down and force myself to smile. "You know what it's like with a new baby. The first few weeks, they're hard." I hold her gaze unwaveringly. I will *not* look as though I'm lying. "We're getting used to it, that's all."

She's going to pry further—I recognize the purse-lipped precursor—but instead she nods. "Go and sit down, I'll put the kettle on."

6.

As the weather warms up, I take Ren out as much as possible, escaping the house which is becoming a prison. The rumble of pram wheels soothes her, and she sleeps with an angelic look on her face. I revel in the peace—I listen to birds singing, to the chatter of people at bus stops, to my own thoughts.

Sometimes we walk to Asda and have lunch in the café, or I pack a sandwich and we go up to the industrial estate and sit on the grass verge and gaze between the buildings toward Dartmoor. Ren sleeps while I read a book or simply watch the planes flying high overhead and imagine their exotic destinations. Or we stand on the curb and wave at lorry drivers heading to and from the factories.

When old ladies coo at her, I feel like a proper mother, proudly showing her off. They ask how old she is and if she sleeps well. I lie and say she's a delight, and her name is Ren.

"Oh, how unusual," they always say. "It suits her so well."

Yes, it does. It *would have*. Ren plays to her audience, practicing her new-found ability to smile and blow bubbles of saliva.

"Isn't she perfect?" they twitter to each other before I'm allowed to continue my journey.

We catch the bus into the city center and go up to the Hoe, passing the registry office where Neil and I were married. It's just a building, but every time I come this way I'm overwhelmed with sorrow. I see us all there, lined up for the makeshift photos, the laughter and conversation among our guests while I was pale and nervous.

Sometimes a wedding party is eagerly awaiting the bride, and I linger to see the dress and the flowers and her joyful anticipation for the day and years ahead of her.

It's a steep climb to the Promenade with Ren's buggy. But the view is unrivaled. The Sound—the harbor protecting the city—is wide and blue, surrounded by green field peninsulas. Behind me is the terrace of large Victorian houses, the statue of Drake, the war memorial, Smeaton's Tower stretching toward the clouds. I'm overwhelmed by the vastness, the calm despite being so close to the chaotic city center, by my ability to block out everything I don't want to think about.

It's an oasis, an escape. Time stands still.

We watch the tourist boats setting off on trips up the Tamar and the ferry from France navigating its way into port and the sailing boats drifting because there's little wind. Other people are doing the same; no one's in a rush to return to their hectic lives.

I stretch a blanket out on the ground and lie Ren on her stomach. She reaches for the blades of grass fluttering around the edges of the blanket, staring at them with concentration and wonderment. After diligent attempts on her part, I pick a daisy and tickle the back of her hand with it.

"Uh, no wonder Neil complains the house is a mess."

I look up and Neil's mum is casting her shadow over us.

"Hello." I scramble to my feet. "We're enjoying the sunshine."

"Hmm." She gives Ren the briefest of considerations, showing no inclination to interact with her granddaughter.

"What do you mean, complains about the house?"

"Well, if you're out gallivanting all the time, it's no surprise really."

"I like her to get some fresh air. It's not good for her to be cooped up while I work."

"You have a garden—a few minutes is enough surely. At this age, she doesn't much care where she is."

But I do. I kneel back down and retrieve the daisy she's dropped, brushing it against her cheek until she smiles. "Do you want to hold her?"

"Her hands look sticky."

"We shared an ice cream." I don't mention I was trying to distract her from crying because she woke from her nap filled with rage at the world.

"Ice cream? Aren't you worried she'll get chubbier?"

"She's the perfect weight for her age. A little bit of ice cream won't hurt her."

"Well. I'll leave you to it. I should get home—*my* house won't vacuum itself."

She walks away; Ren remains unacknowledged.

"Like mother, like son," I murmur to myself.

I gather Ren's toys and pack them into her bag; I wipe her face and hands and strap her into the buggy. The spell is broken, and my angel Ren turns back into a devil.

7.

Sleep when the baby sleeps, says the book, and the health visitor, and my mum.

But I feel guilty. I should be baking scones, batch-cooking chili and curry for ease when Neil comes home unexpectedly. I should be tidying and cleaning so there's no dust for Neil to run his finger through. I should be washing yesterday's dishes and collecting the recycling into their different boxes.

I allow myself to sit while I drink a cup of tea, rather than snatch mouthfuls on the go. My body sinks back into the soft cushions, and three nights of Ren-induced wakefulness pushes down on my forehead.

My eyes close; my mug tips.

The doorbell rings.

I consider ignoring it, but I'm worried they'll ring again and wake Ren. I shuffle to the door, and Janie stands there with a huge box of chocolates. I can barely mobilize a smile.

"I'm so sorry I haven't been before—I'm such a bad friend. Exams and..." Her voice escalates and I hold my finger to my mouth. "Is this a bad time?"

"I was dozing and..." I point upstairs. "She's asleep."

"Oops. Sorry. I didn't think. Do you want me to go?"

Yes, yes, I do. I shake my head and allow her inside.

"I can't believe it's been so long since I saw you. You look great. You were a giant ball last time. Sarah must be so big now."

I wince at her name spoken aloud; I can't help myself. "Yes, she is. She'll be awake soon and you'll be able to meet her." I flutter around, gathering crumbs from the coffee table into my hand, moving the ironing pile from the settee with embarrassment.

Neil's mum's right—houses don't clean themselves.

"Don't worry about that," Janie says. "Let me put the kettle on, you look knackered."

"Constantly." I follow her into the kitchen and lean against the wall.

"But it's good, right? You're happy?"

It's what she asked before Ren was born, as though trying to alleviate herself of the guilt of being careful and childless. On Facebook, she's been posting nothing but how excited she is to be off to Brighton for university in a few weeks. *My life officially starts here*, I believe she wrote.

I nod because I don't trust my words.

Ren cries, and I sigh—just a few more minutes, that's all I want. Tears prickle and I blink them away. The stairs get steeper every time I climb them. Ren's red and sweaty, thrashing at the mattress.

"Oh my goodness, she's adorable. She looks like you."

I scoop her up. Her gaze is fixed on this stranger. "This is your Auntie Janie. Do you want a cuddle?"

Janie takes her but struggles to hold her. Ren's arms and legs flail around. "She's strong." Janie scrunches her nose and hands her to me. "And I think she needs changing."

"Go and finish the tea. I'll be down in a minute."

Clothes off, nappy off, wipe, cream, nappy in bag, new one on, vest poppers popped. All done. I'm getting good at this. The first few times were a long and convoluted disaster.

Ren and I bounce down the stairs and I make airplane noises which startle then fascinate her. Neil and Janie jump when I walk into the kitchen. They were close together, and now they're not.

It happens so quickly I can't trust what I saw.

And when did Neil get home? I didn't hear him come in.

He leers at Janie and slinks down into one of the chairs. Janie looks uncomfortable, smiling awkwardly, and her cheeks are bright red.

"What's…?" But Neil's glare silences me. No questions; rule number one. I try to catch Janie's eye, but she's flicking her gaze away from me.

"Janie and I were talking about university, about how exciting it is for her."

I swallow. "Okay."

"You wanted to go too, didn't you? Clever little Gracie."

"A long time ago," I say quietly.

"Never thought you would. Too scary and so far away. It's a good job you've got me. Me and Sarah and our lovely house together." His voice is slick and nonchalant. On the surface, he's perfectly cordial, but there's underlying menace and I can't work out why.

Janie plays with Ren's fingers; Ren gnaws on Janie's knuckles.

"Did you see Janie's prom photos? Looking good, yeah? That dress was something else." He whistles softly and Janie closes her eyes. Her cheeks are pale now, color drained.

"Neil…" I begin but have no idea what will come next. The word hangs in the air. I have to stand up to him, stand up for Janie—tell him off, tell him he can't say things like that about my friends.

Silence creeps around us. Neil smirks.

"I should go," Janie says, unwinding her fingers from Ren's.

"I'm sorry." Although I'm not entirely sure what I'm apologizing for yet. My words are lost in the rustle of her bag. I reach for her arm, an apologetic gesture, but she brushes me off. I follow her to the door and Neil stands behind me, resting his hand on my shoulder. I wriggle, but he clamps onto me.

"Thanks for the chocolates," I say as she walks down the drive without a word. She half turns but doesn't look at me. I don't blame her. I should have done more.

Neil maneuvers me inside and shuts the door.

"What was all that about?" Ren's still in my arms, her head resting against my shoulder. The side of my face is damp with her perspiration. "You can't treat my friends like that."

"In my house, I do what I want." He kicks the charity shop bag I've left in the hall. "Look at the state of this place. It's disgusting. Janie agrees, she told me."

"She wouldn't say that…"

"You're jealous, aren't you? That she's leaving and you're not, that she's looking hot and you're…" He scoffs. "I remember the way you looked when I met you. Shame I couldn't see into the future, eh?" He grabs me arm and yanks me toward him. "Don't ever think you're better than me. You should be grateful I took you and your kid on."

"She's your daughter too—"

"Ah!" He whacks me with the back of his hand, catching my cheekbone with his ring.

I'm too shocked to retaliate, to yell or hit back. I touch my face, already throbbing, checking for blood. Ren's fine—her mouth engages in voice-less conversation as she dreams contentedly.

Neil barely reacts. He pats his pockets, checking for wallet and phone. "I'm going out."

I check myself in the mirror by the front door. Already, my face is swollen with the tinge of a bruise. The shape of his ring forms a red ridge.

This time, the flowers are pink carnations. He doesn't wait for my thank-you's; he doesn't reach out to hug me and nuzzle into the top of my head. He drops them on the kitchen counter while my back is turned. I arrange them in the jug, throwing the previous bouquet in the bin.

8.

Time passes in Ren-shaped milestones. First da-da noises, first belly laugh. In a haze of insomnia and a freefall of flowers, I barely notice the year vanishing under me.

Janie leaves for university without coming to say goodbye. I read her Facebook statuses, but she ignores my comments—while she responds to everyone else, I don't even get a "like."

It could have been me too. Leaving with excitement and trepidation, setting off on this great big adventure. Ren will never know how much she changed my life. Will she grow up thinking of me only as this frustrated woman chained to the house and caring for an ungrateful husband?

I want more for her, just like Mum wanted more for me.

Ren is inquisitive and mobile, with a lightning temper just like her father. Giggles turn to rage, contentment to vexation, in the briefest glimmer of her eye.

When Neil thinks I'm not watching, he holds her and tickles her, and blows raspberries on her tummy. They laugh together, and she beams for him, her face flushed with delight. I peer through the crack of the door and witness her betraying me with her love for him.

She doesn't smile for me; she doesn't laugh.

I creep into the room, hoping to force Neil to admit his adoration for her, but he's already put her back down on the playmat.

"Sarah needs changing," he says without looking up.

I scoop her from the floor. She twists to see Neil and scrunches her face into a whimper, her chubby hands reaching for him. I stiffen and try to ignore it. She doesn't mean to hurt me, she's just a baby; but a tear falls down my face and I wipe it on Ren's shoulder before Neil notices.

9.

His hand on the base of my spine makes me tingle, a reminder of something I've forgotten.

When he says, "Why don't you sit down for a while?" I see a trap. He hasn't gone to the pub like he usually does, slipping away while I put Ren down. Boots off, he spreads across the settee like a beached whale.

"I was just going to…" I gesture toward the kitchen. Not to anything specific, but if he asks, I'm always just about to do something. He put a glass of wine in my trailing hand.

I haven't drunk alcohol since Ren was born. Only a few sips and I'm relaxed and woozy. Neil's face loses focus. His hand on the base of my spine is warm, firm, familiar. He hauls me toward him, contorting me into a clumsy hug.

"We never talk anymore. We always used to talk."

Funny, I don't remember that. I recall watching him play video games and pretending to be interested.

"I guess things change when you have a baby," I say, because he's waiting for a response even though it wasn't a question.

"Well, it shouldn't. How was your day?"

My insides spasm. A trap. A test.

"We played in the garden, I cleaned the windows, the window cleaner came. Sarah tried some banana for the first time—she wasn't keen."

He nods encouragingly. "Anything else?"

Shit. What have I missed? What does he know? He reaches beside the settee and pulls a bag onto his lap.

"Oh," I say with relief. "I popped to the shop for some stuff for tea. I couldn't resist that cute dress for Sarah."

He tips it out. In the folds of the dress are two bottles of foundation and a palette of neutral eyeshadows. "What's with the makeup?"

"Nothing."

"Who are you trying to impress?"

"No one. I wear it for myself."

A couple of days ago there was a gash above my eye. It's healed, but the bruise persists. It's purple now. It'll be a swamp green soon. I don't want to see either of those colors in the mirror.

A week ago, there was a different wound. A month ago, the whole side of my face was swollen and red, disguised by careful contouring.

He peers closely. "You're wearing it now. Take it off."

"I'll do it when I go to bed." Neil knocks the glass from my hand. It lands by my foot but doesn't break. Wine seeps across the carpet.

"I want you to do it now."

I fetch my face wipes from the bathroom and sit on the coffee table directly in front of him. The light in here is bright—not for us, the muted, soft-focus bulbs or dimmer switches. We have sharp daylight at all times. I clean my face slowly, allowing the purple bruise above my eye and the red graze on my jaw to appear.

He watches, squirming uncomfortably as the truth is revealed. "You've got a bruise."

"Yes."

"You're so clumsy," he says absently. "You really should be more careful."

He kisses my forehead and takes his cans into the kitchen. I hear them clatter into the empty recycling box.

1∅.

I buy an artificial Christmas tree and decorate it with Ren in my arms. She grabs the tinsel and laughs when I try to pull it from her. She holds a star-shaped bauble gently between finger and thumb, gazing intently before trying to eat it. Her eyes sparkle as the fairy lights make our faces green and red and orange and blue, holding her arm out and watching her skin change color.

I want to take her to see Father Christmas, but Mum says she's far too young. I linger at the end of the queue of excited preschoolers and their harried parents. The noise crescendos to the top of the mall, until the whole place is filled with joy and laughter.

"When do kids stop believing?" I ask, because I don't want to miss the window. Ren's only seven months old, but that's seven months older than the last time I blinked.

"Depends. Darren was about seven or eight. Obviously, you were a special case."

I wasn't quite five—one of the older kids at school went around telling the reception class and got hauled in to see the head teacher. A letter was hurriedly sent to parents. I knew before my big brother, sworn to secrecy so he wouldn't find out.

"I want everything to be perfect for her." I gaze at my baby, sleeping contently because she was awake all night. If I could curl into a ball and sleep right now, I would. My layers of makeup don't just hide the yellow shadow of the bruise, but my black, hollow, exhausted eyes as well.

"And it will be."

Mum pushes the buggy away from the grotto, heading down to M&S, for mince pies and Christmas crackers. For every item checked off her list, two more are added. Just a quick trip into town, she'd said yesterday.

"How do I know if I'm a good mum?"

She sucks air into her cheeks. "No one knows that for sure. You figure it out. You'll make mistakes—we all do—but you'll learn together, you and Sarah."

Sarah. The name still jars, makes me judder to a halt, makes me want to correct whoever is calling her by the wrong name. *It's Ren,* I want to say. Like the bird, I'd explain, because she's my little Wren. But I don't want to set her against Neil, I don't want to share the story of how she came to be Sarah. So I keep her real name secret.

We're home before four, of course. Tea on the table by five. Neil strolls in at half-past and the lasagna is burnt and dry.

11.

On Christmas Eve, Neil wakes in a foul temper. He came in late, stumbling and swearing. I pretended to be asleep when he fell into bed and could only make out some of what he was mumbling. I have no idea what happened, but he wasn't happy about it.

Before he's even drunk his coffee, he's in the living room stripping the tree of decorations and throwing them into their boxes. He dismantles the tree haphazardly so the branches twist or break.

"What are you doing? Stop!"

"Christmas is canceled."

"You're not serious."

I laugh because he sounds like Alan Rickman in that Robin Hood film. Neil glares and throws one of the baubles at me. Its sharp edge strikes my temple.

"What about Sarah? It's her first Christmas."

"She's a baby, she doesn't know what day it is. I'm pissed off with all this shit, so we're done."

"We'll still be going to Mum and Dad's, though?"

Irritation flashes across his face. "I *said* we're done."

"They're expecting us. Darren's home."

"I don't give a fuck. Phone them, tell them one of your whiney little lies... But leave me the fuck alone."

"I can take Sarah by myself," I say without thinking. "They were looking forward to—"

He's beside me in an instant and I cower. "And show me up coz I'm not there? Is that it? Poor little Gracie running to mummy?"

He brushes my cheeks with his hand, a tender touch. I want to nuzzle against him.

He scrapes his nail down my face, gouging my skin.

"No, I'm not letting you do that to me. You're going nowhere."

"We haven't got any food in. I didn't buy anything."

He's already pulling on his boots and checking his wallet for cash. I'll have to pop out for a few Christmassy things—it's doable. I can cobble something together. My head whirls with a plan to salvage the day. But when he leaves, he locks the door behind him. I check the key rack. He's taken my keys too.

I dread phoning Mum. I delay as long as possible. I tell her I think Ren has chicken pox and it would be best for us to stay at home.

"Are you sure? Do you want me to come over and have a look? It might just be a rash."

"No. She's got a temperature, and she's really cranky. I'm sure it is. She's sleeping now."

"Okay." Her tone changes, crisp and sharp. She doesn't believe me. "Darren wants to say hello. Merry Christmas."

"Hey sis, what's up with the little one?"

I repeat myself, adding extra details about snuggling up with Peppa Pig and only wanting to drink milk. "Look, I have to go, Sarah's crying. Merry Christmas."

"I love you, sis. Take care, won't you?"

"Love you too," and my voice catches.

The next day, it's just the two of us. We eat chocolate for breakfast and baked beans on toast for lunch. I prop Ren against several cushions when we open her presents, and she plays with the wrapping paper. I take photos of her eager face, because Neil might realize what he's missed and want to see them. I know it's a longshot.

Snap, snap. I catch her surprise at the Jack-in-the-Box, and her delight at the music on her plastic piano. She adores her new green teddy bear and refuses to let him go, even when she's shoving raisins into her mouth or lying on my lap to watch *Elf.*

Neil blunders home after noon on Boxing Day and goes straight to bed. In the kitchen, my jug is full of dead tulips.

2:4Ø A.M.

The mattress is concrete beneath me. I roll to my left, then my right, onto my stomach with my face pushed into the pillow. I lie on my back again, and the mattress punctures my spine. With each movement, the bed squeaks and I get knotted up in the duvet.

Years ago, when I was little, I'd fall asleep to the planes arriving and departing from the airport. Occasionally, an engine would sound different, as though it was in pain, and I'd imagine it would cut out altogether any moment and the plane would plummet onto our house. I'd hold my breath and hide under the duvet—as if my covers would offer any hope of shelter—to avoid the inevitable explosion.

When the airport closed, I struggled with the empty skies—any noise, even the fear of a dying engine, was better than no noise at all. If you listen long enough, silence whistles.

It whistles now, as I strive to hear something.

It's funny how I spent so long yearning for peace and solitude when Ren was born, and now it's the last thing I want.

The Bad Mother

1.

It's my birthday. I'm nineteen. I lie for a moment, enveloped in the frosty February dawn, aware only of my breath entering and leaving my body. A kid at primary school once told me if you exhale long enough, the reflex to inhale again ceases. I breath out for as long as I can.

Out, out… sinking, slowly. Out. Out.

My alarm goes off, and I gasp for breath.

There are no Facebook notifications, no cards in yesterday's post. Nothing to signify it as anything other than an ordinary day. Neil's breakfast is waiting for him to stumble down the stairs. He eats and leaves without mentioning it.

"Just you and me then, Ren. What shall we do? Shall we change your sheets?"

Ren opens her mouth as though she's going to kiss me, but bites into my chin instead and laughs when I say, "Ouch."

Mum takes me for lunch on the Barbican, a café nestled into a Victorian terrace crammed with sofas and two-person tables and pictures covering the yellow walls. Ren's asleep in her pram.

"She's growing so fast," Mum coos, fussing with the blanket.

"She's fine, Mum." *Please don't wake her.*

Mum smiles and slides a small gift box across the table. "Happy birthday, Gracie."

It's a gold locket: my photo sits on one side, Ren's on the other.

"It's beautiful. Thank you."

I stare at Ren's rosy cheeks, her eyes slightly crossed as she focuses on the camera. Her smile is wide and excited. She never looks this happy for me—it seems accidental when she does. My detachment is increasing. I'm captivated by the photo rather than the sleeping child in front of me.

Outside, people unencumbered by prams and baby paraphernalia and responsibilities are skipping past the window, carefree and happy. They laugh as they catch my eye, mocking my reality. I want to run to them and dance in the sunshine with them. I grab hold of the table to prevent myself leaving.

"It's lovely," I repeat, aware of the bustle of the café once more.

Our meals arrive. Mum ordered wine for us, but I don't like the idea of drinking in front of Ren. I take small sips.

"You're quiet. Are you all right?"

"Just tired. Another bad night with madam."

Mum holds her hand to my forehead. "You're a bit warm. Are you ill?"

"No. Like I said…"

"Just tired. Yes." She isn't convinced; I choose to ignore her.

"This chicken is delicious. How's yours?"

"You haven't been yourself for months. And then, there was that Christmas fiasco—"

"What *fiasco?* Sarah was ill."

"Yes. Measles, wasn't it?"

"Chicken pox." When I lie, I always remember what I've said.

She nods tersely. "Of course."

"Do we have to do this again? It was bad timing, I said I was sorry. You all had a good time; I was at home with a grumpy baby."

"You don't have to jump down my throat."

"I don't know what you want me to say. You keep bringing up the same crap all the time, and I'm fed up with it."

We probably look as if we're having a wonderful time. The people over by the wall are watching two women—relationship undetermined—smiling, being convivial.

"I want you to tell me the truth," Mum hisses.

"The truth about what?"

"About your marriage. About Neil. About the bruise on your arm."

My forearm peeks out of my sleeve and I cover it with my other hand. "I fell. I caught my arm on the door."

I see what I'm doing, defending him. If I was watching Jeremy Kyle, I'd be muttering *just tell her the fucking truth, you silly bitch.*

"There's nothing wrong with my marriage," I add, just a moment too late to be credible.

I'm angry because she doesn't already know. I'm angry because I can't tell her.

She takes a deep breath and a mouthful of veg. I drink without thinking; my glass is almost empty.

"Perhaps there are just some things we shouldn't discuss anymore," she says pointedly. "I never thought I'd have to censor conversations with my own daughter, but—"

"You're being ridiculous."

"Am I?" She shrugs and sips her wine. "Maybe I'll have better luck with Sarah. Maybe *she'll* want to talk to me."

Happy birthday to me.

2.

I'm tempted to buy a cake on the way home but can't be bothered in the end.

I consider phoning Mum to apologize, but I don't do that either. We finished lunch with strained small-talk and parted with a brief hug. Perhaps it's best to let it blow over.

The ironing is done and the house smells of curry when Neil gets home. "How was your day?"

"Where were you?"

"With Mum."

"I phoned. Where *were* you?"

"Mum took me for a birthday lunch." *Remember my birthday?*

"Liar. Who is he?"

"I was with Mum. I had Sarah with me."

He snakes his hand through my hair, scrunching it into his fist, and pulls. "You're lying. You always lie."

"You're hurting me."

He twists his hand, pulls harder. I stand on tiptoes to prevent handfuls being ripped from my scalp.

"You can ask my mum." I squeal as he yanks again, then drops me.

Ren, in her highchair, claps her hands and squeezes her toast into her little fist. Just like Daddy.

Neil glares with contempt. We're face to face and I'm frightened. I never say anything, never fight back, never stand my ground. Never tell him how much I hate him when he does this to me.

"You—you can't do this to me. It's not right." My voice is tiny as I try to stop the words seeping out.

"Do what, exactly?"

"Treat me… like this, hurt me."

"You don't get it, do you? It's your fault. You provoke me, you make me do it." There's no expression on his face; his arms are poker-straight by his side. "I give you everything you need, don't I? A house, money for food, clothes. But you go out of your way to make me angry." Mock compassion crosses his face, the *this-will-hurt-me-more* of my childhood. "If you behaved, I wouldn't have to punish you."

"I'm not a child."

"Oh, look at you, getting all riled up now you're a tough nineteen-year-old." He emits an ugly laugh. "What're you gonna do anyway?"

"I'll—" I don't know. "I'll leave. I'll take Sarah and I'll—"

"No, you won't." Each word is eased out and substantial. His voice resonates. Once, it was sexy and moody, now it evokes uncertainty and terror. "You wouldn't last one day as a single mum. You barely cope now. You're useless. You need me."

"That's not true." But it is. Every day is a struggle. Tears prick my eyes, but I keep them in check.

Neil bends toward me so our noses almost touch. "If you ever think about leaving, you'll regret it. Do you understand?"

I swallow and nod.

"Good. Now…" He stands up straight again. "I think the curry's burning. How about we have a couple of beers, to celebrate your birthday?"

Because I can't fight back, because I'm angry and confined and weary, I take money from Neil's wallet and hide it in an old pig-shaped biscuit jar.

I want Ren to stop whining, to sleep through the night so I can rest, to start walking so I don't have to carry her. I want time alone. I want Neil to stop flaunting his freedom while I'm trapped here like Cinderella.

So I take his money because he won't miss it, and it's a tiny act which puts me in control.

A few days later, I take some more.

The next day, when I'm food shopping, I choose the bargains—the 2-for-1 offers, the 2-for-£2s. I put the savings I've made in the pig barrel as well.

The following week, I do the same.

I laugh with childish glee because he has no idea what I'm doing. I've got no plans for the money, but I think I'll treat myself to something special.

3.

The pig jar is filling nicely, mostly with coins. I haven't counted it, but there's a gratifying clunk as the metal hits the pile—the tone changes as the drop reduces.

I force myself into a new kind of contentment, demure and obedient. Hiding bruises and marks and scars from the world, from my parents, from Neil. The house is spotless, and the baby is clean and fed. When Neil comes home drunk, I look after him; when he criticizes, I resolve his issue. A chipped mug thrown away, his favorite jeans washed for the weekend, Ren pacified when he's hungover. His tea is on the table when he comes in from work, his favorite lager is in the fridge.

He's satisfied with this new version of his wife—the tantrums have reduced, the attacks less frequent. I'm only young, after all—it's taken me a while to figure out how to make my marriage work. This is the way it should have been from the start.

The woman in the mirror is disheartened. She frowns with a concern not even Mum is offering. She's a thinner, ashen version of herself. I can't look at her anymore.

Ren-shaped time. First crawl, first tooth. All that's gone before is forgotten. I don't recall a time when her bites didn't pierce my skin and draw tiny droplets of blood.

The sun is warmer; days are dry, rain infrequent. At the park, her bare toes scrunch on the grass. She hates not being able to walk. I put her a quarter of the way up a big-kid slide and guide her to the bottom. She squeals and wants to go again and again, until my back aches. I put her on the swing, but she shrieks with rage.

"You've got a determined one there," says the woman pushing a little girl on the swing beside us. The child stares at Ren with big blue eyes.

"Yes. Hopefully she'll tire herself out."

"How old is she?"

"Almost eleven months."

"Charlotte's fifteen months. She's just started walking."

"How lovely." I move the swing back and forth, not quite letting go. Ren digs her nails into my knuckles.

Charlotte screeches and tries to stand. "Time to go, I think," her mum says, although I'm unsure if she's talking to me or her baby. She pulls the child from the seat and kisses her cheeks with mumumum sounds. Charlotte giggles and puckers her lips in response. "Nice to meet you. I'm sure we'll bump into each other again."

"Yes."

"I'm Kirsty."

"Grace."

A friend! It's been so long since I've had anyone to talk to, apart from Mum and the lady at the newsagent who gives Ren a Freddo bar sometimes. I watch Kirsty walk away, pushing her buggy and letting Charlotte wander. Charlotte picks weeds and Kirsty bends to help her.

Ren holds her hands up to be removed from the swing, and then cries when I lift her out. She squirms from my arms and lands heavily. She pushes herself up onto her hands and feet but can't maneuver herself upright. She falls back and screams, staring at me with dark eyes as though it's my fault.

4.

I'm exhausted, swollen, tender.

I bought a pregnancy test yesterday, hiding it beneath a bunch of grapes in the trolley, and now I'm staring at it in shock. I took the test to *rule out* pregnancy, not confirm it.

Yet a flow of delight trickles over me. I never realized, until this moment, I want another baby. I need one. Because this is the baby who'll love me; the baby who'll make everything else right.

"Oi, Grace." Neil bangs on the bathroom door. "Sarah needs you."

No she doesn't, I mutter to myself. She needs a pair of hands to accommodate her, to do something she can't do herself. It doesn't matter if I'm on the end of those hands or not. They could be anyone's hands. I smile at the woman in the mirror, our secret intact.

"Grace!"

In the kitchen, Ren's standing at the counter trying to reach her cup. I rinse it out and fill it with fresh milk.

"Ta," I say, and she attempts to copy—*aa.* "Are you hungry? Do you want some lunch?" I gather cheese and grapes from the fridge. "You could've done this for her." *It's not hard,* I want to add and bite my tongue.

"How'm I supposed to know what she wants?"

"It's lunch time." *It's bloody obvious!*

I brush my hand against my stomach, and shiver with the thrill. I hug Ren as I lift her into the highchair, and she levers herself away from me with her feet against my hips. I must have done something very wrong— what child avoids cuddles with their mum, or sits in contented solitude to play? What child wants to be so independent before their first birthday? I watch as she carefully places the sandwich into piles of component parts, totally occupied.

The next baby won't be like this. I'll make sure he isn't.

Each time I pass the mirror in the hall, I inspect my stomach. If I push my hips forward and stand at the right angle, a small protrusion is already visible. I don't want to tell anyone; it all goes wrong when other people know. I fold myself forward and the bump vanishes.

I sit in the garden and watch Ren crawling around, squashing bugs between her fingers before I can reach her to say *No!*

Neil stands at the kitchen window with his arms folded and a stern expression. What does he see, I wonder? What's he thinking? I know he loves Ren, but he can't love me, can he? Does he even notice I'm here?

He comes out after a moment, and crouches to see what she's doing. Her face shines, and she offers him the dandelion in her hand, and they discuss the flower in depth—Neil pointing at all the tiny petals, Ren's tongue poking out in concentration. I take surreptitious photos, pretending I'm scrolling Facebook instead. If Neil knew, he'd walk away. I lie on the grass, close my eyes, and listen to the joyful sound of their giggles. Happier without me.

It's not the end of the world. I have a house, security, someone… just someone so I'm not alone. I try to be a good wife, and sometimes he's a good husband. Sometimes I think things are turning a corner, that he's getting used to married life and one day he'll relish it. Other times, the jug in the kitchen is filled with too many flowers.

Neil goes out before tea. Saturdays are different; his evenings start far earlier, and he ends up in the pubs and clubs on the Barbican, losing his friends and himself.

He's back earlier than usual. I've just turned off the light and pretend I'm asleep to avoid him. I wait for the swearing and stumbling and vomiting, but instead, he slips under the duvet and his hand glides across my hips. It's a tender touch. I twist slightly, edging toward him, encouraging his arms all the way around me. He moves closer; his body mirrors mine.

I yield to the hesitant pressure against me. I raise my hips so he can lift my nightshirt. His fingers probe my body until he enters me and pulls me tight against his torso. I sigh and relax into the rhythm, feeling complete.

5.

It looks like rain, so we wrap up for the park this morning. There's no way I'm staying at home with my little banshee. She's pulled the head off a doll, dented the cupboard door under the sink with a saucepan which should have been too heavy for her to hold, and smeared a tube of tooth-paste across the bathroom floor.

Over on the swings, Kirsty's pushing her daughter. I wheel the buggy across the grass and fiddle with the straps, pretending to be distracted so she can make the first move. I'd hate to say hello if she doesn't remember me.

"Hi. Grace?"

"Hello. I didn't see you there—don't they make these clasps tricky?"

I hold Ren's hands and walk her across to the swings between my legs, an awkward and unwieldy action.

"In," Ren says, pointing resolutely.

"Swing," I repeat, and wedge her into the baby seat.

She doesn't want me to push. She forces my hands off the metal bars and kicks her legs frantically, getting nowhere. I approach from behind and give a little nudge.

Both girls get bored at the same time, so we put them on the grass. Charlotte heads for the small flower bed by the railings, and Ren crawls after her. They babble nonsensically to each other, with great concentra-tion.

Kirsty takes a photo. "I'll send it to you."

And we're absorbed with friending each other and cooing over each other's pictures. Hers are filled with smiles and selfies and kisses; mine are blurred, snatched afterthoughts.

I slump back against the bench. My jeans are cutting into my waist. Surely it's too early for maternity clothes—I should at least tell Neil I'm pregnant first.

"Are you okay?"

"Just tired. It hits you like a train sometimes, doesn't it? She's not sleeping well—I was up most of the night."

Ren pulls herself onto her feet using the railings, but they're not even and as she cruises along, she stumbles and falls into the mud. I rush to comfort her, but she pushes me back and crawls away. I remain on my knees for a moment to conceal my mortification.

"Independent thing," I say once I've composed myself, and Kirsty nods sympathetically.

Tears rise, pressure develops in my temples as I try to prevent them. Ren's trying to stand again, this time in the middle of the grass. She topples forward. I stay where I am; I won't be humiliated by my own daughter twice.

Later, while Ren sleeps on the settee, I look at the other photos Kirsty sent to me. Ren's a stranger to me in these pictures. I wonder if I'll recognize her when she starts school, if she'll merge into all the other little girls in her class and I'll bring the wrong one home. Am I a bad person? Is it not her at all, but me? Will I be void of emotion for my next child as well?

Ren stirs, frowning and serious, but doesn't wake. I move on, scrolling through my timeline, liking a couple of statuses of people I barely remember, following a couple of links. Mindless, wasting time. I could be reading, or folding yesterday's laundry.

I'm on a clothes shop site now, coveting beautiful things I'd never wear. All my money goes on Ren, of course; all my clothes are old and baggy and fraying.

Still, there in front of me, is a red dress—a grown-up version of the dress I wore when I met Neil. Elegant, knee-length, in a slinky fabric that would skim my waist and disguise my bulge. Even Neil would approve. I buy it on a whim and log off immediately.

6.

"What's this?" Neil holds the dress above his head.

Shit. "I don't know."

"*You* bought this." He has the packaging in his other hand.

It arrived yesterday. I panicked and shoved it into the cupboard in the living room without thinking.

"You opened my post?" Stupid girl. That's the least of my worries.

He steps forward and pushes the dress into my face. "Why are you buying slutty clothes? For your boyfriend?"

"I thought you'd like it…"

His eyes darken. His fist clenches around the dress. He throws it to the floor, and it lies like a dead body at my feet.

"Where did you get the money from?"

"I… When I go shopping… sometimes there's a bit of money…" I take a shaky breath.

"So you're scrimping on food to buy things for yourself? Using *my* money?"

"No! It's not like—"

He wraps a hand around my neck, squeezing. I gasp for breath and he shoves me to the floor. I land on my knees beside the dress. I hate that dress. I try to get up and he pushes me down with his foot, pressing against my pregnant stomach.

His foot grinds against my hip, his face knotted into disproportionate rage. He shifts his weight until I yelp.

He's a giant looming above me with ferocious scorn. He kicks.

Once, then again. With all his might. Cracking against my pelvis.

Pain seers through me like a hot knife.

The life inside me dies.

He leaves me on the floor. He goes into the kitchen and grabs a lager from the fridge. The can hisses open. I listen for his footsteps returning, but he remains there and shuts the door.

I haul myself up, steadying myself against the settee, unable to stand straight. Blood trails down my thighs and seeps into my jeans.

I don't cry. I clean myself up; I change my clothes. I check on Ren, fast asleep in her cot.

I don't cry later, when I'm browning the mince and peeling potatoes for tea. Or the next day, when Neil leaves for work and the hours spread out in front of me.

My anguish is too vast. If I start crying, it'll engulf me.

The woman in the mirror is hollow, alone. She gazes as though she doesn't know me. Her eyes are dull and haunted. I witness the moment her heart breaks. My heart. My break.

Ren's oblivious. She plays with her bricks and her dolls, neither needing nor wanting me. Barely noticing I'm there. When Neil comes home, he drops flowers on the kitchen counter, and Ren holds her arms out to him to be picked up and hugged.

I'm overwhelmed with grief. I can't be here. "I'm going to the shop. We need milk." And I walk away, leaving Ren behind. If she wants him, she can have him. I limp to the shop and stand outside.

What am I doing? Am I really just buying milk and going home? I've got nowhere else to go. I could keep walking. I could catch a bus to Totnes or go north and get lost on Dartmoor. People disappear all the time; no one would miss me. In a few months' time, someone might realize and say, "Have you seen Grace?"

In the end, I buy milk and go home.

7.

The house is clean, dusted, polished. I cook but can't face eating. I dust the tops of the cupboards and move furniture to vacuum underneath. I wash the curtains. I'm restrained and obedient. Meek and compliant. I remain at home, anxious someone will detect the remnants of pregnancy around me and the soreness with which I'm still moving.

The emptiness doesn't wane. It grows more potent, nestling deep within me, colonizing the space my child has relinquished.

One night, unable to bear the bleakness any longer, I take one of Neil's lagers. Bubbles gurgle to the surface and froth fizzes over my hand. It's a harsh taste, strong and sharp and cheap. I prefer vodka or rum, things I can add cola to. I force myself to swallow, and it slips down my throat with a shiver.

It should have been the answer; it should have made my world rose-tinted and untroubled after one drink. But there's no difference. Still ugly and desolate. I fetch another one, gulping it down in case Neil returns early, and disposing the evidence.

I'm not mellow like Neil is when he's had a few. I'm not calm or jovial. I want to cry—a single tear lingers on my cheek, an icicle. Then a stream of them prickle my face. I surrender, allowing a torrent to overpower me. I gulp air between sobs, lungs inflamed. I press my face into a cushion, so I don't wake Ren.

When the tears stop, I'm drained. I go to bed and drift into a restless, dream-riddled sleep.

8.

For Ren's first birthday, I bake a cake. I've never done it before, and my first attempt is soggy—it slops over the side of the tin and covers the oven in gloopy gunk. I prod it, and it wobbles like jelly.

The second is rock hard and the edges are crispy. I've run out of time, so I put a candle on top and cover it with flakes of chocolate and red icing—the only coloring I had. It looks like it's been stabbed to death.

Neil sneers when I bring it to the table and light the candle. "What the hell is that?"

I lean forward and help Ren blow it out, preventing her from grabbing the hot wax.

"I ain't eating this crap."

I cut small slices. "But it's her first birthday cake, you have to have a piece."

He pushes his plate away, propelling it across the table and onto the floor. *Crash!*

Ren does the same, copying Daddy, but I catch her bowl just in time.

Neil stands and I flinch as his arm brushes the top of my head. I watch him cautiously, in case I need to duck out of his way. He grabs his jacket and leaves. Ren gurgles and coos. I spoon cake into her mouth, but she sucks off the chocolate and icing and spits out the rest.

So, I eat it, her slice and mine. Chewing steadily and swallowing it down with gulps of water. It swells in my stomach and I unbutton my jeans. It's disgusting, but I won't have Neil finding our barely-touched pieces stuffed into the bin. After I've bathed Ren and tucked her in with her Christmas teddy, I cut another slice. Eventually, I find a Tupperware box and put it away for tomorrow.

In the living room, I tidy away the wooden train set Mum and Dad gave Ren earlier. I think Dad had more fun with it than she did. Ren delighted in unwrapping the box and throwing the paper into the air. Dad made up the track, filling the room.

I didn't ask them to stay. Mum made pointed remarks which I ignored. Dad played with the train track long after Ren had lost interest.

When the room is Neil-approved tidy, I snap the tab off a lager and switch on the TV. The more I drink, the easier it is to tolerate the taste. I rest my head against the back of the settee and listen to an old episode of *The Big Bang Theory.* I didn't mean for the lager to become a regular thing, but the evenings are long, lonely places. Waking with a fuzzy head isn't ideal, it makes Ren's whining harder to bear, but I manage. I have several mugs of tea, while she eats her breakfast, to edge myself into the day.

When my eyes start to close of their own accord, I go to bed. It's only half-past eight, but for at least one more day, my sorrow is deflected.

3:1Ø A.M.

Here's something I've never told anyone—one of those memories you bury deep down and hope you'll realize it was never a real event but something you once saw on TV.

I abandoned my daughter in a supermarket.

She was about five months old, I suppose, asleep in her pram—her fingers entwined in the white crochet blanket Mum had just given her. She looked so angelic, but I was already dreading her waking again.

In the home baking section, I clicked on the buggy's brakes and put the basket down on the floor. I don't remember what I was looking for, but I was engrossed by various bags of sugar for a second—icing and caster and granulated. I side-stepped as the enormous variety of sugar gave way to tubs of hundreds and thousands and tiny bottles of flavoring and coloring.

The farther away from Ren I was, the more relaxed I became. I shuffled toward the flour, barely paying attention to the items on the shelves, until I reached the shoe polish and laces on the display at the end. It was a quick pivot into the next aisle entirely.

Now I was looking at rice and pasta, at sauces and condiments. I waited, perhaps hoping for intervention, for someone to notice Ren all alone and raise the alarm. No one did. There was no loudspeaker announcement, no staff hurrying to the spot. Farther away. Closer and closer to the tills, to the exit.

A child started to wail. Mum once told me you recognize your own child's cries, a secret language between the two of you, but I never could. It echoed around the shop, coming from everywhere at once. Suddenly, a woman walked around the corner, the screaming baby clasped to her chest and an apologetic smile on her face.

Not Ren after all. Not my baby.

But I realized what I was doing, what I was about to do. I ran back, wracked with guilt and panic and the fear of being exposed as a terrible mother. Worse than terrible. I'd left her. My own daughter. I was going to walk away and pretend she'd never existed.

As I reached the buggy, a member of staff was approaching from the opposite direction. She looked at me with curiosity, smiled briefly, and continued on her way.

Ren was asleep, looking angelic, with her fingers woven into the crocheted holes of her new blanket.

The Runaway

1.

I haven't seen Kirsty for a while; I'm avoiding her. Each time I reach the park, I scan for her, veering away if I spot her cerise raincoat. I catch up with her on Facebook, like her photos and comment on memes she shares, but I can't be friends with her now. I haven't got the strength to be happy.

Today, Ren runs into her by accident before I have a chance to steer her away.

"Look at you, walking all by yourself." She ruffles Ren's hair and Ren toddles off to find Charlotte. She straightens up. "Hi Stranger, I thought it had been a while, but…" She indicates toward Ren.

I pull my sleeves down to cover the green and purple bruises on my arm—one recent, one less so.

"I was starting to think you were avoiding me." And she laughs.

I wish I was Kirsty. So joyful and relaxed, secure enough to make jokes and not worry they're true.

"I've had a lot going on." In comparison, my voice is dull and quivering. I think of something to add but draw a blank. "Busy," I say inexplicably.

She pauses with curiosity, then chats amiably about the weather and the unkempt state of the park. I only have to nod or make encouraging noises for her to continue, and I'm more grateful than I can explain to her.

As she talks, I reach into my bag for my phone, scraping around the edges. It's not there. I retain my smile, but this isn't good. Neil sometimes phones or texts, and I need to reply.

"I have a confession," Kirsty says.

I don't think I've kept up with the flow of her conversation. "Oh?"

I pat my back pocket—sometimes I put my phone in there when Ren distracts me.

"I'm…" She stops and sighs. "I know this is none of my business and tell me to butt out if you want, but I'd hate myself if I didn't say something."

My expression is blank. I am blank. I slide my hand into my jacket pocket. Shit—I must have left it at home.

"Are you okay? Sometimes you look sad, and I've seen... some..." She nods toward my wrists.

My sleeve has ridden up, showing off the raw wound where Neil twisted my skin a couple of nights ago. I'm wearing foundation to disguise swelling around my eye, but I don't think she's noticed. I hide my hand behind my back.

"It's nothing. I'm clumsy. And I've been upset recently because"—I inhale, preparing for the horrible words I'm about to say—"I miscarried."

Her eyes widen and her cheeks turn deep crimson. "Oh shit, I'm so sorry." She rests her hand on my shoulder. "Oh God, you must think I'm such a prat."

"No, it's nice to have someone who cares." But I'm withdrawing, sinking back into my skin. Heavy makeup hides a multitude of wounds. How closely is she watching me? Can she see all my flaws? I thought I'd been so discreet, but obviously not.

First the phone, now this. The world is balancing on a tightrope. I want to leave. I wait for a pause in her dialogue to extract myself. I don't want to be rude, but in a minute, I will be—I'll stand abruptly and call Ren over, and say I'm so sorry but I've remembered an important appointment. And I'll wave goodbye with a promise to call her, knowing I probably won't.

2.

Neil's at the front door when I get home, waiting for me. Scowling, simmering.

"Where've you been?" His voice is graveled and foreboding.

"I met a friend."

I unclasp Ren's buggy straps and she clambers out. She grabs her beaker from the tray underneath and waddles into the living room.

"It's quarter to five."

"I didn't realize it was so late. Sarah was playing with her little girl."

"You've never mentioned this *friend* before."

I don't tell you everything. I wheel the buggy into the corner of the kitchen. "I bump into her sometimes and we chat."

He holds my phone out. "You didn't take this. I didn't know where you were."

"I know, I forgot it today."

"What are you hiding? Where were you, really?"

"With my friend. In the park." I glance at the clock. "I need to get tea on."

"How can I trust you when you sneak off all the time?"

"I wasn't sneaking. I was with Sarah, for God's sake."

I don't notice him lunge. I'm not braced for the slap. My cheek stings. The impact jolts me backwards. I duck from the next one.

He grabs my wrist and twists my arm behind my back, pushing me onto my knees. Pain shoots through my elbow. I wriggle to escape. I lash out and he laughs. In my fury, I bite his forearm.

Shit. Shit. Shit.

I scramble to my feet and run to the living room. He follows. He throws a mug; it grazes my head and smashes against the wall. I dash to the patio doors and out into the garden.

Neil pauses, his face contorted and puce. I shuffle backwards, keeping distance between us, a step away for every one he takes toward me.

He grabs the rake leaning against the house. We both stare at it, fore-seeing his next move.

"Neil, please…"

He leaps with the prongs raised. I turn and shriek. He brings the rake down, digging the rusted metal into my back, and drags it along my spine.

Skin tears like chiffon.

Blood drips like sweat.

My howl reverberates along the line of gardens.

Neil drops the rake, shock etched into his face. He trembles—from rage or panic, I don't know. We're motionless, rooted. Birds tweet, the air ambulance speeds toward the hospital. One or two faces appear at windows. He flees inside.

The ragged edges of skin catch on my shirt as I stagger to my feet and wince.

A neighbor appears at the fence, then another from the garden further along.

"You okay, love?" asks the first, tentatively.

I don't know her name—I don't know any of them. Neil doesn't like me talking to them, so I don't.

"I'm… fine. Thank you." Words guarded, emotions reined in and subdued.

"You need help, love. You need to get away with that babby of yours."

"No, no it's not like that."

"I can hear through the walls, you know, love—they're not that thick. I know it's not the first time."

Neil's watching from the house, his expression indecipherable, his arms crossed. I prickle with fear.

"You have to leave me alone," I whisper to the neighbor at the fence. "Please. Just leave me alone."

I walk rigidly upstairs to the bathroom and lock the door. I collapse against the sink and catch sight of the woman who lurks in the mirror. She's tormented and petrified. The wounds throb; streaks of blood smear my slashed shirt. I lift it and twist to check the deep punctures in the reflection.

"Grace, come on, come out."

"I'm washing my hands."

The woman in the mirror can't stop trembling. Water runs red as it cascades over her hands and splashes up her arms.

He's blocking my path when I open the door. He bends and rests his forehead on mine, skin grinding against skin.

"One day, my darling," he says in a wretched, agonized tone, "you'll go too far. You'll make me so angry I won't be able to stop. I won't *want* to stop. Do you understand?"

"Yes."

"Is that what you want?"

"No," although I don't even make a sound this time.

He stands straight and, with his forefinger under my chin, tilts my face up. He kisses me softly, pats down his jacket pockets, and leaves.

This isn't right. I've been fooling myself, pretending this is normal. But it isn't, is it?

3.

The woman in the mirror is misshapen. Her cheek bulges, her eye is swollen shut, painful when she blinks. The cuts on her back are deep crevasses and inflamed welts.

She's fractured. Her whole existence crushed into tiny pieces. We've both been stripped back to essentials.

I pack without thinking. Too late for anything else. Once Ren is in bed, I shove as much as I can into the two holdalls I find in the cupboard under the stairs. One will loop over the handles of the buggy; I'll carry the other.

The frayed layers of skin on my back catch every time I move, drawing spots of blood.

I pull the pig jar from its hiding place behind bottles of pasta sauce and cans of soup. I sit at the dining table and count.

There's less than two hundred quid. Hardly anything. I count again, stacking coins into one-pound piles, bunching those into groups of ten. A hundred and sixty-two pounds, thirty-two pence. I brush away frustrated tears. It's far less than I thought, far less than it *ought* to be.

Neil must have discovered it—stealing back the money I've been taking from him.

How can I do anything with a hundred and sixty-two quid?

And yet, I must.

Ren wakes early the next day, so I dress and feed her hastily, glancing over my shoulder the whole time. We creep out, clicking the door into its frame so the slam won't wake Neil.

The soft *pud-pud* of the wheels as they pass over cracks in the pavement sends Ren back to sleep. She's dreaming, her hand reaching to grab invisible things. Her face crumples into a smile and a little giggle erupts. Then she's snoring again, sucking her thumb.

She keeps me walking. Alone, I'd turn back, or sit on the curb and give up. The further I walk, the heavier the bags become. The striped wounds shear on my cotton vest. I stop and switch the load around every so often, flinching as the developing scabs split.

We live on a hill. My parents—where of course I'll end up because I've got nowhere else to go—live on another hill. Between us Forder Valley is a deep groove in the landscape. I cut through the sleepy housing estate, checking over my shoulder, and brace myself for the steep climb.

I ring their doorbell, too exhausted to find my key.

"Gracie. What a surprise. Come in." She casts her eye over my bags. "What's going on?"

Ren rouses at the sound of Granny's voice. "Ga-ga."

"I've left him." And as I say it aloud for the first time, I break down into tears.

Mum takes over. She brings the buggy into the house, removes the bag from my shoulder, fills Ren's cup with milk and puts the kettle on. It's all so swift and comforting. I curl up on the settee and exhaustion hits me.

Ren drinks her milk and chomps happily on a rusk while Mum sits on the floor beside me, stroking my cheek. Ren thinks it's funny and pats my head too, getting damp, biscuity fingers caught in my hair.

"You should have said something. I asked. You never said."

I shrug. "This is me saying something."

"How did Neil take it?"

"He doesn't know. He was in bed when we left."

The gravity of the situation thunders down on me. I've left my abusive husband and gone to the first place he'll think to look. What am I doing?

"I shouldn't be here." I try to sit up, but my top catches on my back. I grimace.

"Show me," Mum says, and I obey—staring into the corner of the room so I don't meet her eye.

"Oh, Gracie…"

Mum fetches her first aid kit and tends to me gently, washing the cuts with water, dabbing with antiseptic which stings so much I bite into a cushion and Ren laughs. She slathers cream and dresses it properly, wrapping bandages around my torso. The relief is immense.

I lie down and close my eyes. The noises in the room and outside the window dissolve. I relax fully, not with one ear open, not with my arms folded to protect me, or balled up tightly to make myself innocuous. But I dream of Neil chasing me, so much faster than I can run. On a merry-go-round, the horses come alive and rear up. Ren's an adult and telling me how I've ruined her life.

I was just doing my best. I was doing it for you.

When I wake, the room is familiar and warm—I'm home ill from school, tucked up with a mug of hot chocolate, and *This Morning* on the telly.

No, that's not right…

Ren!

Where's Ren?

I struggle to my feet, heart racing, a dense knot of panic in my stomach. Then I hear a giggle from the kitchen while Mum sings nursery rhymes.

"She woke about an hour ago," Mum says when I stand at the kitchen door. "You were zonked so we left you alone. We baked some fairy cakes for lunch." She points out the cake mix slopped all over the worktop, and all over Ren's euphoric face. "She's so adorable, so much like you at that age." She smiles wistfully.

"Well, let's hope she doesn't screw her life up like I have." I don't need to be reminded of what could have been, I know. Right now, I should be starting my second year at uni. I could be meeting exciting new people, planning my travels and future life. I'm not. I'm here.

Mum's lip twitches but she remains silent. Sorrow, exasperation, trepidation—it's hard to tell what she's thinking. She fills the kettle, takes the buns out of the oven and turns them out onto the cooling rack. Ren's fascinated, peering to look, but holding back when Granny says, "Hot."

4.

My bedroom still has remnants of my life from before. Boxes stacked against the wall to be collected, but ultimately forgotten. Clothes Neil wouldn't approve of hanging in the wardrobe, two sizes too small now anyway; History textbooks and nineteenth-century novels with tiny print on my shelves alongside folders stuffed with notes, as if I'm going to continue where I left off.

My last-year self floats around the room, ghost-like, reminding me of my choices and my mistakes. If I was at university, this room would be just the same, permitting me to fall back into its easy rhythms. But my return would be anticipated. It wouldn't be a failure.

As it is, it's repelling me.

There's commotion when Dad comes home, as he sweeps down on Ren with delight and smothers her with noisy kisses. I grip the edge of my bed, pretending for a moment I haven't heard him return—but I can't hide here forever.

He says, "I'll kill him," when I explain everything, and I think he means it. His eyes are hard and fearsome.

"It doesn't matter now, we're here, and we're okay." I lean my head against his arm. "I just want to forget him."

We don't tell him the full extent of my injuries. It's for the best, we decided—and based on his reaction, we were right.

"We can decorate Darren's old room for Sarah," Mum says lightly, as if she's only just thought of it. I can tell her brain's been busy all afternoon. "Unless you want it, Grace?"

It's the bigger room, he was the older child. I shake my head.

"Something pink," she continues. "You can make a four-poster bed, Mike—a little Sarah-sized one, like you did for Gracie. Remember?"

"You don't need to go to any trouble. She's just a baby, she won't notice."

"Rubbish. We want to spoil her, don't we, Grandad?"

Dad gazes into the conversation with confusion. His eyes are distant and pensive. He'll be confronting Neil, in his head; they'll probably be fighting, Dad will have him pinned against a wall. "Um…"

"I'll start packing up the room. It's only a few boxes. We'll have it finished by Sunday." She leans back and frowns. "We'll need a solicitor, I suppose, for the divorce. Will he cause problems, do you think?"

Solicitors? Divorce? "I haven't thought about it. I don't know." Too much, too soon.

"Not to worry. We'll get you settled first, then make a list of what needs to be done." If nothing else, she loves making lists.

I put Ren down in a drawer, emptied out and heavily padded with blankets—she wriggles too much to sleep in bed with me. She's snug in there, tucked up with big brown eyes peering over the top of the blanket, listening to Grandad singing a lullaby.

Mum works her way through the soaps, and I scroll through Facebook beside her. Kirsty has shared a parenting meme on my timeline, but I don't reply. I don't want Neil latching on to the conversation. I consider messaging her, but I don't know her well enough—I don't want her thinking badly of me.

Occasionally, Mum scribbles something in her notebook, or mumbles to Dad or raises her voice to speak to me. Her mind is racing, just as mine is slowing down.

It's only nine when I go to bed. It's been the longest day. I creep around my room in the pitch black so not to wake Ren. She's breathing harmoniously and knocking her dummy on the wooden side of her drawer as she sucks. Mum and Dad go to bed soon after, turning off lights, taking their mugs into the kitchen, checking the doors. All the reassuringly safe sounds of my childhood.

5.

I don't sleep well. Tossing and turning, dreaming I'm back home and Neil's discovered my plan to abscond. I wake almost every hour. Once familiar sounds are foreign now—houses speak different languages, and I've forgotten this one.

Dad leaves for work and I eat my breakfast at the living room window, staring along the street. Ren hasn't stirred. Already she's more settled here than in her own home.

Mum takes the day off, even though I tell her we'll be fine. She says she's owed some hours so it's not a problem.

"We can go for a walk," she says, and I shake my head.

"Can't we stay here? Just... here?" Inside, behind the curtains, hidden where no one will find me.

"If you like." She makes a clipped sound with her tongue. "You did the right thing."

I nod. "I know."

"What's wrong, then?"

"I don't know."

The first schoolkids make their way to school. With every shriek or skidding bike wheel, I jump.

"Come and sit down," she says when I meander back to the kitchen. "You'll give yourself indigestion."

I raise my eyebrow, with a smile. "I'm going to turn into you, aren't I? I'll be telling Ren that eating her crusts will give her curly hair and carrots will help her see in the dark."

I head for the hall. Mum follows.

"Are you really so worried?"

"I don't know."

"He'd be foolish to come here, with me and your dad around."

"I suppose." Not foolish, but arrogant—an innate belief he's always right, that he can do what he wants to me.

Ren calls out and Mum fetches her. She makes scrambled egg and cuts toast into soldiers. Ren eats the bread and squishes the egg between her fingers.

I return to my lookout at the window. We shouldn't have come here. There are refuges for women like me—I should have waited, planned properly. *This* was foolish.

There's something effortless about being in my childhood home. It lacks the discomfort of Neil's house, the sense—even now—of not belonging. Ren becomes easier. She brings me her dolly to rock to sleep and passes me a cup of tea she's pretended to make. She chatters to herself, lyrical muttering I can almost understand.

This is how it's supposed to be, and it's nice. It's how I thought mother-hood would be.

I can't help but peer outside, though. Just in case. I bristle occasionally, as though Neil's watching us. I feel his finger scratch down my spine, although it's just the scabs starting to heal.

6.

I'm turning into my mother, writing lists—of things I want to do, of things I need to do, of things I'd like to do in the far-flung future:
Get a job
Burn everything that reminds me of Neil
Do fun things with Ren
Go on a foreign holiday, on a plane!
Make Ren love me

The doorbell rings just as Ren climbs onto the settee and curls up to sleep. Now her eyes are open and alert. My heart pounds. I'm alone; I should ignore it. It rings again, and I open it.

Neil stands in front of me, stony-faced. "Hello Grace."

I try to slam the door, but he's quicker and stronger than me. He puts his foot in the way, and it bounces off him. He strides inside.

"My dad's upstairs—"

"No, he's not. He's at work. And so's your mum. It's just you and me." He shuts the door behind him. The tiny clunk reverberates.

"I'll scream."

"Is that anyway to greet your husband?"

I shake my head demurely. I know I'm demure, that's how stupid he makes me. I know I fall back into the same pattern and can't fight my way out. I picture all the things I want to do to him, all the ways I want to hurt him.

He struts into the living room and winks at Ren who's climbing down from the settee and holding her arms out to him. He doesn't pick her up. He slumps into the armchair.

"What have you been telling mummy and daddy about me, then?"

"Nothing." My voice trembles.

"Good girl. I'd hate them to think badly of me after I made an honest woman out of their pathetic daughter. They should be grateful." He fixes me with a stony glare. "You should be grateful. Do you think you are? Do you think walking out on me shows gratitude?"

"You need to leave."

"Not without you and Sarah. You're coming back with me."

Ren gurgles and smiles at her father. No matter how threatening, how scary and severe he is, she's always happy to see him. It's a disloyalty which cuts me. Neil sweeps Ren into his arms with a smirk.

"Give her to me."

He won't hurt her. She nuzzles her face into his chest, and he kisses her forehead. But all the time he's watching me, gauging my reaction.

I hold out my hands for her, but she turns her head away. "Sarah, come to Mummy."

I want to rip her from his arms, run, run away. But I'm rooted to the spot.

"Oh, Grace, you'll never learn, will you? No one wants you. No one loves you. I'm your best hope."

He wraps Ren in a bear hug, and she giggles. He holds her above his head and makes the noise of an airplane, swooping her in a figure of eight. They rub noses, and Ren blows him kisses.

"Don't pretend you love her. You don't."

"It's funny, isn't it, how you can love someone so much, someone you never thought you would?" He flicks his eyes toward me. "Sarah, I mean. Not you. You're just some knocked-up bitch who trapped me. But Sarah…" He smiles and it's genuine. I've never seen his eyes light up before—soft and playful and indulgent.

Her head rests on his shoulder, her eyes closing. Neil kisses the top of her head and her little hands brush him away. He lays her down on the settee, extracting his arm carefully so not to wake her.

"So, you see, I can't let you take her away. I'd miss her too much."

He sighs, weighing up this hefty conundrum, and sits down again. It's half-past one. Hours until Mum and Dad come home. He pulls a hip flask from his jacket pocket and offers it to me. I keep one eye on Ren. If I was quick enough, I could snatch her up, I could run.

"I thought you loved me," he says, "and yet you don't trust me enough to take a drink from me. It hurts, you know that? Right here." He thumps his hand against his chest, but as ever a smirk is lurking.

I don't move. He unscrews the lid and takes a gulp, then offers it to me again.

"I should go. You don't want me here, you never wanted me at all, did you? Prissy little goody-two…" He breaks himself off and forces a smile. "Just a sip, for old times' sake, and then I'll go. I promise."

He won't leave it alone. If I don't take it, he could be here all day, here when my parents come home. I take the flask, pretending to sip, but he tips from the bottom and pours it into my mouth and down my chin. It's not the vodka I was expecting—it's hot and sharp, catching the back of my throat.

"That's it. Good girl."

"You have to go now. You said you would go."

He edges forward in the chair, then stops. "Nah. Not without you. You're my wife, and you're coming home with me."

My fists tighten behind my back. My shoulders hunch. Enough. No more. I'm standing, he's sitting. I lurch downwards and lash out, kicking and punching hard into his chest. Not hard. Not at all. He pushes me away with his foot into my stomach.

Stands and towers over me. Grabs my throat and holds me at arm's length

I can't reach him. I twist and grapple and kick and scrap.

My hissing maternal instinct comes surging out of me. My fight for survival.

He tightens his grasp and I struggle to breathe.

Ren stirs. One day, she'll remember this as the day her father killed her mother, and it'll destroy her.

He laughs and releases me. I crumple to my knees. He kicks out, catching my lip.

I grunt. Metallic blood fills my mouth, and everything is black.

When I come to, Neil's carrying me upstairs. I'm flipped over his shoulder and my head bounces against his back. It's such a long way to the bottom of the stairs. I tighten my arms around his waist to prevent him throwing me.

"Ren? Where's Ren?"

"Sssh," he says tenderly.

He opens the doors in turn to find my room. He dumps me onto my bed, and I fold into a heap.

"Where is she?"

He covers me with my duvet and kisses my forehead. He runs his fingers around my lips and pinches my cheeks to open my mouth. He pours the liquid from the hip flask and I choke on it. His hands circle my throat, like all the times before, and this is it. This is the moment he kills me. I wait for the punch, the kick, the hands closing in and stealing the air from me.

Nothing happens. He walks away. It's dark again.

Wake up, wake up… Tiny hands prod me, shake me. Ren? I groan and pull away. It's too early. *Wake up, it's not time for you yet.* I'm so tired. Just let me sleep.

7.

"Grace. Gracie!"

Mum's beside me, shaking me, rousing me. A heavy beat pulses around my head. I try to move, but my body is swollen and painful. Mum opens my eyes with her fingers and wipes my face with a tissue.

"What's going on?" Dad's here too. "Where's Sarah?"

I see his lips moving; the words don't make sense.

Sarah? Ren. I was dreaming about her, about Neil. Neil was here. Neil took Ren.

"Gone… Neil… Ren gone." My tongue is thick and uncooperative. I brush my hand over my face—the left side is distended and sore.

"He did this?" Dad's fury propels him toward the top of the stairs and back. "I'm going to kill that son of a bitch."

"Dad. No."

He kneels beside me and strokes my forehead. "Look what he's done to you." I think he's crying, but I can't be sure. "He's abducted my grandchild."

"His daughter…" What the hell! I'm still defending him?

My heartbeat drums into my skull. My head swims. I feel sick.

Mum and Dad are animated, silhouetted against the sunlight pouring in. Dad leaves; Mum stands stock-still and scared. The front door slams.

"He'll get hurt," I whisper.

"I couldn't stop him." She grabs her phone and dials 999. She garbles through the events and gives my address. Neil's address. "Please hurry."

Mum helps me stand, taking my weight. I'm dizzy looking down the stairs, remembering the bumping motion as I clung to Neil, terrified he'd simply let go and watch me tumble.

My bloody handprint should be on the wall. Pictures should be dislodged; coats from the rack should be strewn across the floor. Vases should be smashed, and furniture pushed out of place. I remember. My frantic struggle. My scramble away from him. My blood everywhere.

But there's no hint of anything amiss. Everything in its place, everything clean and neat and tidy. The bastard tidied up. I laugh at the irony. I laugh and laugh until tears stream from my eyes and I can't stop.

"I'll put the kettle on. We should probably sober you up before the police come," Mum says.

"I'm not drunk."

"You reek of it, Gracie."

"No, Neil made me drink something. He had a flask."

He had a flask. He did. I remember.

The only time I've ever seen Dad cry was when our dog Benny died. Not torrents, but not a solitary tear either. He came from the vet's and sat in the garden beside the plot he'd dug in preparation. He couldn't bring himself to put the body in the hole. Darren and I watched helplessly from Darren's bedroom window.

When he comes back from confronting Neil, he sits heavily in his chair in the living room without acknowledging us, blank and shattered, gasping with raw sobs.

Outside, a police car idles while the officer inside talks on his radio then drives away.

"What happened? Where's Sarah?" Mum demands, and he mumbles a reply.

From my fetal position on the settee, I can't make out what he's saying, but Mum gasps and holds her hand to her mouth. I strain to listen, to concentrate.

"Where's my baby?"

Dad exhales. "The police checked her over—she's fine."

"Why didn't you bring her home?"

He rests his head in his hands, his fingers latticed together as if he's praying. "It's not that simple."

He mumbles something to Mum. They lean in close, excluding me. Their conversation is insistent and frenetic. Then Mum kneels beside me.

"Neil says he came to talk, and you were drunk—"

"He had a flask. He forced me to drink."

"He says you've been drinking a lot recently. He's counted the bottles and cans."

"One or two. Hardly anything." My voice is getting smaller. They're not listening to me.

"He put you to bed, for your own safety, and took Sarah because you weren't in any state to look after her—"

"He hit me. Look at my face."

"He said you fell while he was here. You caught your cheek on the coffee table."

I didn't. That didn't happen. They're not listening to me. He hit me. I remember.

"I want my baby."

"Social services are going to visit, and if they're happy, she'll stay with Neil for the time being."

Waves of nausea pass over me. I stop listening. My eyes are heavy, and I rest my head on the cushion, shuffling to get comfy.

In place of my parents, Neil's bearing down on me, telling me I'm a bad mother and Ren doesn't love me. Ren skips past, older, six or seven. She points and screams, "I hate you." Then Neil's beside her, and Janie and my parents, and my brother Darren. And they all hate me.

3:43 A.M.

Intermittently, car headlights streak across the ceiling; shadows elongate and fade. The noise of the engine lasts longer, and I try to guess whether it's turning left or right at the end of the road. Where do people go at this time of night? Are they coming home from an evening out, a taxi full of revelers giddy with alcohol? Or are they going—an early airport transfer, perhaps, to Exeter or Bristol, heading somewhere exotic?

I scroll through my Twitter feed, glancing apathetically at the 280-character ruminations of strangers—millions of disconnected people searching for someone to bond with.

I type something about not being able to sleep but discard it rather than post it. No one cares what I have to say. I want to put something meaningful, something worth sharing and liking. But most of the time I talk about the weather and what I had for lunch.

What could I write today? I have so much to say, my life still unraveling—I just want it to stop. Telling strangers would be easier than telling my parents. I picture sitting around an enormous table, sharing coffee with countless people, as we all spout our two-sentence soundbites.

I picture myself standing on a mountain and shouting into the vast valley below. That's more like it. We're all standing on our own mountain, striving to be heard.

The minutes pass like hours.

When my hands go numb, I drop the phone to the floor and my mind is blank. I'm deluged with darkness, swamped by the pitch black pre-dawn sky.

The Ghost

1.

Ren cries at four every morning. She kicks off her blankets while she sleeps and at four o'clock, she's cold enough to need tucking back in. I smooth her hair and stroke her cheeks until her tiny thumb jams into her mouth and her eyelids flicker. I watch the glimmer of a dream on her face.

Tonight, when I wake at four, Ren's drawer is redundant beside my bed. In bleary-eyed confusion, I wait for her to cry out. The silence of the room is punctuated with the spasmodic drone of traffic on the main road, the trickle of next door's water feature they forgot to switch off, my mother sobbing in her room.

But Ren isn't crying.

Ren isn't here.

I skulk downstairs, glancing into the shadowed corners in case she's hiding, playing peek-a-boo—in case we've been accidentally overlooking her for hours. I search for a packet of biscuits or a bar of chocolate to distract me. In the fridge, there are several stubby bottles of lager. I take one, without thinking.

Wrapped up in my duvet, I sip the lager, the cool liquid trickling down my throat. And it's not enough. It's not nearly enough.

I wake up. When did I fall asleep?

I dreamed about Ren, of course. She was sitting in her cot, in her blacked-out room, in an empty house, all alone. Neil was out, because he's *always* out.

Always out... He is! How can he look after her when he's always at work or in the pub? He has no idea what she likes to play with, what her favorite CBeebies program is, when she naps, that she likes scrambled egg but never omelette. Did he have any idea what he was doing when he took her?

I dress quickly, gulp a mug of tea and bowl of Shreddies, and leave. I need to see Ren. I have to get her back.

It's peculiar to walk without a pushchair, to swiftly maneuver around obstacles and get on a bus without struggle. My arms hang by my side, superfluous, limp. My body is lighter and more agile. Yet, my legs are sluggish; my head filled with shadows weighing me down.

Outside my own home, I'm an impostor. Inside are my books and clothes, my washing-up gloves and my towels and my ironing board, my duvet, my favorite chocolates in the fridge. And my child.

The door's locked. My key doesn't work. I bang against the glass.

"Neil. Neil!"

I stand on the boundary, where the grass bleeds straight into the pavement, and scan the windows at the front of the house, in case he's hiding in the corners of the rooms. Curtains twitch in several of the neighboring houses, but I don't care.

"I want Sarah. I want my daughter!"

I'm brave, now, when it's too late. I'm invincible. I can do anything I want. I can stand up to him when there's a locked door between us. I beat my hands against the door again, yelling for Neil to come and admit what he's done, rising into hysteria and anguish. Rage surges. I want to kick the door down; in this mania, I think I could.

My energy depletes. My arms tire and drop to my side. I rest my head against the door, giving in to tears of frustration. My legs quiver. I sit on the doorstep and draw my knees to my chest. They should be here; Ren should be settling down for her afternoon nap. Where are they? What has Neil done with her?

"Think he's out."

I look up. The neighbor who was so kind, so concerned, is stood at her door. Now, she's wary and terse.

"Was he with my baby? Have you seen her? Is she okay?"

"Better now than with you, perhaps."

"What do you mean? I'm her mother."

She shakes her head. "Yeah, but sometimes it's not for the best, is it?"

"You said you heard our fights. You said I should leave."

"Guess I didn't know what I was talking about. You should go before someone calls the police." And she withdraws back into her house.

I peel myself from the step. I don't want to face him anymore. I can't be here when he comes back. My body is rigid and painful as I shuffle down the road. I pass the twitching curtains and hostile front doors.

The bus is hot and clammy. The tiny windows are open, but ineffective. People steam and sweat. We jolt to a halt at every bus stop. Passengers jostle past me with shopping bags or thrust backpacks into my face as they turn to sit. Before the bus turns left towards the shops, I press the bell and get off outside the pub.

Cider in the sunshine—how perfect that sounds. It's dim inside as my eyes acclimatize. Several people in suits are sitting around one of the tables. A couple of old men are watching golf on the TV.

"Stowfords," I order, and watch my fingers tapping the bar.

2.

The front door shields me from the terror within. On the driveway, I pause, safe from the Grace-and-Neil ghosts re-enacting their fight over and over.

I wish I smoked—I'd have an excuse to hang around in the garden. Nonsensically, I pull up some weeds and throw them onto the pavement. A woman walking past scowls snobbishly but doesn't say anything.

Mum flings the door open. "Grace, get inside."

Heart beating like a battle drum, breathing rapid, I obey.

"Where've you been?"

I fidget under her gaze, unsure what to do with my arms, tugging the bottom of my shirt, deflecting scrutiny.

"Okay," she says brusquely. "Strong coffee for you. Mike?"

Dad appears. He holds my shoulders and steers me through the wibbly-wobbly hall to the kitchen. He sits me at the table and Mum boils the kettle.

"We want to believe you," Mum says without looking at me. "We wanted Neil to be wrong. We *knew* you wouldn't drink with Sarah around. But here you are…"

"Sarah's not here."

"Drinking's not the answer," Dad says, stroking my hand. "Not if you want to see Sarah."

I only had one… a couple. I was thirsty.

"You can't go to the house, you're not allowed, for a little while." He squeezes my hand now, making me focus. "Do you understand?"

"I didn't."

Mum humphs; Dad sighs. "We know you did," he says, narrowing his eyes to warn Mum to back off. "Neil called. Said you spoke to one of the neighbors."

"You're ganging up on me."

"No, we're trying to help."

Mum puts a glass of water in front of me. "Drink this." She fusses with the coffee, adding three spoons of sugar to the mug. "Now this."

"I don't take sugar." My mouth is uncontrollable. It's an effort to get the muscles to work in unison.

"Frankly, I don't care."

I wrap my hands around the mug. It's too hot; I almost drop it. I rest my head in my hand, the weight of it unbearable. I alternate between the water and coffee, aware of Mum's scowl, grimacing at the sweetness. As soon as I finish, she whips the glass and mug away.

"Now, go and sleep it off. We'll talk about this later." She doesn't smile. She turns away. The threat of the impending lecture makes me feel five again.

I silently beg Dad for support, but he nods in agreement with Mum, unable to hide his disappointment in me.

The walls and floor conspire to make the journey upstairs tricky. I hold on to everything I pass, to steady myself. I only had two, I remind myself. Or maybe it was three.

In my room, Neil leers at me, callous and triumphant. His hand on my throat. The smell of his breath in my nostrils. I lie face down, suffocating myself in the duvet. He was right here, beside my bed, and pressed his cold, glassy lips to my forehead. I shudder. And he does it again and again.

3.

Mum stops decorating Ren's room. She bundles up the dust sheets and leaves them on the landing. I watch impassively from my bedroom door.

When she goes downstairs, I rest my hand on the handle, mustering the courage to go in.

The walls are only half-done—fresh rosewood pink suddenly gives way to Darren's pale gray, mid-stroke. The edges haven't been filled. The animal-themed mural Dad suggested is just a pencil outline. The curtains remain folded in a neat pile. Paint pots are stacked, brushes have been rinsed and left on top.

"You've given up," I say, not turning but sensing Mum at the door.

"So have you."

I'm ready to launch a robust defense of my actions but fail to form any cohesive sentence. My head teems with argument, with rage and contempt; yet I'm composed and languid on the outside. I shrug. Because, really, it's all she expects of me these days.

I don't want to talk—I want to lash out and accuse. I want it to be someone else's fault, not mine. Never mine. And yet it is. She's my daughter, and I allowed her to be stolen from me.

"We'll get a solicitor; we'll get access."

"I don't want *access*; I want her. I'm her mother; she should be with me."

"It's not that simple." She looks around for somewhere to sit, but there's no furniture, we never got that far. "I've been looking into mediation—things can be discussed, arranged. You have to understand how serious the allegations are."

"He attacked me with a rake." The wounds are still red and raised, catching on my clothes whenever I move. The bandages have gone; the long, deep cuts remain. "Do you want to see them again?"

I lift my t-shirt as if to tug it over my head. Mum stops me and pulls it back down. "No, I don't," she says quietly.

"He doesn't love her. He'll hurt her like he hurt me."

"I'm sure he won't."

"You don't know him."

She sighs and fiddles with the cuff of her jacket. "We saw them, in the street. Not to talk to," she adds quickly. "He crossed the road before we reached them and hurried away." She moves to stand beside me. "She looked clean and cared for. She was wearing the blue dress I bought her. I think he's trying his best."

Trying his *best?* I don't have the words to argue, I gawp with bewilderment. "When did you see them?"

"A couple of days ago. I'm sorry, I should have told you."

"So, that's it then. He's happy, she's happy. Everything's good."

"We could do more if you stopped drinking. How many of those have you had?"

I gaze at the bottle I'd forgotten I'm holding. I tip it from side to side and take a sip. "Just one."

4.

I'm at the window when Mum leaves for work, staring into the street like a ghost gliding through time, and I'm there when she returns. Days pass—strands of time catching on gate posts and blades of grass and scraps of rubbish being tossed on the breeze.

Normal people do normal things as though my life hasn't just detonated. Shouldn't they know? Shouldn't there be some seismic shudder underground causing birds to jolt from the trees in unison and shockwaves to billow across the country?

It's a quiet road, a wide residential thoroughfare connecting the two busier roads at either end. Neighbors come and go—to work, to shop, to school and back. Some of them catch my eye, if I don't duck back in time. They judge me; I see the repulsion on their faces.

Quiet is good. There are no surprises in the silence. I position myself on Dad's armchair, so I have full view outside and of the TV, and this is how I spend my day. The familiar daytime voices are reliable—local presenters share the news with a sparkle as though they're sitting at the dining table to gossip about fugitive deer on the A38; game show hosts direct their questions at me.

I don't answer the doorbell if it rings. I don't even peer from the window to see who it might be. I sit very still as if any movement will have them storming inside. Bad things happen when you open the door.

"You should think about getting a job," Mum says when she comes home, tidying away the detritus of my day, collecting mugs and glasses, folding magazines and piling them on the table.

It's been two weeks since I lost Ren, and she wants me to forget her already, to pretend the last eighteen months never happened. No husband, no child, no scars or stretchmarks.

"Or at least do some bloody housework—look at the state of this room." She has a stack of dishes now, balancing on her arm. "And do you really think that's the answer?" She points to the wine glass in my hand.

Just as when I was a child, the stream of misdemeanors is unending. Once she starts, she can go on forever. *What about...? And don't you think...? Why don't you...?*

"It's just one." It rose-tints the memories; it softens the pain.

"You have to pull yourself together."

I snort. "Says the woman who's had it all so easy for the last thirty years. When did your husband lock you in the house or rename your child or make you feel like he could kill you at any moment?"

Her mouth falls open. I've said too much, shared things I never wanted to.

"You know what, I don't care. Pretend Neil's a great dad, doing a fantastic job. Pretend I'm the problem. I really don't care. I'm going out."

"Where? Gracie?" She throws her hands up in despair.

She's still calling as I walk down the drive and out onto the pavement. She may be calling when I meander along the main road and past the shops and stand outside the pub. She sends a couple of texts which I ignore, and finally my phone goes quiet.

The noise from inside is a gentle drone of voices rather than pumping music, a quiet mid-week vibe. When I walk in a few people glance across at me but turn away quickly. Mostly, they're in small clusters of work colleagues or couples out for an early dinner. One guy is playing darts by himself.

I order lager, cheap and pale with a dirty aftertaste. I sit by the window and let the chatter drift over me and allow two girls to sit beside me as the room fills up.

When the bell rings for last orders, I haul myself from the table and shuffle obediently to the door.

5.

The house is a cage, the walls close in on me, replaying all the evil things which happened that day, and there's no escape. They replicate and amplify. I crouch down in the corner of my bedroom with my eyes squeezed shut and my hands over my ears to avoid the memories, but it doesn't work. It loops over and over.

Being out of the house is less intimidating than in.

The world is gigantic, and I'm so very small—I secrete myself away in the bustle of busy pubs, and nobody cares.

I'm vague about what I'm doing and who I'm with. "Kirsty," I yell over my shoulder, the first name that comes to mind when I'm pressed for one. Or sometimes Marie or Andrea or Jess.

"I'm not at school anymore, you don't have to vet my friends."

Mum sucks the inside of her cheek. "It would be nice to at least meet them."

"I think your mum just wants to make sure you're okay... happy," Dad says. We've never needed an interpreter before, but these days we can't say two words without it being a drawn-out argument.

"Happy?" I laugh incredulously. "Yeah, of course she does." I stab my fork into the pork chop, small and hard and overcooked.

They lean back in their chairs, and I feel them having a soundless conversation above my head.

I push my plate away. "Gotta go. Marie'll be waiting."

"I thought it was Kirsty tonight?" Mum says casually.

"Nope. Marie." I *always* remember.

On good nights I move from the local pubs on to the Barbican, and there's always some friendly guy willing to buy me a drink. Sometimes, without money left over for a taxi, I walk home. August nights are twilit and golden, heat infuses the tarmac and the walls and the wide open spaces. I feel invincible, untouchable, as if I'm gliding on air, as if carried by magic.

On very good nights, I'm not home until just before Dad gets up for work. I sneak in and bury myself in my duvet, pretending I've been asleep for hours. He always checks.

My phone beeps. I fumble through my discarded clothes to find it, trying to focus on the blurry icons on the screen.

Neil.

I drop the phone; it lands heavily on my chest. What the hell? I steady it with both hands and stare at his name, my stomach freezing solid. It's been weeks. I hover my finger above the icon but can't quite press. I should ignore him. I should block his number or change mine. But he's my only link to my baby. What if there's an emergency?

I know what u been doing, naughty girl

With another beep I'm looking at myself holding a pint in each hand, apparently drinking from both. Another beep and I'm slumped over a table covered with empties. Another and another. I'm lifting my top at some guy in a sombrero. I'm leaning on railings, struggling to stand.

Interesting eh? Missing ya kid are ya? Nah. Looks like ur having too much fun. These pix will come in handy ;-)

My heart thumps against my chest. He's been spying on me? No, he can't have—I'd have noticed him. But someone took these photos. His mates. I've seen a couple of them around—they've bought me drinks. Stupid, *stupid* girl.

They're hideous. I'm hideous in them. Splayed across tables and bars and pavements and men. But he's wrong—I'm not having fun. Look! I'm empty and haunted. They're photos of a woman who's given up.

This is what it looks like when you don't feel anything anymore.

I open the locket around my neck and gaze at Ren—six months old, cross-eyed, kissing the lens. I should have been a better mother. I should have protected her, stood up to Neil, left sooner. I should have been better.

6.

"We need to talk," Dad says one day. Which day? No idea, to be honest. I roll onto my stomach and hide my head under my pillow.

"Go away." I can barely open my eyes. It must be early. Dad must be on his way to work. Waking me before he goes is a new level of cruelty.

The mattress dips as he sits down. "It's half-past four."

"Too early, go back to bed."

"Half-past four in the *afternoon*. You've been asleep all day, haven't you?" I stifle a giggle. "No."

He sighs. If I open my eyes, he'll be exhaling into the room and have both hands clasped behind his head, arching to stretch his back. "You've got to sort this out, Grace."

"I'm tired. Leave me alone."

"You don't remember coming home this morning, do you?"

I wait, fearfully. Dread and shame in equal measure.

"You walked in when I was getting ready for work. You threw up on the front step and collapsed in the hall. I had to carry you to bed."

I snigger. A dull pain circles my head.

"You're not a child anymore. You're nineteen, and you're a—" He stops abruptly, but his words find their way into the room anyway.

You're nineteen, and *you're a mother now*.

That's what he was going to say. That's what I hear.

"You think I need to be reminded?"

He reaches forward, but I push his arm away.

"Gracie, I'm sorry. I didn't mean…"

"Leave me alone," I say, so quietly I can barely make out my own voice.

And he does. Downstairs, I'm sure they're talking about me as they make dinner together. Each with their own job—chopping onions, boiling pasta, browning mince—working fluidly.

I sit on the stairs, because I don't want to face them. I'm twelve again.

I've left unfinished homework on my bed and Darren's yelling at video games in his room. I rest my chin on my knees and pretend my only problems are acne and Mum not letting me buy the jeans I really *really* want.

"She hasn't mentioned Sarah for weeks," Mum says. "She barely speaks to me anymore. I don't know what's going on in her head. It's like she's stopped caring."

"I'm sure she hasn't. She's in a bleak place right now. You can't expect—"

"She seems to be having a great time, actually."

"Irene..."

"Oh God, I'm sorry. I don't know what I'm saying. I just—I can't stand the drinking."

"I know."

"It's not how we brought her up. It's not *her*. She was always so sensible, before Neil. I should have put my foot down. We should have banned her from seeing him."

"She wouldn't have listened. She'd have resented you. We just have to support her now."

"But she's making it hard for us to do that."

The stair creaks as I fidget to get comfy and the kitchen door closes. I wish I knew what was happening. Is Mum crying, is Dad hugging her? I've been sucked into my own world and I'm making their lives a misery because they can't understand. I was a mother, and now I'm not. I'm a bad person because I've been trying to forget my own child. They'd be better off without me. Everyone would.

I slip into the bathroom and probe around the cabinet for Mum's sleeping tablets. I grab two boxes and pop a few out into my palm. What am I doing?

"Dinner's ready," Dad calls.

Could I do it? Could I swallow these pills and allow them to steal my life? There's a bottle of wine in my wardrobe—I could lie in bed and watch a film and simply fall asleep.

And my parents would find me. And they'd live with the guilt and regret. I slump against the door and the tablets tumble from my hand. I dress quickly and run downstairs.

"Not hungry," I call, evading questions and slamming the front door.

7.

The bar is sticky. I sit precariously on the wobbly stool and reach out to steady myself. I gulp the first half of my pint straight down.

"Looks like you needed that."

The nearest bloke is hunched over his own drink, focused on it as though it'll vanish if he looks away. I've seen him here before, always in the same spot. At first, I'm not even sure he said anything, he's almost inert.

"Long day. Long year," I say with a shrug, sounding like the OAPs who hang out here in the afternoons.

He grunts, agreeing, commiserating, whatever. He doesn't say anything else though. We descend into sociable muteness. The TV behind us is showing darts. Randomly, the only bloke who seems to be watching shouts or swears at it, making us jump.

My stomach is still churned up from last night and the lager doesn't settle well. Normally by now, I'd be on my second, or third, getting as wasted as possible, as quickly as possible. Because then, I don't notice I'm alone in an empty pub watching darts.

It's like she doesn't care. That's what they said. That's what they think of me.

Another sip, and another. I can't raise a smile. I gaze distractedly at the foam clinging to the inside of the glass. I picture how I'd look right now, if someone took my photo and sent it to Neil. Would he see the real me? I turn swiftly to catch my imaginary photographer in the act. But of course, no one's there.

I slither off the stool, my drink still half full.

No hangover.

No headache, no dry mouth or nausea. I lift my head, and the world isn't spinning—it's crisp and defined, stark and icy. Ren calls for me. I see her shadow as she rushes around the house. It'll never go away, will it? The loss and anguish will always be with me.

Dad looks up with a smile when I sit at the kitchen table. I spot the surprise in his half-raised eyebrow, but he doesn't comment. "Bacon butty?"

I nod vaguely, and he adds more rashers to the pan.

"You were home early last night."

I shrug and pour coffee from the pot. Saturday morning means real, fresh coffee.

"Did you fall out with your friend?" His tone is light, casual—*breezy* is Mum's word for it when she's light and casual.

"No. Just... came home."

"I see." He puts my sandwich in front of me and sits opposite. There's no escape now, no avoiding his concern. "Have you spoken to Neil at all?"

I choke at his name. I recall the photos on my phone I deleted immediately. He'll still have them, biding his time to use them for maximum impact, like if Mum and Dad persuaded me into mediation.

"Why would I?"

"Because you need to get something sorted, for Sarah's sake. She's missing you."

"I doubt she's noticed I'm gone."

"Of course she has. She's..."

I hold my breath, waiting for his next words. In turn, he glances at Mum who's yawning at the door.

"We saw them," she says. She pours herself coffee and leans against the sink.

"Again? It's becoming a bit of a habit."

"We were shopping."

I put my sandwich down, dimpling the bread with my finger because I can't think of anything else to do.

"She's looking happy... clean. She's got two new teeth and—"

I stand and my chair thuds against the wall. "How does this help? You think I'd be glad the man who hurt me is being so good to my child? You think I'm glad to know he could have been helping me all the time I was with him, but instead he *chose* to torment and terrify me?"

"That's not what—"

"He is a bad man. He was, and he'll show it again. If my baby gets in the way, if he hurts her, it'll be your fault."

I rush upstairs, two at a time, and punch the door shut. I spin around, grabbing clothes and shoving them in my holdall, grabbing my toothbrush and soap and my old sleeping bag from the landing cupboard. I have no plan, but I can't be here with them.

Bag packed and straining at the seams, I slump onto the floor and sob furiously until I'm purged of tears.

8.

My bag waits by the front door. I squeeze chocolate bars and apples into the gaps and wedge a dusty half-full bottle of vodka between jumpers. All of this without thinking, without considering the implications. When a sliver of doubt enters my head, I brush it aside, because this is the right thing to do, for all of us.

I check in each of the rooms to confirm the house is empty, void of witnesses to my departure. I deliberate between my two jackets, and choose the thicker one—even now, as the year slips into September, the evenings are getting chillier. I lock the front door and post my keys through the letterbox.

When I was eleven or twelve, I ran away with Janie. We didn't get far—I wrote a detailed plan, with a carefully drawn map, and left it on my desk. Darren found it and came in search of us in the woods down the road. He took us home before our parents found out.

I stop at the junction. Cars trundle past. One slows down, allowing me to cross, but I'm not ready. I step back and wave him on. I zig-zag the maze of sleepy residential streets, with the anxiety of bumping into someone I know who'll want to trap me into conversation, and duck into the footpath which creeps between back gardens.

Mannamead Road is long and anonymous and takes me all the way into the city center. Cars whizz past, people walk with purpose, no one notices the troubled girl with her life on her back.

The bag strap cuts into my shoulder. I stop to switch sides ever so often, resting it on the ground and feeling so light I could float away. I take stock of where I am, where I'll go from here.

It's getting hotter. I take off my jumper and tie it around my waist. I hit Mutley Plain and already there's a gathering of lunchtime drinkers at the pub. I consider stopping, but mentally count the meager amount of money in my pocket.

Onwards. At the top of North Hill, the sea glints on the horizon, beckoning me. My gait increases as I head downhill, bustle past the old library and museum, through Drake's Circus and onto Royal Parade with its ceaseless line of buses and bellowing horns as drivers vie for space and pedestrians ignore the traffic lights.

Beyond that, the hill I've pushed Ren's buggy so many times, this time weighed down by my holdall and my nervousness. Is this my option, running away? If I caught a bus, I'd be home before Mum as though nothing had happened. Torn between continuing and returning, I set my bag on the paving slabs.

People nudge past me—foreign students in a long, snaking line, families walking four-abreast, office workers with packets of sandwiches and reusable coffee cups. And I'm just here, standing, uncertain, watching the buses arrive and depart. I posted my keys into the house; I've already made my decision.

I bow my head as I pass the registry office. I don't want to see happy faces and lives full of promise. I speed up, as though their happiness will pour from the walls to taunt me.

The sea is almost turquoise when I catch my first glimpse of it, rich and overwhelming. The sky is peppered with candy floss clouds. The headlands of Rame Head and Heybrook Bay push themselves out past the Breakwater. I drop my bag on a bench and sit, pretending this is just another normal day.

Dusk takes the place of the evening sunshine. This, right here, is comfortable. Sitting is easy; daytime is safe. Where do people sleep? I've seen them in shop doorways with blankets tucked around their legs even on warm days—I've sometimes bought coffee for a couple of them. Do they stay there all night? Is it their forever place? Are they allowed to move to other doorways? Is there a clandestine etiquette I should know?

I haul myself from the bench and heave the holdall onto my shoulder, grumbling at the heaviness. I plod across the road and down the steps toward the water, navigating the mash-up of stone steps and tarmac paths crisscrossing the cliff face. It's a labyrinth, great for hide-and-seek when you're little, perfect for fishing or paddling your toes in the water. It's tired and derelict, battered by successive storms over the years, yet concealed and protective.

Cut into the rock are old buildings, tucked directly under the road, boarded up. And below one of these buildings is a large recess with stone arches providing a semblance of shelter. The day's heat is reflecting off the rocks and with the sun glinting on the water, it feels Mediterranean. The corners are harboring puddles from this morning's high tide, but it's as good a place as any.

Noise from the road lessens, then ceases altogether. There's romance in the sound of the waves rippling against the shore. Without the sun, the warmth doesn't last long. I put on my jumper and minutes later, my jacket too. I slip into my sleeping bag, pitifully thin, bought for mid-summer festivals not bedding down on hard concrete slabs—a chill pervades from below.

A small sip of vodka warms me and isolates persuasive thoughts of catching the last bus home. I made my choice; this is it.

The rhythm of water lulls me into a slumber, and I try to ignore the grumble of hunger. I consider the chocolate and fruit in my bag, but when I move my arms, I shiver uncontrollably and pull them back inside, curling my knees to my chest and sucking my hands into my coat sleeves.

Arms wrap around me. Or, at least, the sensation of arms draped heavy on my shoulders and the closeness of a small body against mine. A child's body. Ren's body. There's no one here, but it comforts me.

3:59 A.M.

Ren used to cry at four o'clock every morning.

Perhaps she still does. It's been forever since I watched her fight sleep, her chubby arms beating against me or her mattress. It's been so long since one full undisturbed night felt like a miracle. But it hasn't. It's been all too short.

I hold my breath and wait for the time to flip over to the next minute, into the next hour. I open the curtains a little, creating a small slice to peer from. The moon is adorned with thinning clouds, casting a glow across the sky. None of the houses have their lights on now, although soon early shift-workers will be stirring. I wonder if I'll be asleep, or if I'll witness their exodus.

Ren still cries in my head—her pitiful, anguished sobs never cease up there. And I can't console her; I'm powerless. I want to snuggle her into my arms, to nuzzle against her freshly-washed hair, to have her fingers pulling on my earlobe.

I unclasp my birthday locket and smile at the photos inside—at me and Ren. I don't look at them often because I hate the memories. I hate my optimistic, naïve face, and I hate all the things this poor girl has yet to experience.

Run, run away. If only it were possible to reach into the past and pull her away from it.

Ren's just turned six months in her photo—before her hair grew long enough for pigtails, before her first tooth splintered her gum and changed the shape of her smile. She's making an Ooh shape as she tries to kiss the camera.

I want to go back to those sleepless nights, to the two o'clock feeds and the subsequent pacing to settle her down, to having the whole night to ourselves while everyone else slept.

I want her arms wrapped tight around my neck. I want her to smile and call me Mummy. I want to turn back time.

The Missing

1.

I'm sprinting through a field of vivid buttercups. My boy runs alongside me, holding my hand tightly, afraid to let go. Ren holds my other hand, albeit looser, her fingers barely laced with mine. Several times, she wriggles free and skips ahead. She bends to pick flowers and clumps them together in her fist.

We're at the top of a slope, hand in hand in hand. *Now*, says the boy, and we sprint to the bottom, the air tingling with laughter. Our lungs ache with the exertion. Faster, faster. Falling and picking ourselves back up. Ren lets go, and when I turn, she's gone.

Ren! No!

I scour the field frantically, calling for her, brushing through the tall flowers in case she's hiding, stifling the delight of the surprise when she jumps out.

The boy lets go too, keeping pace with me for a second, then vanishing. And I'm alone in a sea of fiery yellow. I lie among the buttercups and watch bright white clouds zipping past in the azure sky. Everything's vivid and yellow. Far too yellow.

The sky is white and overcast when I open my eyes; there's drizzle in the air making my face and sleeping bag damp, but not unbearably so. Already, the sea is busy with trawlers and a lone swimmer who stares when she catches sight of me. I tighten the sleeping bag around me, cold, shivering violently for a moment despite the moderate air.

Ren let go. She wouldn't hold my hand. The boy—brimming with tenderness and love—tried his best to catch up with me, but his legs wouldn't carry him. I'm filled with sorrow at the memory of him; I knew him, I loved him. But he left too.

Wind rattles the loose balustrades and waves slop over the rocks. Water flows toward me and I shuffle back to avoid my sleeping bag getting soaked. My back is stiff, and my legs are cramped. I try to slide from the sleeping bag, but my body is alien and uncooperative.

2.

I watch my phone die. Twelve percent, eleven, ten—the amber bar turning red. Critical.

I could put it on ultra-power-saving mode, I suppose, but what's the point? I'd be forced to listen to Mum ringing and texting, frantic efforts to make sure I'm okay. There are several missed calls already. Several texts I can't bear to read.

They'll have picked my keys off the doormat. They'll have noticed my toothbrush and some clothes are gone. They'll have seen the items missing from the fridge.

They'll know I'm not just out late.

I imagine Mum texting how we can work this out, and I don't need to do anything drastic. She'll say we've still got options and I should be at home because that's where Ren needs me to be. She'll call her Sarah without realizing it'll make everything so much easier. *Sarah* isn't my daughter: Ren is.

And she won't repeat the conversation I overheard, she won't say she doesn't think I care, or that I'm having too much fun. She'll already be pretending she didn't say anything of the sort.

The morning passes in front of me. Tourist boats, more swimmers, a few canoeists and kayakers. The sun rising from the right and prodding through the dispersing clouds. It gets warmer and I wriggle out of the sleeping bag, fold it, and sit on top of it.

I'm hungry. I eat an apple and one of the chocolate bars, but they don't fill me for long.

Three, two, one. My phone buzzes as it switches off. I catch sight of Ren's photo on my home screen for the final time.

At lunch time, or at the time I think is lunch time, I pack up my bag and walk into the city center. The closer I get, the more hostile the noise becomes. My shelter beneath those strange little arches on the Hoe was so serene and relaxing. I tuck my bag against my body to defend myself from the onslaught.

I buy a sandwich for lunch, but with each mouthful, I'm nervous and sick. I wrap it back up and put it in my bag for later.

On a different day, I might be here with Ren, pushing her buggy like all the other mothers are doing. I might pop into Boots for nappies and stop for a coffee while I give Ren a snack. I might check the time and wander up to the Hoe before catching the bus home. Normal things I took for granted last month, last year.

Now I don't quite belong. The streets have taken on a foreign appearance. Among coffee-drinking, bag-laden shoppers who woke in cozy beds and had hearty breakfasts in front of the TV, I'm detached. They push past while I saunter without purpose; when I sit to rest, they ignore me.

It's not too late to go home.

Except it is.

I reach for my locket and immediately smell Ren's soft hair straight from the bath, and her warm breath on my neck as she snuggles into the towel. I don't look at the photo inside. I don't want to.

3.

Within a couple of days, I'm hungrier and more tired than I thought possible. I catch sight of my disheveled appearance and baulk. I weave among the crowds, surprised how simple it is to become invisible, and wonder how long it will be before I'm completely expelled from the streets once so familiar.

Sharp, autumnal cloudbursts soak me. I wedge my hands into my pockets and wander around to find shelter. The best places are taken, in the subways at North Cross roundabout, the covered area next to the old Littlewoods shop, in the doorway recesses of abandoned buildings.

Vacant eyes watch my search before losing interest. I copy the way they sit on their folded sleeping bags or blankets to avoid the cold concrete paving slabs and put a small towel out for spare change. *Spare change, sir? Have a good day.* Others have hats or plastic pots, more organized, more established. I'm mired with the impression I'm pretending, none of this is real. I have a home and a roof, a family, an out whenever I want.

Except I don't.

Suddenly there are far too many people. Too many legs walking past, blocking my view, close enough to accidentally trample me; too claustrophobic. I pack up and walk away, with my meager coin collection. On the other side of Royal Parade, I watch skateboarders fail their jumps and peer through long fringes to check if anyone was watching. I don't count.

I'm heading back to the Hoe, but I don't want to—it's too early. Crossing the road, I sit on a bench beside the large anchor—Plymouth is a naval town, so I've never questioned why there's an anchor embedded into the ground, just like I've never wondered why we plucked a lighthouse from its seat out at sea and brought it onto the Hoe. It's just there.

Far enough away from the shopping crowds but before the ascent to the Promenade, this is a good place. A few people are dotted around, with their possessions wrapped in plastic bags or wedged into large rucksacks.

One woman parks a rusty supermarket trolley and yawns loudly as she sits.

Their faces are blank, waiting for nothing to happen. Which it does, again and again. A couple of them are talking, their backs against me, although every so often one will turn to catch a sly glimpse or the other will look over the top of his companion's head.

"Don't worry. It takes time." The woman with the trolley scoots along her bench, coming close but maintaining an appropriate distance.

"Sorry?"

"We keep to our own. We haven't seen you before."

"Oh. No."

"It's like a club, you see. We watch out for each other. But we're particular, we don't like strangers. We don't trust them." Her voice sounds relatively young, but her face is weathered and lined.

I nod, signifying my understanding but having nothing to contribute. *I don't belong here*, is the message.

"How long have you been on the streets?" she asks.

"Not long."

"I can tell." She cackles and coughs, displaying several gaps in her teeth. "Oh boy, can I tell."

I sit straighter, insulted.

She stops laughing as suddenly as she started. "Two years, for me. Time slips by without you realizing."

Two years? I can't imagine what that would be like. Twenty-four months. A hundred and four weeks. Two birthdays and Christmases.

"Where you sleeping to?" She pulls the sleeve of her ragged jumper down over her hand and pulls at a thread.

"Around." I'm not giving away my spot. I like it there. I have a sea view.

"There are shelters, you know, if you need them when it gets colder." She delves into her coat pocket.

Colder? Of course it will be. Autumn's barely begun. The winter stretches out in front of me. Last year, it snowed.

"They can help you get back on your feet." She hands me a torn, crumpled leaflet. "Too late for me, I wouldn't fit anymore—but you're young, you must have family, people who are worried about you." She's perched on the very edge of her bench now, leaning toward me. I slide away.

"No," I say too quickly, and she raises her eyebrow. I hold the leaflet out to her, but she refuses to take it back. "I'm fine. I don't need…"

"What are you trying to avoid?" she asks softly, maternally.

I grab my bag and stand.

"I'm Sandra, by the way. In case you need… someone. Just say Sandra to most of these folks and they'll know where to find me."

I don't want to know her name. I don't want to share mine. I don't want friends; I want to be alone. "Thank you."

"Well," she says grudgingly. "See you around then." She reaches for my arm. "There's a soup run on the Hoe, half-nine every night. I'll look out for you."

"Thank you," I say again and hurry away.

4.

I fold up my sleeping bag and walk into town. I stop outside House of Fraser and peek at my reflection while pretending to look at the weirdly poised mannequins. My hair is matted, my fringe plastered to my forehead.

I sit in my usual spot and place my new plastic bowl on the ground. I don't make eye contact with anyone. I trace the path of a spider as it disappears down a crack in the concrete.

I fold up my sleeping bag and walk to the shelter for a shower. I have a coffee too. I wash my clothes and change into the spare stuff at the bottom of my bag. The jeans feel damp and there's a peculiar odor, but I don't have anything else. I'll wash this next week. I do all of this automatically, as if I've been doing it forever. I remember putting on the washing at home, sitting with Ren in her highchair and watching the laundry going around and around.

Is Neil washing her clothes, and bathing her, and brushing her hair? Is he loving her the way I do… did… no, do?

I fold up my sleeping bag and walk into town, into a fight between skateboarders. A group gathers around them, jeering and yelling. I veer right to avoid them. I sit in my usual spot and listen to change being thrown into my bowl. I'm starting to learn the tone of the coins—light and musical means coppers and five-pence pieces, a clunk is normally a pound coin. I buy myself a hot chocolate and a big sticky bun, and still have some left over to tuck away in the pocket of my bag for a rainy day.

I fold up my sleeping bag and walk into town in the rain. There are fewer people when the weather's bad, but they must feel sorry for me because I still get a few coins in my bowl, and a white-haired lady who reminds me of my gran holds out a coffee for me. She's nervous and almost apologetic, as though she's responsible for my current turn of fortune.

I walk into town and see Ren in the middle of the plaza. She's running and jumping and chasing pigeons—hair bouncing, arms waving, face full of smiles and mischief. My heart misses a beat.

Neil.

Neil must be with her.

I scout around in panic, scanning the shoppers for his familiar, arrogant stride.

It's not her. A completely different father picks her up and twirls her into the air, and a different mother follows them with a buggy laden with shopping bags.

Not her, but it could have been.

I've been walking around these streets and sitting in full sight without a thought that at any moment I might see Mum or Dad or Kirsty, or Neil.

It's not too late to leave. I could catch a bus to Exeter—I'm sure I have enough for the fare. I could truly disappear. From there, I could go on to Bristol or London, Manchester or Leeds. There'd be endless possibilities.

But I'd never see Ren again, I'd never find my way home.

5.

There are too many people. Too many little girls who look like Ren. I grab my bag and head past the shops and the Pannier Market, down toward Frankfort Gate, and across the busy road. The bag's too heavy and awkward to run with, it bounces against my hip.

I amble down the road, turn into another, and walk until I reach a park. My direction is all mixed up, and I have no idea where I am. I sit under a large tree on the perimeter of the park; branches creak overhead, shadows of the leaves flit across the grass.

This is all too hard, and it's only the start. I think of Sandra's two years. I wonder if she has kids or family she ran away from. Everyone has somebody, I suppose, even if you don't realize it. I wonder if she regrets it.

I squeeze the locket and reach for the vodka in my bag. It's empty, just dregs which offer no comfort

The sound of children laughing from the playground carries on the wind.

"Hello, lady," says a little voice.

I ignore it.

"I said hello. It's rude not to say hello back—that's what my mummy says."

I tilt my face toward the sky. A child, about five years old, is standing beside me, slightly bending forward to peer intently.

"Didn't your mummy tell you not to talk to strangers?"

He giggles. "You're not a stranger, silly."

I frown. I don't recognize him—is he the son of someone I know, someone I've spoken to at the bus stop or in the supermarket perhaps? I squirm and try to secrete myself into the tree. I scan for someone who seems like they're searching for a child, but there's no one obvious. There's no one close.

"You should go back to your mummy now. Do you know where she is?"

"You look sad."

"I'm always a little bit sad," I say without thinking.

"I can help. I helped you before. I hugged you and kept you warm when you slept."

I jolt. "What did you say?"

He covers his mouth with both hands, his eyes wide and shocked. "Oops. I have to go." He waves and skips away.

"Wait. Come back."

But he's gone. Not running away, not scooped into his mother's arms. Just vanished.

His voice lingers; the conversation replays itself until it too fades, and all I hear is the wind brushing through the branches above and the shrieks of delight from the playground.

6.

I'm late returning to the arches. The wind's picking up, pushing against me; the sun set hours ago. I hate walking in the muted spots of the streetlights—the shadows conjure danger.

I pass several people clustered around a car, some eating, some with mugs. I recognize Sandra, or at least the shape of her shopping trolley. I halt and change direction as discreetly as possible, but she spots me.

"Hey," she calls, and the others turn to me. I wonder if I should make a bolt for it, but it's too late. "I was wondering what happened to you. Haven't gone home then?"

I shrug sullenly, pulling myself into my jacket.

"Come and eat, get a hot coffee—you're frozen."

It's been the sort of day that if I was home, we'd have considered a barbeque, albeit with jumpers, and by now we'd be toasting marshmallows and warming our hands on smoldering charcoal.

"I'm fine." The aroma of food wafts toward me. Hunger gnaws at my stomach and slides into my throat.

"You don't get bonus points for starving yourself."

"I had something earlier."

She raises an eyebrow. "They're nice people, they don't ask questions. Not like me, eh?" She cackles at herself. "I know, I'm too nosy—you don't have to give us your life story." As she talks, she travels toward the group, drawing me along. "They've got bananas tonight. I can't remember the last time I had one—so delicious."

I smile faintly. I accept the soup offered to me. It tastes like home. I listen to the eclectic discussions occurring around me—moving quickly between some trouble one of the blokes had last night, to the chaos of Brexit, to the best place to get a sandwich contribution from a friendly passerby.

Soup finished, banana eaten, I inch away from the group until I'm outside of the circle.

"How's it going, really?" Sandra's beside me before I can slip away. She must have been watching.

"Okay, I guess."

"Are you safe? Warm enough?"

I shrug.

"You're struggling." She clicks her tongue. "You shouldn't be here."

"I'm fine."

"Some of the lads have been talking about a squat. Above a shop. Been empty for a while, so no one bothers to keep an eye on it. Might be worth checking out."

She explains where it is. I know it. I was sat opposite it for a while yesterday. I got three quid and bought myself a pasty.

"I'm fine," I repeat. "But thanks, it's nice of you."

"Go home, kid. Whatever happened, whatever went wrong..."

I blink back tears. I'm not fine. None of this is fine. I'm alone and I don't want to be. I'm a million miles from my daughter, and there's no way back. It's been almost two months since Neil took her away from me; it's been too long.

7.

The moon casts a silver streak across the water. There's a haze of red around it tonight, dust in the atmosphere, Dad would explain if he was here. We often sat together and gazed at the sky—I'd point out the International Space Station whenever it passed over head and he'd explain the constellations. I never cared about the stars—too many, too far away. How could those tiny pricks of lights be the same thing as our gigantic sun? No, I liked the moon best. Men walked on the moon. I could cup it in my hands.

When the rain comes, I'm huddled into the far corner of the shelter, woolly hat pulled low over my forehead and ears, gloved hands covering my cheeks until they suck up the warmth. Soon it's hammering down, bouncing off the concrete beach and making splashes in the sea. Ferocious winds batter the lamp posts, churning around the arches. One of the wooden doors from the beach huts breaks open and bangs erratically against its frame.

Engines from boy-racers roar across the foreshore and rope clangs against the flagpoles up on the Parade and wind whistles along the paths and rocky nooks. I hunker down and curl around my fears like the long, bony fingers of a fairy tale witch. I take a swig of vodka, and the noise abates.

Those arms are back. I snuggle into them. A small hand brushes my forehead the way I sometimes soothe Ren, and it lulls me to sleep.

The longest night merges into a solemn gray morning. It doesn't stop raining so I remain where I am—I can't deal with every item I own getting wet. Last night's soup is heavy in my stomach, but it won't last.

It's later than I usually hang around. There are many more people milling about. Up the steps and slopes, across to the left, the café's open and conversations filter down. Some people are drawn down to my refuge, stopping short of seeing me but lingering at the railings and watching the stormy sea swelling.

The tide swooshes and swirls, crashing against the rocks and the concrete and the pebbles. I lean against the back wall and close my eyes, pretending I'm on a beautiful Hawaiian beach with the sun beating down and a plate of juicy pineapple and mango beside me.

The fantasy doesn't last. When I open my eyes, the sky and sea are a vast swath of gray fog dipping into the horizon and the temperature plummets.

8.

It's the 23rd of September. The discarded *Guardian* flapping about my feet tells me so. I've been missing for three weeks. No, not missing—I'm right here.

I gaze down at it, noting headlines which make no sense, detached from the world, from the people who walk through me as though I'm not here.

Each day is colder than the last. Every night brings uncertainty. Gales blow in from the sea; the rain is persistent. My clothes are perpetually damp, and I've got a gritty sore throat.

"Hey, Kid."

I hunch down and continue the way I'm going. I don't want to speak to anyone, not even Sandra.

"Or do you prefer Grace?"

I stop. My skin tightens.

"I always wondered what you were called. Now I know." She wheels her trolley toward me and wafts a newspaper in front of me. When I don't immediately take it, she shoves it into my hand.

It's the local *Herald*, with my picture on the front page.

"Shit."

I'm pixelated in black and white, sitting on the floor with Ren, stacking bricks for her to knock down. It's the one Mum took the day I went back home. She's been cropped out of this photo, but my brain inserts her back in.

Sandra's watching me closely, saying nothing.

There's an article alongside, but I can't bring myself to read it. I can't bear to know what Mum and Dad are saying. I stroke my top lip and feel tears sliding down my face.

"I knew you had someone," Sandra says so gently it makes me cry even more. "What are you going to do?"

"I don't know. I can't go back. It's been too long."

"Oh, kid, it's been the blink of an eye."

"Would you go home, if you saw something like this?"

"I don't have a home. No one waiting for me. You got family."

I pull my woolly hat down to cover my forehead, to hide away. "They took his side, my husband's side. I left him. That day." I indicate the photo and scoff. "I'm bruised all over in this photo, the other side of my face is cut. I've got slashes on my back from a rake." I pause and stare at my picture until it blurs. She has no idea what's to come. *Stupid girl.*

"They took his side," I repeat quietly, "and said I should talk to him, to work something out. Not to bring her back home, but to ask him to let me visit her, to plead with him. They listened to him…" More tears, huge blobs splashing onto my jacket. "They didn't believe me anymore."

I hand the paper back to Sandra.

"So, thank you for caring, but I don't want to go back to them."

She takes it from me and folds it carefully. I drift away from her—first an apologetic step backwards, as if about to say more, then turning fully and leaving her behind. My legs are unsteady. My feet hit the ground like lead.

4:47 A.M.

I pad around the house. To the kitchen for water, then tea, for biscuits to fill my sudden hollowing hunger, then a bowl of cereal when the biscuits fail.

I stand in the hall, in the living room; I creep back up the stairs and pause when the step mid-way creaks. How did I forget which one to avoid? All those late nights and giggly returns home, it should be imprinted on my mind.

My fingers are icy; my toes are numb. Back in bed, I wrap a fleece blanket around my shoulders. I've been much colder than this, of course—those nights on the Hoe when I could barely move in case the freezing draught overwhelmed me, when I woke with snow sprinkled across my face and breath which was solid, when I wondered if I'd survive another night, and I thought of my parents and this house and all the love in it, and how much I'd longed to replicate it with a husband and family of my own.

They'd always known it was a mistake, but I couldn't see it. I wouldn't listen. I wish I had. How different everything would be now.

The chill air snakes up my fingers, over my wrists. My bones ache, my forearms, elbows, shoulders. I pull the blanket farther around me, burying my face in the cocoon I've made.

Nobody

1.

"How much, love?" calls the man in the car pulling up alongside me. He leans across the passenger's seat.

I gaze blankly, processing the question: *How much?*

He thinks I'm a... But it's daytime, why would he...?

My sleep-deprived head prevents me from imparting a sharp retort or storming away. I'm immobile. He's got a sleazy smile on his face and a glow of sweat on his upper lip. His hair is slicked back. A strong whiff of aftershave floats into the air.

"Get in, love."

I've heard the stories, when I've fallen into stilted conversations at the shelter—about the women who've been propositioned, about the men who watch out for them like knights in the darkness. Some go with them; some need the money too desperately to say no.

This guy reaches further across the seat for the door handle, and sense overwhelms me. I slam the door against his knuckles, and he yelps. I run. I don't know why—there are people around, there's no immediate danger. But running feels like the right thing to do.

Across the road, past the anchor, all the way along Notte Street until I'm at the entrance to the Barbican. I lean against the railings and gasp for breath.

"You just gotta watch out, keep one eye open," Sandra said at some point, and I do.

Every car is a threat, every man who brushes past could grab me and drag me down some small alley. It's getting dark; not quite night yet, but rainclouds will conceal the sun before it sets. I walk along the Barbican, eyes on the damp-shiny paving slabs and irregular cobbles. I follow feet along the pavement, and watch feet approach and move around me.

2.

It's the same day, different day, yesterday—stumbling toward winter. Frost lingers on the roofs and pavements; it catches my breath on the air. It covers me as I sleep, and I wake stiff and numb.

I wander around, trying to keep warm. I sit in the subway at North Cross, bowl on the floor in front of me, but the wind whistles through it and I'm shivering before I realize.

In the lull before Christmas, the city is bereaved. Before the decorations and funfair and festive music is piped from the shops, the streets are angular and exacting. People move in faltering lines. When it rains, they gather beneath the concrete canopies, flitting to the next when the downpour lightens however briefly.

As twilight falls, lone footsteps echo around the streets and you can almost hear the lights in shops being switched off. It's too cold to go back to my arches on the Hoe, the air is already crisp and dense. Instead, I search for the squat above the shop-for-rent Sandra told me about. As instructed, I slip through the crow-barred back door and climb the stairs.

Several pairs of eyes fix on me when I reach the top. I feel the air bristle.

"Sandra sent me." My voice squeaks; I haven't used it for a few days. I cough and repeat myself.

They're unmoved, continuing to ogle.

"You know Sandra, don't you?" Perhaps it's the wrong place, the wrong name. Perhaps everyone here hates Sandra, perhaps she keeps sending them gullible fools as some kind of long-standing prank.

"Yeah," says a gruff voice from the gloomy corner. "Sandra's cool. Come in, find a spot."

I scan the place. It's been derelict for a while. Windows are whitewashed and rusty. Some are broken and shards of glass have been swept into the corners. The lino floors are grimy, dusty, sticky. Sleeping bags are spread out, along with a couple of thin mattresses—too heavy to drag around the streets, but perfect when you have a dry, permanent spot.

There are doors leading off this large area—into small rooms which would have once been offices and stock rooms, I expect—and stairs leading to the floor above. There's an odor of wet denim, sweat, and urine.

Some of the squatters are alone, sleeping, eating, or in one case reading a worn copy of Harry Potter; others are assembled in muted conversation. In the darkest corners, they snort and smoke and inject.

There's a discussion about Brexit, initiated by a man they call Del reading a newspaper article aloud. There's joking and laughing, and a dispute about whose tin of baked beans has been eaten. It's all so normal. I close my eyes and think of home—Mum and Dad discussing the news, Darren poking me repeatedly in the arm because I ate his Wagon Wheel.

More people are arriving. They pause when they see me. Several women eye me with interest and disdain, while the men—mostly—nod and move on. I smile, but don't offer anything. I want to be alone.

I roll out my sleeping bag and secrete myself inside. Around me, the voices become more boisterous, occasionally bubbling over into argument, escalating to a fight. Scraps, really. All over before it's started, until the next one heats up. Inside my bag, I push my fingers into my ears and imagine waves crashing against the concrete beach and the engines of dawn fishing trawlers. I try to hear the busy silence.

3.

"How much, love?"

It's early. I couldn't sleep. Mist hangs in the air, but dawn is pushing through.

I turn with a cold, rigid glare. A bloke of about fifty sits on the far end of my bench, his eyes shifty and jittery, his lips slobbering. He's in a suit, although his tie is loose and there are stains across his shirt.

"I'm just leaving, mate." I pause. I remember nights like that—they never actually ended, and morning arrived abruptly. "You should go home and sleep it off."

"Aw, come on. You can show me a good time." He edges closer, reeking of ten-hour old alcohol. He grins and wipes his mouth with the back of his hand.

"Leave me alone." I pick up my bag and hold it against me, creating a barrier.

"You know you want to—"

"No, I don't." My voice echoes around the walls.

He grabs my arm and pulls me toward him. I twist to get away, but he has purchase and drags me close, nose to nose. I push, and he staggers backwards.

"Fuck off!"

I run, again. But with more urgency than before. The streets are empty; I'm exposed, and there are no crowds to absorb me. He won't be following—I doubt he even remembers seeing me, given his state—but I keep going, twisting this way and that, finding backstreets to duck into. In a lane behind a terrace of houses, I sit on gravel and lean against a garage door.

The little boy from the park appears beside me and rests his head on my shoulder. I see him as clearly as I see Sandra pushing her trolley along the road and Del sitting cross-legged on his bed at the squat. I squeeze my eyes shut and rub them vigorously until they're itchy and watering.

He's still there.

"Did the man scare you?" he asks.

I won't reply to my hallucination. My hands shake. I'm hungry. I was sitting on that bench waiting for the bakery to open. Sometimes, the woman who opens up saves one of yesterday's pies for me.

"I'll protect you. Mummy says I'm big and strong."

"You're not real," I mutter.

My gaze rests on his frowning, angelic face and soft blond hair. I smile. I've conjured up a beautiful child.

"I'm hungry." He jumps from the floor and pulls at my sleeve. I swear I feel the gentlest of tugs.

Stupid, hungry, deluded girl.

"Come on, it's breakfast time. I like Coco Pops. Do you?"

We walk together, my invisible friend and me. At some point, he's not there anymore.

4.

She was called Eleanor. She'd been in the squat since it was discovered, she said; on the streets a few years before that. She shook her head when I asked how long exactly. *How long* was always my question—I wanted to know what was in store for me. She'd made her corner a little piece of home. On her wall, she'd stuck crumpled photos of her daughter and husband, and she had a collection of birthday cards for them both, never sent.

One day, an indeterminate number of years ago, they'd gone to Exeter for the day—just the two of them. It was the summer holidays. Eleanor was working, but her husband had the day off, and they went. But never returned. There was an accident. The police came to her workplace and they sat in the boss's office to tell her life as she knew it was over.

She couldn't cope. She couldn't pay the rent on her part-time wage, couldn't rally herself to go back to work anyhow or look for something with more hours. She went to live with her elderly parents, but her father died, and her mother went into a home. The house had to be sold.

She lost everything and ended up homeless, she said.

She shrugged when she told me her story, I guess she'd had years to prac-tice, to keep her voice from wavering, to keep her thoughts from straying. But she cried at night. We all heard her sobs. She cried for people who died so many years ago, and I rarely cry for Ren.

She was called Eleanor, and now she's lying motionless on her thin mattress, cold to the touch. She must have died some time yesterday, and we never even noticed. We came in and sat in our own worlds. We ate from cans and maybe said a few words to each other.

When I first met Sandra she said, "We keep to our own."

But we don't. We keep to ourselves.

No one does anything for a long time. We sit in trepidation. Del and one of the other guys says we should call the police and have her collected. At the mention of the police, several people scarper.

"It's the right thing to do," Del calls after the ones leaving. But I know none of us will be here when they arrive, not even Del.

5.

"How much, love?"

Tonight, I'm exhausted. My entire body is aching.

Tonight, I'm walking back to the squat.

Tonight, I just want all of this to stop.

"Twenty?" I say, because surely he'll baulk when I step from the shadows and he sees me properly.

"Ten."

Foggy and weary, my thoughts tumble over themselves. *Run, run away.*

"Sure," I reply with hopelessness, crawling into the car and pushing away the cavernous pit of dread in my stomach. Whiffs of cigarettes and greasy burgers and BO greet me. There are polystyrene cartons and chip bags in the footwell, a cold slimy feel to the upholstery.

He drives a couple of minutes along the road and turns into a side-street of industrial units and garages.

"In the back," he barks.

I glance behind me but remain belted in place. I try to say something, to explain this is a terrible mistake, to please let me go—but my voice croaks and the words fade. I rummage for the door handle but can't find it in the dark.

"For fuck's sake, I haven't got all night."

He unbuckles me and heaves me through the gap between our seats. I fold into the back and he follows. I don't think to fight or wriggle from his grasp. I chose this; this is my fault. He pulls his jeans down over his hips and crushes his mouth against my neck, his warm breath damp on my skin. He unzips my thick jacket and slithers his sweaty hand under my jumpers, his fingers getting tangled in the layers. He shoves his mouth onto mine, and I pull away. He pushes my head into his groin.

I think of the sea, deep and green. I think of bobbing in a boat on the sea, deep and green. I think of having sun on my face as I bob in a boat on the sea, deep and green...

I think of the sea...

I'm back on the street, two grubby fivers wedged into my fist, as the car drives off. Tears pour down my face. I pull at my clothes because they're constricting and suffocating. They're dirty, tainted. Their filth stains me, creeps across me like mold, envelopes me like a second skin.

Got to feel clean. Got to be clean.

I vomit. Right there in the middle of the pavement. Gasping with horror and repugnance.

It's a frosty, clear night—stars glimmering, the crescent moon frowning at me. Ice hangs in the air and a chill wind pushes against me. I begin to unzip my jacket, to let it fall from me, to remove every debauched layer.

The boy's arms are around me, stopping me, taking my weight, so big and strong. If not for him, I'd crumble. I'm small and splintered.

There's a late-night off-license close by. I lumber along the road, my mind blank, operating solely on instinct. The lone shop assistant follows me around the shelves vigilantly. I buy vodka. I hold out the hand with the money but it's not enough.

"Another four pound fifty, love."

I flinch at the word 'love,' and gaze at my hand. He has to repeat the price before I look through my bag for more. As soon as I'm around the corner, I drink. The liquid coats my lips and trickles down my chin. It takes the edge off my sordid shame, my guilt, my loss. My thoughts fragment. I'm at peace.

6.

Dawn is pink and hazy; the sky is luminous with snow-feathered clouds. I'm in the center of town, staring down the broad length of Armada Way. I was on my way to the squat; I must have stopped walking. The vodka is half gone.

Office workers in suits and clip-clop heels decant from buses and trudge to the multitude of coffee shops. Lights go on in banks and shops. Students amble to early lectures. The street cleaner whistles as he sweeps, and delivery men trundle their trolleys. They avert their eyes when they notice me. Because I'm not here. I'm invisible. I'm nobody.

I want my arches back. I want to curl up into my corner and smell the sea when I wake up and watch the seagulls float, waiting for fish. I don't want to return to the squat where people argue about trivial things and get stoned to run away from their lives and die in the middle of the day.

Someone comes out of Costa with two takeaway cups and hands me one while avoiding my eye. Later, someone offers me a breakfast bap.

And then I see her. In this wretched state, I see Kirsty, my almost friend. She's walking alongside her daughter and pushing the empty buggy. Charlotte's so big now—her hair in shoulder-length bunches, her face elongated, her movements purposeful. Old enough to be trusted not to abscond when Kirsty lets go of her hand.

I grip the bench to prevent myself rushing across and begging for help. Look at me—I'm polluted. I'd disgust her, if she recognized me at all, that is. She'd pull Charlotte close and hurry away.

I wonder if Neil brings Ren into town, if he buys her toys and treats her with sweets when she's been good. I wonder if he lets her dress up with fairy wings over her coat.

My little apparition is skipping beside Kirsty and Charlotte, although they can't see him of course. He waves at me, smiling brightly, beckoning me over, but I shake my head and absurdly whisper, "No, I can't."

He turns to Charlotte and covers his eyes, playing peek-a-boo. The little girl giggles with surprise when he shouts, "Boo," and holds her hand out to him. She's babbling earnestly and he's replying.

No, she can't be. *They* can't be. He's mine. The boy blows me a kiss and fades away. Charlotte's mouth opens wide as she searches for him between the legs of all the adults walking past, and bursts into tears.

I head for the respite of the Hoe. It's quiet, save for a few locals walking dogs or jogging along the foreshore. The row of parking spaces which stretches the full length of the sea front is mostly empty. Good. I don't want crowds or people staring with repulsion. I want to be left alone to drink the rest of this vodka and fall into a dreamless oblivion.

If I close my eyes tight, I'm twelve again, on holiday in Cornwall with my parents. The sea is splashing against the beach and seagulls are squawking and fighting over abandoned chips. I can hear Mum calling me for the picnic she's setting up, and Dad and Darren playing cricket with a tennis ball.

Here, now, the feeble October sun warms my face and the swooshing waves ebb in time with my breathing. I unscrew the top of the vodka and take a long swig which stings the back of my throat.

"How much, love?" calls a man from his car.

It takes a moment for my head to tilt toward him, for my eyes to follow and focus.

Not again?

But what else can I do? One time was always going to lead to the next. I want to sneer in distaste and walk away. But I don't. I think of the money and get in the passenger side.

I barely notice this stranger. I block out his face, his voice, his touch. I push back my tears and try to unclench my fists. I stare out of the window at the derelict buildings he's taken me to and hope no one's watching. I shut my ears to his grunts and moans.

When I'm returned to the same spot, I hardly remember anything. I still vomit. I still have the same gnawing abhorrence as before. I swig my vodka and wait for it to pass.

7.

The air has been dank and gray for days, the vast sweep of cloud makes the world dismal and monotonous. Underfoot, brown leaves mulch into the pavement. I drift through the days as though they no longer exist—or as though I don't. A ghost. Ignored, overlooked, walking along roads I don't recognize because if I sit in one place, I'll grow thick tentacle roots into the pavement and never leave.

"Who the fuck are you?"

A tall, Amazonian woman—all makeup, big bleached hair, and garish, gold jewelry—looms over me. I take in her tiny skirt and thigh-high stiletto boots with abstracted attention, taking a moment to realize she's not another hallucination.

In my stupor, I've drifted far from my usual haunts. I look for a road sign or landmark.

Such high heels! How does she walk in them? I rise onto my tiptoes to emulate her.

"And what the fuck d'you think you're looking at like that, bitch?"

I half-point to her boots, but she slams her hand into the side of my face, catching my chin with a chunky skull-and-cross-bone ring. I gasp and step away, holding my hands in front of me.

"I don't want any—"

There are two women behind me. They grab my arms and restrain me. I squirm, and their long false nails dig into my wrists.

A punch to my face. Blood gushes from my nose and mouth.

A fist in my stomach. I crumple forward, winded and groaning.

They drop me to the tarmac, filling the air with harsh, cackling laughter.

The first woman crouches beside me and grabs my hair to turn me toward her, her face inches from mine. Her gum-minty breath brushes my cheek.

"Stay away from our fucking patch. If I see you here again, I'll fucking slice you. Got it, princess?"

She stands and, almost as an afterthought while I flounder on the ground, stamps into my stomach and grinds her stiletto into my skin until I shriek.

The boy tries to help me stand, but pain sears through me.

"You have to move, you can't stay here," he says.

He manages to prop me against a fence. Cars pass by. It's getting dark, and I'm concealed from the road.

"You have to stand up."

I close my eyes and shake my head. "I can't. Leave me alone. Please."

8.

"How much, love?"

How long have I been here? Minutes? Hours? It's fully dark and the streetlights are spot-lighting the pavement. My joints have seized; my fingers feel as though they'll snap off. My breath billows on the freezing air. I need a warm bed, a warm car, anything at all.

"Ten," I mumble automatically, without looking up. Why bother? They're all the same.

I stand, using the wall to jimmy myself up, wincing at the stiletto-induced agony in my abdomen. My head is sluggish and disconnected. I taste blood and wipe it with the back of my hand, fascinated by the smear it leaves.

He recoils when we're face-to-face, this guy, as though *I'm* the monster. He jumps out of his car and rushes across to me.

"Shit, what happened? Let me see your face." He takes my hand and pulls me toward the light. He touches my cheek and I flinch. "Does it hurt?"

"What do *you* think?"

"Sorry." He backs off, holding his hands in submission. "Just trying to help."

"A *Good Samaritan*, eh?" I snigger. I snarl more than smile because my lip is swelling up now. My words are sticky and mumbled. "You're all the same, aren't you?"

"Pardon?"

"Forget it. Still wanna fuck?"

He considers me warily. "Sure. But I'm hungry first. You want to come with me?"

My stomach growls, the thought of food is enticing—I don't recall my last meal. But the offer of anything besides money makes me suspicious. There's a catch.

"You've eaten?"

"Seriously?"

"No, I didn't think so." He seems so concerned. He smiles kindly. "My treat?"

I hesitate, weighing my options, searching for an escape. Everything about this is wrong, yet he's being so nice. My instincts are dulled, I can't make this decision.

"Here," he says, holding out a ten-pound note. I take it. "See you round."

I wave the money at him. "What's this for?"

"We agreed ten, so that's what you've got."

"That's not how it works."

He shrugs. "I changed my mind—there's no need for you to miss out on the money. Have a decent meal, or… whatever."

I shift from one foot to the other, still holding the money in the space between us. "Are you coming too?" I hold my breath, wide-eyed. Shit.

"Do you want me to?"

I swallow, not trusting myself. *No, no I don't.* I need to walk away—he said I could. He was going to leave himself. I stopped him. I should take the money and go. But I'm already nodding. "Sure."

"I'm Marco, by the way."

I haven't said my name aloud for a long time—no one's asked. *Grace* feels wrong—too homely and pure. After an inept pause, I say, "Charis. I'm Charis."

9.

We're in a small, back-street pub. Evidently this guy knows the landlord because when we walk in, he asks for a bowl of warm water and some cloths before we even order a drink. The landlord makes a flippant jibe I don't understand.

We sit in a corner, and while Marco cleans blood from my face and hands, he asks about Charis. And Charis smiles...

"I've lived all over the world. Paris, California, India for a time." She sips lager while Marco inspects the scratches on her forearm. "I was born in Italy. My parents moved around a lot, traveled, never really settled anywhere. It was a strange childhood, lonely, you know?"

The landlord brings their meal, and Charis dives into the chunky chips and removes the gherkins from the burger with a "yuck."

"They both died a couple of years ago, a plane crash." She smiles, imploring him to collude in her fantasy.

"A plane crash," he confirms sympathetically. "You're an orphan, then." Charis nods. "I guess I am."

People are staring at them, at *her*, disparagingly. She doesn't belong. They're trying to decode the uneven relationship between a thirty-something man in a business suit and a girl dressed in tat. They're wondering why she's bruised and bloody, and if he's the guy who did it.

Marco drinks his red wine—classy, Charis thinks—and watches her attentively. "So, how did you end up on the streets?" He's going to say more but stops himself.

"Like I said, I've got no family. No friends, either. Just me." She shrugs, pushing away all the memories which are no longer hers. "It's okay. I get by."

Marco isn't fooled. He knows it's all bullshit. He lets Charis talk and bury herself deep in her lies. But *I* know. I see the skepticism in his eyes, the amusement on his lips.

She takes large bites of her burger, filling her mouth—the decadence of gluttony after surviving on scraps.

"Why did you get beaten up tonight?" He pushes his untouched chips toward her. "Does it happen often?"

"I was on the wrong street at the wrong time," she says, mouth still full. "I usually keep myself to myself. I don't like trouble, it's inconvenient."

"How long's it been?"

"On the streets?" She smiles wryly. "It feels like my whole life."

"It's going to be a cold winter."

"Yeah."

His phone vibrates on the table. He glances at it and his lip twitches. "It's late," he says, finishing his drink swiftly. It's only half-past ten. The night hasn't even started yet. "I have to go. I'll see you round."

"Thanks for the meal."

Marco pauses at the bar to pay the tab. Charis thinks she sees the flash of a fifty. Without him, I'm me again—claustrophobic and fearful. In a room full of strangers who have normal lives, I'm conspicuous. I finish off the chips, and my lager, and start to gather my things.

"Another one?" asks the landlord, clearing the table. "Marco left a bit extra, be a shame to waste it."

I smile coyly. "Why not?"

1∅.

"Hello, there."

My eyes are closed. I'm asleep. Don't wake me up. "Go away."

"You can't sleep here, it's not safe."

I was dreaming I was someone else.

"Come on, I'll take you to my place." I'm lifted from the pavement onto my feet. "Had a good time, did we?"

"No, I don't want to go to…"

My head floats beside me. Sharp lights pierce my eyes and I close them again. So sleepy. Just let me sleep here, I'll be fine… But I'm pulled along by this new savior. I reluctantly lean on his arm to prevent me from tumbling to the ground. My legs can barely keep up with him.

I'm moving but not walking. In a car. This is bad. I try to sit up, to find the handle, to escape. But my fingers are rigid and disobedient. The streetlights flash past like flickering Christmas decorations, and I'm flying on a magic carpet.

Hands wrap around me and pull me into the cold again.

"Who're you?" I try to ask, but the syllables jumble in my mouth.

He snorts. "I'm just a Good Samaritan, honey." He turns us around sharply, and my head flops to one side. It hurts to retrieve it. "Another couple of steps, that's right, up we go."

We've left the street; we're inside. He props me against a wall while he fiddles with keys, then I'm scooped up again.

"Up the stairs, keep walking. A few more, good girl. We'll get you into a warm bed, shall we?"

Charis

1.

There's a noise. Unusual and perturbing. Anything that doesn't make immediate sense is a threat. I open my eyes, ready to spring to my feet and flee.

I don't move. My head is detached, swimming in dense fog. My arms and legs are raw and weak; my mouth is swollen and dry. My left eye throbs every time I blink; I can barely see through it.

I've no idea where I am. I'm in a bed, a *proper* bed. I haven't slept on a soft mattress for so long. I'm naked. Where are my clothes? I spread my arms out and tentatively explore the space beside me. It's cold. I'm alone.

I remember… I remember… nothing, nothing at all. Where am I?

I try to sit up, but the movement makes me dizzy and sick. I find a position which doesn't make the room spin and lie very still.

"Good morning, honey. I wondered if you'd surface today."

That voice… I recognize it. I peer from the duvet as he walks around the room and opens the curtains. The light pierces me, and I bury myself under the covers.

"You haven't eaten. You've got to eat something—it'll make you feel better."

On the bedside table, there's a plate of buttered toast and a glass of water. I reach for the water and sip painfully. He sits on the bed and holds the glass with me.

"It's you."

It's the weird guy from last night, the one who paid me not to have sex and bought dinner. He takes the glass and puts it on the side. He's not smiling—shouldn't he be smiling?

"How did I get here?"

"I found you in the road. You were in a bad way. Seems you had yourself a bit of a party after I left."

"You came back for me?"

"Nigel, the landlord, phoned me. He thought you needed someone to look after you. I felt responsible."

I say nothing, still wary. I've lost sight of what typical behavior is. I can't decide if this is something everyone would do, or just random psychopaths looking for their next victim. I grip the duvet.

"I bought you a toothbrush, shower gel, some other stuff. I didn't know if you had any..." He sneers at my holdall. "The bathroom's across the landing when you're ready."

"I—I..." I stop. A shower? I haven't had one in ages—I stopped going to the shelter a while ago. I've been wiping myself down with wet wipes in the public toilets. "Thank you."

Alone, I nibble at the toast and drink more water, trying to alleviate the queasiness—I'm not sure how accommodating this guy would be if I puked all over his house. It's a bare room with no pictures on the walls and no unnecessary furnishing, like cupboards or a chair. The home of a bachelor. Shit.

The window faces onto another building, close-set, so I can't determine where I am. I can't formulate an escape plan if I don't know where I am.

My stomach begins to settle as my unease rises. The smell of toast reminds me of Dad cooking breakfast at the weekend, rousing Mum and me with the fragrance of bacon wafting up the stairs. It's a homely, reassuring smell, despite being cold now with the butter congealing on the surface.

The room spins when I stand; my head teeters from side to side. I steady myself with the wall. It doesn't make sense—how much did I drink last night?

In the bathroom, the woman in the mirror is hideous. Her face is bruised along one side, her eye is fused shut and swollen. Me. My face, my eye. I look worse than when Neil was hammering me. I open my mouth and my jaw spasms; the cut on my lip splits.

Small memories are returning, random and scattered. I try to grab them, but they vanish. There were women. There was a man in the pub, after this guy left. Or before. Or *was* him?

I brush my teeth. The taste of mint, the freshness, fills my mouth. I brush until my teeth squeak.

The hot water discolors immediately, rinsing street grime from my body.

I lather shampoo into my tangled hair, feeling the softness cascading over my shoulders. When I rinse, it squeaks too. The gel fills the cubicle with rich coconut, but it stings. I'm speckled with purple and green bruises, with burning abrasions and deep cuts. Old and new injuries combine until my skin is camouflaged. My stomach has a raised blemish of rough, red flesh, and as I graze my finger over it, I recall the sharp stiletto which caused it.

I scan this broken body, these scrawny arms and protruding hip bones. Skin hangs from my waist, off my thighs. Raw husky sobs echo around the bathroom, relieved and vulnerable in equal measure, until I'm depleted. The woman in the mirror is expressionless.

The robe left for me is fluffy and large, dropping almost to the floor. I go in search of my Good Samaritan, following the sound of the radio and movement to the kitchen downstairs. He's making coffee. I want to leave. I *would*, if I was dressed for it.

"Feeling better?"

I assess the dazed feeling, the hunger and dehydration. I nod. I shouldn't nod—my head spins.

"Coffee? More toast?"

"Yes. Please." I side into the chair at the tiny bistro table. "Um, sorry, you'll have to tell me your name again. I don't quite remember."

He raises his eyebrows and smiles. "Ah, I'm not surprised. I'm Marco." He puts a mug in front of me and holds my gaze. "And you're Charis." I frown, and he adds, "At least that's what you told me last night."

Memories. More memories. A trickle of them. I strain to maintain a neutral expression.

"That's right. Charis."

And Charis is a strong woman, a fighter, a better person than me. She hasn't been crushed yet; her life is just beginning. I am Charis, and Grace fades into the shadows.

Marco takes Charis's chin between his thumb and forefinger, moving her head left and right, up and down. Nausea rises, her head hovers above her. She pulls back, and he lets go.

"You scrub up quite well. Not bad at all." He glides his hand along the collar of the robe and strokes her cheek. "Once the swelling goes down, you could be quite pretty."

Charis recognizes the slimy arrogance. She closes her eyes, disappointed she didn't notice the signs earlier. She thought he was different, someone who truly wanted to help. But that's not how it works anymore. She lowers her head, peeking through her eyelashes, and pouts seductively. Because this is what *Charis* does. She leans toward him, encouraging him.

"You're wasted on street corners, you know," he whispers in her ear.

Charis's eyes flicker, but her smile remains glued to her lips. She twists so the robe falls from one shoulder and her breast is exposed.

"Not right now, honey." His fingers play with the edge of the robe, brushing against her skin, then steps back. "I'm going out. Make yourself at home."

"Wait. You're not leaving me here." She stands. "Where are my clothes?"

"Relax, enjoy yourself."

"Thank you for your help, but I want to go. I want my clothes."

"No. I'm looking after you now."

His severe expression prevents her from arguing back—it reminds *me* of Neil. He pockets his phone and leaves. Charis hears him locking the front door, but she follows to check.

2.

Charis plots her escape. She's on the first floor, so jumping would be ill-advised but conceivable. Directly in front is a row of old stone buildings, four stories high. It's probable this building is in a similar terrace. Between them is a narrow-cobbled passageway—not a street, definitely not a road. Flags fly from poles, so close Charis could steal one.

Opening the window, she leans out and hears cawing seagulls and the bustle of people. She breathes in the scent of the sea. She's on the Barbican, in one of the tiny alleys snaking off the main road. At the end of this lane, there'll be shops and restaurants and pubs the full length of Southside Street. And people milling around. All she needs to do is yell and they'll come running.

But then what? Back to the squat, to asking strangers for money, and the uncertainty of the next car to pull up beside her? Back to being Grace?

Charis makes another coffee. She watches the steam rise and marvels at the simplicity of her joy—hot water, a soft bed, being unburdened with worry. She sits by the window, drinks coffee, feels the warmth of the house all around her.

A woman wanders beneath the window, taking photos. She crouches and angles her camera toward the stone doorway and hanging baskets. She tilts the camera further, contorting her body to get the right shot—she must be aiming at the rooftops and the radiant blue sky.

This is Charis's chance. *Help me, I've been kidnapped.*

Their eyes meet. The woman stands and smiles self-consciously. She looks like a student, from the art college perhaps. Or maybe it's just a hobby, a way to fill her Instagram feed. She looks like someone who'd help, if she was asked.

Charis raises her hand. It's supposed to be a distress call, but it looks like a wave, and the woman waves back.

She lifts the camera and aims it at Charis, and Charis ducks into the shadows of the room, recalling the swollen, bruised mess of her face. How visible are these injuries, she wonders. Were they obvious as the picture was being taken, or will the woman be sickened when she enlarges the image on her computer later and realizes what she missed?

The photographer's still there, her camera turned to the cobbles and the pink flowering weeds which spring up along the curb. Charis can still shout down to her. She stands and scrolls through the photos she's taken, covers the lens with its cap, and walks back toward the shops. She'll probably treat herself to a hot chocolate now, sit in one of the cafés, and watch people amble past.

3.

Make yourself at home, Marco said. So Charis explores.

The house covers the top three stories of the building; the ground floor is a mystery she's been locked away from. On this floor is the kitchen and living room, with a dining table and a tired, brown three-piece suite. Upstairs, the bathroom and two bedrooms—one Charis slept in and a smaller one, furnished just as sparsely. On the third floor is Marco's room and another, locked room.

Charis peers inside but doesn't enter. The curtains are closed, and his bed is unmade. It's as bleak and functional as the rest of the house. There's an odd vibe—it doesn't feel lived in. As though Marco's just passing through. Not a home. Not a place where you could kick off your shoes and drink wine in front of a good film. It's like Neil's house when I first moved in. History repeating itself. Or perhaps that's just my memory of it.

After being outside for so long, the walls are clingy and restrictive. Charis pictures herself as a tortoise, as though everywhere she goes from now on she'll be dragging this room with her.

Her nausea is spiking, although her throbbing head is subsiding. Back in the kitchen, she searches for something to eat. She fills a bowl with muesli and makes a mug of tea. In the living room, she puts the TV on—the silence is too loud—flipping through channels which are alien to her, as though watching in a foreign country. Even the news is remote and bewildering.

It's getting gloomy, clouding over to unleash torrential rain. Yesterday, I was out in this weather, and today Charis will be warm and dry, snug in her fluffy robe. She curls up on the settee and lets the noise of the TV, and the driving rain on the window, lull her to sleep.

She doesn't dream. Charis has no daughter to fret for, no family to miss. So she drifts off easily, peacefully.

Someone's in the room. "Marco?" she mumbles. No answer. "Ren?"

"Shhh, it's just me, silly."

"Are you checking up on me?"

"I thought you were lost."

"No, everything's going to be okay now."

"You've got a different name."

"I'm a different person."

He takes Charis's hand, and turns it so her palm is exposed. He traces the lines and sighs. "No, it's okay. You're still you." He snuggles down beside her and kisses the top of her head.

4.

"Wake up, *honey.* Time to pay your dues."

Charis stretches out slothfully and scowls. "What's going on?"

"I've got a job for you."

"What d'you mean?"

"Well, if you're staying here, you have to pay your way."

"Who says I'm staying? I never asked for your help. Just let me leave and—" She tries to sit up and swivel herself off the settee, but Marco uses her robe to pin her down.

"No, honey, that's not how this is going to work. You're staying here. You need me. You need someone to look after you. You're just a kid, you won't make it through the winter. You have no idea what it'll be like."

She glowers. He's right. The nights are already long and foreboding; the days dreary and damp. She resigns her anger and forces a syrupy smile. *A strong woman, a fighter; remember this.* There's a tightness in her chest she's trying to ignore, heaviness in her stomach. *My* tightness, *my* heaviness.

"What's the job?"

"I've got a friend—he wants to meet you."

Charis nods with dismay. "I should get dressed then."

He doesn't move, keeping her confined.

"Would you mind letting me get up? And telling me where my clothes are?"

He scoffs. "Those things? I threw them away. Here."

He thrusts a large bag, stuffed with clothes in varying sizes, into her arms. All of them are from charity shops with the tags still attached. Slinky dresses, flouncy mini-skirts, strapless tops. In a token attempt at day-wear, there's a pair of jeans and an oversized sweatshirt.

No underwear though, not a single bra or pair of knickers.

She holds out several items which are near enough her size. "What should I wear?"

Marco points to a short, blue dress with cut-away waist and sequined hems, and she leaves the room. In her bedroom… No, not *her* bedroom, *the* bedroom. This is temporary; she won't be here long enough to call it hers.

In *the* bedroom, she dresses quickly and gazes miserably at her reflection. Her bruises are conspicuous and incongruous with the outfit. She touches each of them in turn, watching the skin turn white then become the previous green or purple.

Marco leads her downstairs and out into the street. The ground floor has a large window, like a shop front, but blacked out. A small, unobtrusive sign says *Private Shop*. Of course it does, she mutters to herself.

They walk to the end of the alley and onto Southside Street, and a car's waiting for them. Marco opens the passenger door and guides Charis inside.

"Have fun. Be good," he says, waving cheerfully as if he's sending her off on holiday.

Charis swivels around to watch him, her Good Samaritan, disappearing into the distance. She hasn't done this before. Instead of my vodka-induced acquiescence, she's powerless and terrified.

She wonders if she can reach over and grab the steering wheel to cause a crash, to escape in the chaos.

Or slip away while this guy is collecting the room key.

Or lock herself in the bathroom and refuse to come out.

But it's too late. They're already in the room. Charis is already perched on the bed. This guy—"Call me Dominic"—is already lying naked next to her.

She exhales and edges closer. It's nothing we haven't done before. It's just another bloke, just another day. She'd kill for a drink right now.

Her hands roam his body; she cringes. He rolls toward her; she cowers. There's a cavern of repugnance burgeoning in her stomach. She shudders. Dominic's bulk is fully on top of her, suffocating her.

"I can't," she pleads, pushing his face away from hers.

"*Can't?*"

She flinches, but he doesn't lash out as she expects. He just stares.

"I don't think you understand how this works. This isn't about what *you* want. It's about what I want, what I'm *paying* for."

He clutches her wrist and twists her arm to keep her from wriggling. She gazes out of the window, watching the sea mist rolling over itself on the damp air, curling around the building opposite. Her stomach churns with every excruciating thrust, with every revolting and repellent grunt.

When it's over, Charis is overpowered with despair. Dominic gathers his clothes—Charis barely noticed him rolling off her. He's almost as stricken as she is, bearing similar dejection.

"You're married?"

His ring glints as he runs his hand through his hair. "Yeah."

"So, why do you do this?"

Why am I here if you've left your wife at home alone? Why do you pay so much to feel so shit? Tell me this is right. Tell me this is the way it's supposed to be, that this is the way you want it to be. Tell me lies, if it'll make me feel better... if it'll make you feel better.

"Why d'you care? You're getting paid, aren't you?" He checks his watch and throws her dress onto the bed. "Come on, we've got to go."

5.

It's four o'clock in the morning. Charis hasn't slept yet. The night presses down on her. When she closes her eyes, I'd like to think she's dreaming about Paris and California, but I know she's not. Her head is full of my baggage—of a husband running after her with a rake and a screaming baby she can't console, and a mother and father standing over her telling her how disappointed they are with her.

There are other reasons she can't sleep.

It's hot. Despite the plunging temperature, she opens the window and leans out, grateful for the crisp air and stiff breeze. Everything is still. Four in the morning is too late for even the hardiest of stragglers from the pubs and too early for café owners to be stirring. Breakfast won't be required for several more hours.

She's lonely. Since sleeping in the squat, I've got used to the snoring, coughing, weeping, tossing and turning—and therefore, so has Charis. Now, she can only hear her own breathing, her own weeping.

She can still feel Dominic's hands on her skin. She showered when she got back, turning the water as hot as she could handle, scalding his fingerprints off. But they're growing back, swarming over her.

She wonders if she's been kidnapped. Marco locked the main door on the ground floor when she came in, and then the door to the house when they walked up the stairs together. So he doesn't want her to leave. But if she's been kidnapped, she'd *want* to leave, and she's not sure she does. The parts of yesterday when she was making herself coffee and watching TV were fun. Falling asleep on the settee was nice, she'd forgotten what a good nap felt like.

When I was little, my parents would lecture me on the dangers of getting into cars with strangers, of wandering off when we were Christmas shopping and getting tangled among the legs of strangers. Madeleine McCann went missing when I was six or seven—my parents sat me down, again, and reiterated their rules.

Both Charis and I have broken those rules—I wonder if they still apply.

It's four in the morning. On the other side of town, Ren will be crying like she always does.

Charis feels the boy lying beside her, the slight dip and roll as he manifests.

She stares at the ceiling until there are no more thoughts or memories or dreams to distract her, until there's a dark, empty space where all those things were.

6.

Charis is awake. Has been all night. The sun rose, the birds chirped, cars and vans began to drive along Southside Street. She lies in bed, wondering if she's allowed to get up. After a while, she tiptoes downstairs, nervous of waking Marco—she doesn't even put the kettle on, she sits at the window and waits.

It's past ten when Marco appears. In the kitchen, he makes coffee and toast. Charis isn't sure if she should go to him, so she waits, albeit a little less relaxed, a little less composed. He goes back upstairs without even saying hello. In days to come, she'll learn this is normal —he's not a morning person—but right now, she panics. What's she done wrong? Will there be punishment?

The wait for his return is long; the creak of the stairs to signal it nauseates her. He pokes his head into the room, nods and goes downstairs to the shop.

Charis spends the day right there, relishing the novelty of the average and mundane. She watches a severe rainstorm flood the cobbles, relieved she's not out there but thinking of all those who still are. Thinking about Sandra.

Later, she curls up with a book she finds under the bed. Every so often, uneasiness creeps across her. Is this normal? Would someone else accept this situation? Would Grace?

But she's not Grace. She's Charis. And she can take care of herself. In fact, she's pretty much landed on her feet here. There's food in the fridge, hot water in the taps, and right now she's sprawled out with a book, safe from the elements. It couldn't be more perfect.

The next few days pan out the same way. Eating, drinking, reading. Over lunch, Charis switches on the TV and watches the news. She's slowly reconnecting with the world. When you're on the streets, the only things that matter are the next meal and surviving the bitterly cold nights. While others, collecting their hot soup or sitting around in the squat, could debate the latest cuts to benefits or if the country needed a second referendum, Charis could not. She was a shadow, slightly out of step with everything around her.

Marco locks up the shop between six and seven—it changes on a whim. He orders pizza or Chinese food, which they eat wordlessly in front of the TV.

Tonight he says, "It's time to get ready. You've got a client."

He brought pie and chips from the chippy, and it lies heavily in her stomach. She takes a breath and fusses with the gravy in the tin foil tray.

He nods his head toward the stairs. "You'd better hurry."

Charis changes into another skimpy dress and waits nervously at the front door.

Marco, as he did on the first night, waves her off.

7.

"You should go out," Marco says one morning.

He's stopped disappearing back to his bedroom. He lingers in the kitchen or living room, and Charis has overcome her urge to hide from him. He's leaning against the fridge, checking emails on his phone, and Charis is drying last night's dishes. It's unnervingly normal.

"What?"

"You've been cooped up since you got here—well, mostly"—he winks—"you should go for a walk or go shopping, whatever. It's not like you're a prisoner, is it?" he adds, though his tone darkens, the glint of a threat in his eye.

She glances out of the window. From here, she's looking out onto the squashed-up backs of houses and shops into a courtyard—sanitized remnants of nineteenth-century slums.

"I'm happy here." Her smile falters.

"No, you're not."

Sometimes, there's a softer side to Marco, a sweet, kind one—a side who visits his mother with bouquets of flowers and checks on neighbors during blizzards. He takes a key from his pocket and puts it on the counter in front of her.

When Charis leaves the flat, it's *me* who emerges onto the narrow-cobbled lane. I pause, expecting Marco to drag me back inside as though it was all a cruel joke. I don't know what to do, where to go, how to blend in with everyone else.

I'm playing a role. I'm pretending to walk down this street and look in the shop windows. I'm observing other people and copying them. I want to go into one of the quaint little coffee shops with tablecloths and china cups and saucers and cream teas, but I don't know how to. I envisage a large arrow pointing me out as different, not normal, not like you.

I'm worried. Of being recognized by a client—now I have a pimp, I have *clients*, not sleazy men who approach me from the shadows. Worried of being outed as a fraud. Of bumping into Mum and Dad, or Neil and Ren. I contemplate what Charis would do—confident, unbroken Charis. She'd swagger along these streets; she'd face them all, especially Neil.

I pop to the tiny supermarket and buy chicken breasts and vegetables for dinner—Charis would cook, just to watch the confusion on Marco's face.

"Hey, Kid. Long time, no see."

Sandra's rusty trolley rattles toward me, shuddering over the cracks in the pavement.

I try to smile.

"Oof, had some bother?" She indicates my cheek, still slightly discolored. The cut under my eye is still ragged.

I touch it self-consciously. "Just a little. How are you?"

"Meh." She brushes the question aside. "You cleaned up. You went home?"

"Not exactly."

She nods as though she understands, muttering to herself under her breath.

"It's good to see you. How are you doing?"

"Same old."

I hesitate, then pull a ten-pound note from my pocket and hold it out.

"Keep your money."

"But you're my friend. You've been so good to me. I want to help. Please."

"It's *your* money?"

"Of course it is."

She looks as though she's going to refuse again, then takes it. "Thanks." She tucks it into one of the dirty, decomposing supermarket bags wedged into the trolley and continues to rummage.

"Well, I should—"

"Wait. Just a sec." Her face contorts as she feels her way to the bottom of a bag. "Ah!" she exclaims, holding a small, wooden-handled thing aloft. She offers it out to me.

It's a knife. One where the blade is concealed in the handle. It's not wooden, but plastic with a grainy pattern and engraved DAVID.

"Who's David?"

She wafts her hand. "Doesn't matter. But I want you to have this." She closes my hand around it with both of hers, as though praying.

"Oh, no." I try to break free from her grip. "I—"

"I want you to be safe."

"I don't need a knife for that." The dangerous times are over. I've got a house, someone to watch out for me, security.

"Grace, please."

Her demeanor alters—serious and sincere—an expression in her jaded eyes which stops me dead.

"Okay. I will. Thank you." I put it in my pocket. When I get home, I'll hide it somewhere, so I never have to look at it.

She nods with relief. "You'd better go. I don't want to get you into trouble."

"Trouble? With who?"

She smiles sadly. "You should've gone home."

She walks away without another word, struggling with the chaotic wheels. People take a wide berth around her, and I see her as they do. In another life, I think I might have crossed the road to avoid her too.

8.

October crumbles away. The rain is incessant, and the days barely brighten.

Charis's client list has expanded, and without realizing it she's got a steady "job" and an income. She has money saved in a small tin hidden in her holdall—it reminds her of my pig jar, but she brushes the memory aside because it's not hers, it's mine.

Most of the clients come to the house now. Marco cleared out the spare room and tasked Charis to furnish it. She bought mirrors and lamps and cushions and thick fluffy throws. She painted the walls deep purple and swathed voile panels over the curtain pole.

Dominic still collects her in his beaten-up Focus and drops her back two hours later. He still barely talks; still looks haunted and sullen as he drives away.

The days are her own. She sits in her room and reads, or watches TV, or listens to music while she vacuums or does some laundry. As though this is a proper house and she's a proper housewife. Sometimes we go shopping, Charis and I, leaving the house side-by-side as though we're the same person; sometimes we stop somewhere for lunch.

Christmas decorations appear in the shops; Christmas music blasting around the stores on a loop. We go to watch the lights being switched on and wander around the wooden huts. We eat hot chestnuts and drink mulled wine. Father Christmas appears in his grotto in the mall. I wonder if Neil will take Ren, if they're here tonight.

Then I remember last year, when Neil canceled our plans and locked us in the house, and know they probably aren't.

I hold my locket, and the small hand of my darling delusion nestles into mine. We stand for a while, awestruck by the lights flashing red and blue and green across our faces.

Charis sees her before I do. I duck behind the corner of one of the huts and peer out. It was Ren; Charis is positive. I scan the street, my eyes lingering on every little girl skipping alongside her father. Too old, too blonde, too tall, not old enough… She's gone. No, there—heading to the merry-go-round.

I hold my breath, ready to run toward her.

Oh.

No.

It's not her. It's never her.

My legs weaken, and I cling to the hut, pretending to admire their scarves. In reality, I'm immobile, overcome with lethargy and grief while shoppers sweep past me. I can barely breathe, sucking back tears.

"Are you okay?" asks the stall owner, and I nod vaguely before shuffling away.

I need Charis. I need her detachment and independence, her lack of baggage weighing her down.

On my slow, winding way back to Marco's house, there are several pubs all teeming with seasonal spirit and jollity. It spills onto the streets and drags me inside. Better to be here among strangers than at home alone. I order a pint of cider and the guy next to me puts tinsel around my shoulders, and I am Charis.

9.

It's just the one.

That's what Charis tells Marco.

It's what she tells herself.

She goes out for lunch most days now, the house increasingly oppressive. And with lunch she'll order a glass of wine. She reads books and feels sophisticated. She's bought herself a journal and sometimes she'll be inspired to write a line or two of poetry. Nothing decent, just jotting down her thoughts—she won't show anyone. She chews on the end of her pen and enjoys the idea of other diners assuming she's a famous author and wondering who she is.

Who is Charis?

That's what she wants to know.

Dominic gives her a Christmas tip. He hands it to her in his usual brooding way and tells her not to mention it to Marco. He says she's upped her game recently, and he likes it.

A glass with lunch turns into a second one as she stretches the afternoons to avoid going back to the house. Her journal is filling up. She writes about her dreams and her previous life in Paris and Rome and India. She allows me to write about Ren, to draw little sketches of her. And occasionally, I write about a strange little boy who stands beside me and holds my hand.

There's a Fisher Price activity center in the charity shop window, and I buy it. There's no box with it and some of the buttons are worn with use, with love. I picture the previous owner crawling up to it, mesmerized by the beeps and buzzes and whirling shapes.

"What age would this be for?" I asked.

The assistant shrugged. "Two? Eighteen months?" She picked it up and turned it over to check. "That information would have been on the box, and we don't have the box."

I bought it anyway, along with a cute green corduroy dress.

They're both under my bed, wrapped up in paper with Christmas trees all over it.

The hangovers worsen. Her lie-ins sprawl into the afternoons. And the world is a lovely, fuzzy muddle. Charis is sure Marco hasn't noticed. She's skilled at covering her tracks, at having mints in her pocket, at holding onto the furniture when she's unsteady, at drinking a pint of water and taking a pain killer before bed.

She leads a succession of men into the spare room—all of them are regulars now; there are no more strangers. Charis makes up back-stories for them, to keep herself amused. A couple are nice guys, she'd consider a relationship with them—walking in the twilight to their favorite restaurant, curling up in the back row of the cinema. But once they've had their fun, they leave without a word. She pulls a bottle from the bedside table drawer and swigs to relieve her disappointment.

Her usual haunts are busier in the week before Christmas, so Charis buys a few bottles and hides them in her room. Just a couple. And Marco doesn't have a clue.

You idiot, Charis—of course he does. He's watching you, waiting for you to slip up. I'm watching you. In your stupor, you're oblivious.

5:14 A.M.

My limbs sink into a mattress abyss. Every part of me is exhausted, hitting the depths of emotional fatigue. My head is crammed with unwelcome recollections, no matter how much I squeeze my eyes shut and cover my ears to block out the sounds. Moments I want to forget, each worse than the one before. Spiraling, tumbling. All the way to the bottom.

Once you hit that, all you can do is climb, isn't it?

I lie poker-straight, swaddled in my duvet. I imagine floating, flying. I breathe as deeply and slowly as possible.

I make each breath slightly longer and slower than the previous one. I picture my lungs as a large tree in the middle of a field, with hazy blue sky overhead and birds chirping. I try to get each inhalation to reach the tips of the branches, inflating the buds of new leaves with oxygen as though they're balloons.

The little boy who no one can see hugs me tightly. "Don't cry."

I wipe my face with the sleeve of my pajamas; I didn't realize I was.

"I like it when you laugh. You're pretty when you laugh."

I smile through my tears, through my runny nose.

He crawls across my bed to look out of the window. "I can see the man in the moon." He points with delight. Sometimes he can be so wise and sensitive, I forget how young he is.

"Did you know," I say, kneeling beside him so my face is level with his, "there are still footprints on the moon from all the astronauts who've been up there?"

His mouth gapes; his eyes widen. "Will I be able to walk on the moon?"

I smile at him, this beautiful figment of my addled imagination. *No, because you don't exist, you're not real.* And yet I say, "You can do anything you want," because it's what Dad told me, and it's what I want to tell Ren one day.

The bed bounces as he shifts to get a closer look, his arm brushes against mine and my skin bristles, goosebumps appear. We sit together and gaze at the moon.

The Prisoner

1.

It's starting to snow, not the proper stuff—sloppy wet sleet that melts as soon as it hits the ground and slips inside your collar. But it's Christmas Eve, so it counts, right?

Marco stands at the door of Charis's bedroom, dressed up, fiddling with cufflinks. "Right, I'm off. Have a good Christmas."

"What?"

"I'm off—"

"I thought that was just for tonight. Aren't you coming back?"

"Boxing Day, probably." He inspects his jacket and brushes a fleck of dust from his sleeve. "Why? What did you think was going to happen?"

Charis bites her lip. She thought maybe they'd spend the day together, and she'd give him the gift hidden in her bag, and maybe he'd give her one, too. She thought they'd eat together. Not a proper Christmas lunch, but something pulled from the freezer. She thought they'd watch a film in the afternoon and maybe, after protesting a little, they'd go to bed together.

"Nothing," she says tightly. "Have a good time."

This used to be my favorite time of year. The decorations, the lights, the real tree oozing the aroma of pine around the house. The family gathered, the magic, the traditions.

Now I picture Neil out drinking, and Ren alone; my parents side-by-side in a sparse, gray house unable to contemplate dressing the tree, deep in thought and regret.

I force myself to recall happier times—the delight on Ren's face as she cuddled the teddy I gave her last year, her mouth sticky with the chocolate we'd eaten for breakfast, the screwed-up wrapping paper we folded into hats. Good memories, precious ones. I squeeze my locket and tears prickle my eyes.

A bottle of vodka's in my hand without me realizing. I drink, filling my mouth with the comfort of it. I hold it up to my eye and tilt it one way then the other, watching the liquid cling to the glass, admiring how it distorts the room beyond.

Alone again. At Christmas. It's wrong. What did I do so wrong?

Tears drip from my nose and chin.

I drain the bottle and let it slip through my fingers. It smashes onto the lino. Broken glass glints in the fluorescent light. I pick up the jagged neck and toss it from hand to hand.

Just a quick slash across my wrist is all it would take. A gush of blood trailing down my arm; a bubbling, dripping wound. Sleepy and content, I'd simply drift away. I graze the cool, sharp edge against my arm. The skin depresses as I push harder and leave a tiny pinprick.

Just do it. What's one more death?

Marco would find me when he comes back on Boxing Day. He might feel a bit sad, but nothing more—he'd be more concerned about the stains I left. My parents would simply never know. They'd anticipate the day I returned; they'd grow old waiting.

The glass punctures my skin. A bright red droplet emerges.

The boy, silently in front of me, shakes his head slowly, a distressed frown on his face, a furrow between his brows. He wipes a tear from his eye and reaches out for my hand. I relax my grip on the bottle and it rolls across the counter.

2.

Charis wipes blood from my arm, washing it gently with warm water. She searches for a plaster, but the bathroom cupboard is empty save for a few toiletries and boxes of condoms. She wraps a towel around it instead and settles to watch the Christmas Eve matinee with a glass of wine.

We ignore the arm, the whole incident. Neither of us wants to take responsibility for this deteriorating body.

Charis drinks until the bottle's empty and the film has finished. Now, she thinks, I want to dance.

In the middle of the Barbican at half-past five on a crisp, dark evening, many people have been embracing the Christmas spirit for some time. Charis rambles behind a group of twenty-somethings, loitering far enough away they won't notice her, but close enough to be caught in their slipstream.

The more they drink, the more they draw Charis into their throng, incorporating her into their rounds, pulling her onto the dancefloor. In-jokes follow them from place to place; Charis herself instigates some of them. They move to the clubs, and the group disperses, seeping into the tangle of people.

She's drinking a blue cocktail.

She's dancing with someone who has too many arms snaking across her body.

She's gripping onto the bar to avoid losing her place and being buffeted by people either side.

Dancing again, with a group of women waving their hands and shrieking to the music.

Resting against a wall while someone talks earnestly about something she can't hear. He gestures going outside, but she's not sure if it's an invitation so she stays where she is, and he leaves.

Kissing someone. Wrapping tinsel around herself.

At the bar. Mumbling her order. The barman shaking his head. Her infuriation rising.

She's outside. Escorted by a bouncer. The world spins as the fresh air hits her.

Time to go home, love, the bouncer says, maybe. His mouth makes awkward shapes, and she stares at his lips.

She sits down against the wall and rests her head, just for a moment, until the dizziness stops.

The little boy pulls her to her feet. She can barely stand, and her head is heavy, falling to one side. He guides her along the road, steering her around obstacles and pulling her back if she strays too close to the harbor-side.

She walks along two pavements; two pairs of feet stagger forward. She pauses regularly, to balance herself against a wall or lamppost, or leaning over to vomit into the gutter.

The boy propels her forward, narrating the journey, just as Marco did the night they met.

"Keep going, up this step, mind the cobbles. Left now, and again. We're almost there."

"No, no, I don't want to go that way. I want to go..." Her words descend into a mumble. Even I can't understand what she's saying.

"You need your key. Where's the key?"

She finds it and fumbles it into the keyhole. They walk upstairs together. The boy helps her into bed and lies beside her and kisses her cheek while she sleeps.

3.

I splutter awake, as though I'm drowning. Marco stands over me with an empty glass, and I'm drenched in ice-cold water.

"You're not dead then," he says. "Look at the fucking state of you."

I peel myself from the sheet, from the dried vomit and saliva. My lips are split; my eyes sticky. I hold my head with both hands cupping the base of my skull, splintered with pain.

Marco sneers and goes downstairs. I stagger after him, inching myself down the steps on my bottom because my legs feel like they're going to buckle. In the kitchen, he's lining up bottles on the counter.

"You came back early. I wasn't—"

"No," he says. "Actually, I came back when I said I would." He doesn't turn around. He rotates the bottles, so the labels are facing the same way, like a well-stocked off-license. "Still like to party, then?"

"Didn't drink all that," I mumble. One or two are in my room, waiting to be put out for recycling. Not these, not six. A wave of nausea hits me. I hold my hand against my mouth until it passes and fill a glass with water. My hand trembles. As soon as it's finished, I drink another.

"Funny thing," he says, in the same calm, ominous voice. "When I got back and you were comatose, I had a look round. And do you know what I found?" He turns, swooping his hand across the display of bottles. "These. In your cupboard, and in the bathroom, under your bed. Why do you suppose that is?"

I lean against the wall, my legs quivering, too unstable to hold me. I consider my options, wondering if I could flee. He grabs my shoulders and spins me across the room to face the stash—vodka and wine and cider. I avoid his eye, but he forces my head up, the velocity making me dizzy. I want to throw up, lie down, drink water, sleep. I can barely keep track of what he's saying.

"You know, this"—he nods toward the counter and shrugs—"couldn't care less about." He points at me, his finger skimming up and down the full length of my body. "This… is a problem. I took you in. Gave you a home. You'd have been dead on the street if I hadn't. And you exploit my trust, laugh at me behind my back."

His voice is deep and precise and intimidating. His words seethe and hiss and battle each other.

Where's Charis in all of this? Why isn't *she* here to take the flack? It's her fault. She's the one who orders wine instead of coffee, who heads for the pubs instead of the cafés. I need her resolve and intellect, her charisma and composure. I'm not enough by myself. I'm stark and cold, and defenseless.

"I didn't—"

"I have people, checking up on my interests. They tell me things, things about you."

"It was Christmas. What was I supposed to do, stay home alone?"

Marco slaps me; I recoil, taking a moment to regain focus.

"I gave you too much, maybe? Let you think this was a free ride?"

He cups my face with both hands, squeezing my skull. He's not going to stop; he's going to shatter me. His face contorts with rage, mutating into Neil for a second.

"You're hurting me."

His face is pressed against mine briefly, his grip tightening. That's the point, I realize; he wants to. My pulse quickens; a scream builds inside me.

"Bitch," he snarls and pushes me aside.

I crash into the wall and slink to the floor, lacking the energy to remain on my feet. I draw my knees to my chest, curling into a ball. I watch his legs walk toward me. He crouches with a snarl. Charis would kick out, knock him over so he'd sprawl across the floor. I don't. I hold my breath, anticipating the worst.

He sniggers and stands. "You're not worth it. You stink. Sort yourself out."

4.

And so, I'm here again. In a hot shower, severely hungover. History repeating itself.

I rinse the past few days from my skin, watching the suds swirling down the plughole. I don't feel better. I don't think I feel anything at all. I turn off the water and let myself drip. I grope for the towel on the rail and wrap it around me. I go through the motions one after the other, pausing between them.

Brush teeth, comb hair, moisturize.

In my room, I strip the bed and throw the sheets and duvet cover into the corner. I don't have spares; I'll have to sleep on the stained, bare mattress until they're washed and dried. Mum had a schedule for the beds. On Sundays we'd strip and change them, the bedding would be washed and hung out to dry or draped over backs of chairs on rainy days or in the winter. On Mondays, the pillowcases would be ironed, and everything would be returned to us folded and ready for the following Sunday. I never managed it when I had my own house. You don't, do you, with a baby? Ren's sheets were on a constant, almost daily cycle.

My hand grabs the locket instinctively.

I reach into my drawer to grab some clothes, but it's empty. I open another. Empty too.

I check the rest, and then my wardrobe. I scan the floor for anything which might be lying around from the past week. Everything empty, everything gone.

"Marco!"

He's already at my door, waiting with a sneer.

"Where are my clothes?"

"Oh, I don't think you'll be needing them for a while, do you?"

"Why not? What's going on?"

"You've abused my trust. Obviously I have to punish you now."

"You can't do that."

I just want to sleep—blood pumps around my head, I can almost hear it. My vision blurs as pin-prick pain hits the back of my eyes and pulsates into my cheek bones.

The hall light behind Marco shadows his face so I don't notice the shift. He grabs my arm and pushes me into my room and onto the bed. He kneels on my thigh to stop me slithering away.

"I can do anything I want," he snarls. "You're nothing."

I kick out with my free leg and catch his shin. I hold my breath—I didn't mean to do it, nothing I'm doing right now is on purpose.

He strikes me across the face with the back of his hand and my head bounces against the mattress. He hits me again, a punch, his fist knotted with fury. My head thuds; my mouth fills with the metallic taste of blood. I hold my hands above me to shield me from his rage, but he seizes them both with one hand and I'm defenseless.

"You fucking bitch."

He pulls me from the bed, and I fall onto my knees, scuffing them against the carpet. My dressing gown is flung open and he stares at my exposed body with hatred and repulsion.

He thrusts me against the floor, and I close my eyes—I don't want to see what will happen next. I shiver with fear, with the pain across my head, with the blood trickling down my face, with the terror of what's to come.

And then nothing. He releases his grip and moves away. He slams my door and turns the key in the lock. Key?

I scramble to my feet and yank at the handle.

I yell for him to come back and let me out.

I hammer the door until my hands are raw and bruised and there are cracks in the wood.

It's futile. Marco will already be downstairs making himself a coffee with the music blaring, or in the shop, two flights down. I sink to the floor, growling with vexation.

Now my adrenaline has deserted me, my headache worsens, and the stuffy air makes me feel sick again. The small window opens only a fraction, the wooden frames neglected and bloated with the damp air. I need water, but there's only a mouthful left in the bottle beside my bed. I gulp and long for more.

My legs twitch, my stomach churns. Bruises start to form on my wrists. The blood in the corner of my mouth dries. The room swerves and sways. I lie on the mattress and curl myself into a fetal position.

I doze, hovering between delusion and reality. My dear hallucination lies beside me and wraps his arms around me. He soothes my forehead with gentle kisses. So compassionate and concerned. I'm overwhelmed by his love, at peace, lulled to sleep.

My head floats above me, and I gaze down at the two bodies lying together, Charis and the child. I could fly away and leave them to be discovered. I could soar through the fissures in the window frame and out into the night sky. I can't feel my body at all now. I don't taste the blood in my mouth or feel the side of my head swelling. Blackness creeps toward me, its arms outstretched and ready to suffocate me softly.

And I let it. I don't fight, there's no reason to. I drift toward the window.

"It's not your time," says the little boy, pulling me back. "You've got so much more to do. Ren needs you. She misses you."

I snort with derision. "No one misses me."

"They all do. I do."

"That's silly. You're right here with me."

"You don't know how special you are, how important you're going to be."

And we're in that golden field again, the three of us running downhill—Ren on one side of me, the boy on the other. Running and gasping and laughing with exuberance. This time, they don't disappear. We lie among the buttercups together and make shapes in the clouds.

5.

Marco opens the door brusquely and throws a pizza box and bottle of water onto the bed.

It's daytime, some time. Probably just the next day, although it feels as though I've been here for weeks. I pounce on the water and gulp—it dribbles down my neck and chest. I trace the path of the fridge-cold liquid as it surges through me, as every cell soaks it up, hydrating every parched inch of me.

Marco watches with apathy and leaves without locking the door.

"You're letting me out? Can I have my clothes back?"

He kicks a black bin liner into the room without a word, and I drag it across the floor. My legs are clumsy and unwieldy from being idle; I'm sluggish and disorientated. I open the pizza box and nibble on a slice. It's cold and the cheese has congealed, but it's better than nothing. The more I eat, the hungrier I become.

I dress in the first items I pull from the bin liner and lurch down the stairs and out into the lane. It's cold, so wonderfully fresh; my skin tingles with goosebumps. The sky is cobalt, and the clouds are yellowed with the promise of snow. It might be cold enough for it, but every snowfall seems like a miracle, and I don't think I'm ready for one of those.

Marco stands at the door. "You've got a job, *Charis.*"

But Charis isn't here anymore. It's just me. I want to say no. I want to tell Marco to stuff it.

But I'm fearful of being locked in my room again, without water or food, until I break.

"But, but, but…" Mum would say, if she were here. "There's always a *but* isn't there?"

Yes, because *but* allows me to hide away, to avoid doing things which scare me; it provides a barrier, a wall, a fortress. It absolves me of standing up for myself and doing the right thing.

And, anyway, isn't this what I deserve? I'm a bad person, a bad mother. I abandoned my child and ran away. Am I not just taking my punishment like I ought to?

Marco stands outside the bathroom and follows me to my room. He waits for me to eat the last slice of pizza and get changed. He puts his hand on my shoulder to steer me to the spare room where my client is already waiting nervously, perched on the bed with his t-shirt in his hand and his belt unbuckled.

We contemplate each other awkwardly. He's barely more than a kid— my age, perhaps, but so much younger. I smile as seductively as I can, attempting to channel Charis one more time—because this is it. I can't do this again. I wink at the client and slam the door in Marco's face.

I'm leaving. I'm leaving. I'm leaving.
I escort the elated, enchanted kid downstairs and into the dark street. He seems confused, as if he was expecting something else, something different. He half-turns as if he's going to kiss me.

I duck out of his way. "No need for that."

He blushes. "Oh, right. Yeah... sorry." He shuffles on the spot, then saunters away.

I'm leaving, I'm leaving. If I say it to myself enough, it'll slip from my tongue when I'm in front of Marco.

In the middle of the shop, I declare, "I'm leaving."

It worked. I said it.

He glances up briefly with an indulgent smile and returns his attention to his phone. "No, you're not."

"I'm leaving." My throat is closing over. I've forgotten all other words.

"And where will you go? Back to your husband?"

"What did you—? How did you—? I haven't..."

How do you know about Neil? I've never mentioned him. I've never even told you my real name. You're bluffing.

He winks with a sly smile, setting the phone aside and resting his crossed arms on the counter.

"I'll go to the police," I blurt out. "I'll tell them you've kidnapped me, held me prisoner."

"The police?" He feigns horror, cupping his mouth with his hand. "I'm sure they'd love to know about *your* activity over the past few months."

I falter, my shoulders drooping. "You forced me..."

"Like I forced you off the streets and into a warm, safe house with a comfy bed? Or how I forced decent food into you?"

"No." I shake my head and take a step away from him.

He was supposed to be my Good Samaritan, but he's got it all figured out.

I draw myself up. "I could—I could walk out right now."

He crosses the shop floor and locks the door, turning the sign to *CLOSED*. "Could you?"

6.

Marco's back beside me in two strides. "Come on then, this is what you want, isn't it? A final showdown, a big display of bravado?"

He towers over me, blocking out the fluorescent light, a looming shadow. He seizes my throat and pulls me close to him. I turn my head away from his earthy aftershave.

"You're replaceable. But *you* don't get to choose when you go. You owe me. I decide."

I take shallow breaths, which is all his grip will allow. I'm as still as possible in case he realizes all he has to do is squeeze a little tighter and I'd stop breathing altogether. He snarls with aggravation, but there's something more—he's scared. His eyes are wide, his top lip is beaded with sweat. Both of us are uncertain what will happen next. I struggle to breathe.

NO! This is *not* how I'm going to die. I want to see my baby girl again; I want to tell my parents I'm sorry. I won't give Marco the satisfaction of ending it like this.

My fury bubbles. The months and years of it. Him and Neil merging. A guttural yell erupts from within. I bite and punch him in quick succession. I manage to hit him across his smug, slimy face. He pulls my hair to yank me away. I bite his hand, satisfyingly deep into the fleshy part between his thumb and forefinger.

He grunts, slapping me again and catching my mouth, opening the scabs from last time. I push back against his torso and he releases me.

I back away, searching for something to use as a weapon. I'd love to attack him with one of those twelve-inch solid metal vibrators on the middle shelf. I rummage behind my back, predicting how much damage I could cause to his skull.

Suddenly one of them is in my hand.

I'm holding it above my head.

Marco jolts forward and twists it off me. He twirls me roughly, until we're facing in the same direction and my back is clamped against his chest. His arm wraps around my throat, my neck trapped in the crease of his elbow. He could easily crush me, snap my neck.

"Ready to give up?" he whispers in my ear.

I kick back, trying to connect my heel with his groin, but I keep missing. He dances out of my way, laughing vindictively. Oh God, how I loathe him. I gouge my nails into his wrist. He yelps like a dog and lets go.

On the counter, Marco's scissors glint in the stark light.

He moves to punch me—bunching his fingers into a fist, ensuring I'm watching, like Neil used to.

The scissors are in my hand.

Opened out so the sharp edge is at his throat.

The blade grazes his Adam's apple. A nick, a slip, all done, all over. I watch fear flash in his eyes and his lips move wordlessly. He draws his hands away, palms open, arms extended.

Time stops. Time is silent. I ease the blade away from him. But I don't let go—I don't let him even think about lunging for it. I hold it up, to remind him it's there, I can still use it.

Eyes fixed on the scissors, Marco takes a cigarette packet from his jacket pocket and offers me one. I shake my head. He takes a lighter from the other pocket. We watch the smoke rise. Marco sits on the floor, leaning against the glass front of the counter, his legs stretched into the room and crossed at the ankle. He rests his head back, savoring the sensation, drawing deeply and exhaling fastidiously.

I sit, too, my weapon primed for any sudden movement.

"You're not the first, you know," he says. "You might think you are, but…" He taps ash onto the lino. "The first one killed herself—in your room, actually. A bit dramatic, granted… But I should've seen it coming. I could've stopped her." He drifts off, a hint of humanity in his eyes. "The other one ran away." He shrugs—a *what can you do* gesture.

He points at me with his cigarette, jabbing the air a couple of times. "And then there was you. Grace, I believe?"

"How…?"

He bats my question away. "You were an oddity. Just kept on coming back. Couldn't help myself, I wanted to know how much you'd take from me. I guess we know, now." He exhales a slow stream of smoke.

"Fuck you."

"I knew you wouldn't do it. You're pathetic. You had scissors to my throat and even then you couldn't do it."

He's so small and ordinary—why was I afraid? He's no different to Dominic or Ashley or Gavin. I generated his authority, allowed my fear to develop to extraordinary proportions. I created all of this. I could have left long ago. I still have the scissors. Why didn't I use them?

I stand with as much dignity as I can muster and toss them to the floor. "You're not worth it."

5:52 A.M.

I could have killed Marco, that day in the shop. Should have.

In my dreams, I've done it a hundred times, many different ways.

I've stabbed him in the chest and stomach and back and watched him bleed out on the lino floor, leaving a permanent stain.

I've lured him outside at midnight and pushed him off the quay.

I've smothered him with a pillow while he slept and restrained him as his limbs thrashed against me.

I've put poison in his curry and witnessed the slow realization creep across his face and the pleading in his eyes as I sat back and explained all the reasons why.

Sometimes he morphs into Neil—the two of them interchangeable in my subconscious mind. Their eyes and mouths overlapping, their malice clashing together, until I don't know who's who.

I stare at my hands, at Marco's imagined blood pooling into the creases. So much blood. I see Marco on the floor. I close my eyes and see Neil instead.

Daddy's Girl

1.

It's too cold to bed down, and I've forgotten how. It was easy last time because I didn't understand what I was getting myself into. It was an adventure—like going to Glastonbury for the first time—and I was naïve.

Although the streetlights are on, they're competing against a thick fog, so it's darker than it would normally be. In my hat, gloves, two jumpers and coat, I'm shivering.

There's nowhere to go. It's after midnight, but long before dawn. It was foolish to leave Marco now, without sleep, with my head and body throbbing from our fight. Perhaps it was foolish to leave at all. I've run out of options. There's only one—I shake it away, but it creeps back.

Home.

I amble toward the Hoe, my footsteps producing sinister echoes. Once or twice, I turn, expecting Marco to be following me, ready to drag me back. I'm all alone. It's both a good and bad thing.

The sea is mellow, lapping gently against the rocks and the concrete. Already the fishing trawlers are setting out—I watch their lights disappearing into the fog. And for brief periods, it's quiet, all sound pushed aside.

I'm on the steps near my arches without thinking about it. The tide's still high but ebbing away. I lay several items of clothing on the cold ground and sit, hunching over my knees, pulling my hat low over my eyes and my hood up. I yawn and close my eyes, waiting for dawn.

We're lying on the grass after a picnic lunch in the garden, watching clouds lingering in the pale blue sky. Ren's crawling off, investigating— she's loving her new-found freedom. She can't stay still for two seconds together, and giggles when I have to chase after her. Her legs move rapidly across the lawn, her nappy wiggling side to side. Her laughter is infectious as it rises high above the garden fence.

It's her birthday next week—she'll be one. I can't believe the screaming baby I brought home from the hospital is now this mobile, babbling, inquisitive little girl.

"Mamam mamamamam," she sings to herself, finally discovering a sound beyond *dada*.

I crawl after her, pretending to nibble her toes. She shrieks with astonishment, pulling her feet away from me, pushing her fingers against my mouth. I chomp on them instead and she giggles and squeals.

"Gracie, Sarah," Mum calls, and when we turn, she's got her camera directed at us. We pose, and she snaps.

I lie back down, and Ren kneels beside me, resting her hands on my stomach and pushing up onto her feet. She topples forward, head-butting my chubby belly before steadying herself and trying again. Fervent determination blankets her sweet baby face. Today is the day she'll walk for the first time. I know it.

2.

It's light when I open my eyes. The fog has lifted but lingers low over Jennycliff and the horizon. One early swimmer is battling the tide; a few dog walkers and joggers are passing each other on the road above with cheery greetings.

"Are you going to jump?"

I turn with a start. My invisible boy is beside me. He sits on his hands and kicks his feet against the rock.

"No, of course not. What are you doing here?"

"Keeping you safe."

What part of myself conjured this child, I wonder? What need is he filling? He's become such a natural part of my life; I miss him when he's not around—the air is a little less warm, I'm a little less content. Right now, despite my skepticism, I'm glad he's here.

"Who are you?" I ask because I can't not know anymore. I'm unsure why I haven't asked before. "What's your name?"

He smiles ruefully and fixes me with eyes so penetrating and pure. "I don't have a name."

Time pauses the way, in a dream, it bends and slows down and loops around itself. We're frozen, the boy and I. The wind drops, people vanish; a vacuum surrounds us.

"Why not?" I hear myself whisper. A shiver courses along my spine, down my arms and legs, up my neck into the base of my skull.

"You never gave me one."

It's so obvious. How did I not see it?

This is the child who never lived.

The child who was taken from me far too early with one jab of his father's fist.

My *son*, who ran down the hill of buttercups with me and Ren and filled the air with glee.

The baby who would love me.

When he smiles, he looks like his sister. His eyes are her eyes, his curled hair and cherub-pink cheeks are just like Ren's photo in my locket. How did I not notice?

"Hello." I hold both of his hands, his warm palpable flesh against mine. A tear runs down my cheek. "You're an amazing little boy, do you know that?" My voice cracks. "You saved my life so many times. How could you do that?"

Because he's not real. Not the way you and I, or Marco and Neil, are real. He's still just an obsession in my head.

He hugs my arm and snuggles into me. He'd only be a few months old, in real life—he'd be nestled against my breast, feeding contentedly. I wipe the tears from my face as I imagine holding this child in my arms, just once.

"Jacob," I say, the name catching in my throat. "I would have called you Jacob."

He repeats it a few times, letting the foreign sounds roll over his tongue. He beams with pride.

"I'm sorry you never got the chance to live. I'm sorry I let you down."

"It happened the way it was supposed to."

I'm the mother of two absent children now. I'm as empty and desolate as the Hoe around me. I sway with the monotony of the waves, thinking of Ren and the boy I've just named. The locket around my neck weighs heavily, and I squeeze it until the heart shape is embedded into my palm.

It's time to go. I've been here too long. I'm tired and thirsty. I force myself to stand and look back to Jacob. But he's gone. I looked away; I broke the spell.

I climb the steps to the café. I order hot chocolate and toasted teacakes. A couple on the next table peek over their menus at me, and I'm conscious of how I must look after Marco's attack.

But I'm corporeal again. Not a ghost or a whisper, not a drunk or a whore.

3.

It was a long walk home; I can barely believe I'm standing here. I came around the back to avoid the scrutiny of the neighbors. I didn't want them knowing I was home before my parents.

Mum hasn't noticed me yet. She's facing away from me, concentrating on a wad of pastry she's kneading. I watch her because I'm not quite ready. The glass in the door provides distance between us, gives me a moment's pause. I could duck down and scramble away, and she'd never know I was here.

She pauses at the sound of the door opening but doesn't turn around. She takes more flour from the bag and spreads it across the board, ready to roll the dough.

"Mum," I say softly.

She squeezes the pastry and it seeps through her fingers.

"Mum, I'm home." I step forward, stopping short of touching her.

I brought flowers—a foolish gesture, in hindsight. I hold them out to her. She leans across for her rolling pin and pauses with her hand on top of it. She's gone gray.

"You'd better put them in water." And, as an afterthought, she calls out, "Mike, Grace is home," and her voice cracks.

Tears are already streaming down her face when she turns, exclaiming in horror when she sees me.

I haven't seen my injuries yet. Even a moment ago, looking through the window, I fixed my gaze beyond my reflection. Just talking or smiling is painful—I can only imagine the full extent of them.

"Gracie! Oh my God, what happened to you?"

I don't know how to explain. There's too much to say, and I don't know how to start. She hugs me, the flowers crushed between us, and I wince.

"Where've you been? What've you been doing? Why didn't you at least phone us and tell us you were all right?"

Because I wasn't all right. I choke back my reply.

Dad rushes toward me and hugs me too, a little more reserved than Mum, a little more space between us. His arms are stiff, his body upright and cautious. He studies the blemishes and marks on my face, reaching to touch my cheek, but I turn away.

Mum fusses, muttering about drinks and food and how hungry I must be, and why did I leave? Where have I been? Her words circle around the room many times, and the noise is far too much.

She stops, mid-sentence, boiled kettle in her hand. "We thought you were dead."

I say nothing.

"Not a single word for four months."

Four months? I didn't realize it was so long. And yet, those early days are so distant, the first night under the arches is a vague recollection. How naïve and helpless I was.

"Four months and six days. We thought you were…" she starts to repeat. Dad takes the kettle from her and rests his hand on her arm.

The silence envelops us, drifting over us like this morning's fog.

"I'm sorry," I say, too late and too disconnected.

There are no Christmas decorations. No lights weaving through the banister in the hall, no silver lanterns over the table, or tinsel hanging up. Cards are stacked on the dresser rather than being displayed. A copy of the *Herald* with my picture on the front, from all those weeks ago, is brown and crispy beside them.

"Can I stay?"

"Of course you can stay. This is your home." She doesn't look at me. She pours water into the three mugs on the side. The relief has passed; the admonishments have begun. Mum's always turned on a pinhead; as a child, I never knew what reaction I'd receive.

"I missed you." Nothing. "I love you."

Mum leans against the counter with her head bowed. I'm not sure whether to hug her or not. Dad shakes his head.

"You should clean yourself up," she says without moving.

4.

I peel off my clothes and let them fall to the floor. I see what my parents just saw. I'm a hotchpotch of bruises and scars, a kaleidoscope of color, a shadow of myself. Whatever they have imagined over the past... the past *four* months, I probably look worse. Indeed, whatever I've been seeing in the mirror all this time has not been the reality—I've masked the horrors, disguised myself.

In the shower, I scrub my skin, washing away Marco and Dominic and Gavin and all the others. They have no place in my parents' house.

Mum leaves a fluffy towel on the rail for me. I wrap myself up, and revel in the luxury of not sharing myself anymore. I wipe steam from the mirror. The woman in front of me is defeated and disillusioned and exhausted.

My dressing gown and pajamas are folded on my bed, washed, ironed, waiting for me. I wonder how long they've been there, how long it was before she gave up hope. When I put them on, they're far too big for me, hanging from my visible hip bones and gathering at my feet. How pathetic I must appear.

The room itself is disturbingly unchanged, as though I should slip back into the life I had before. Which before? Before I ran away, or before I got married? Neither suit me now.

There's an open magazine on the floor, makeup spread out as though I'm still applying it for a night out, a dress hangs from a hanger on the outside of the wardrobe. Frozen at the very moment I made my decision and left.

The clothes in the wardrobe are skeletons of my previous life, ones I never dared take into my marriage. It should have been a clue. The man I married should have accepted me as I was, and yet I molded myself—from the age of fifteen, when I met Neil—into what he wanted me to be.

I'm lost in grief and regret and distance and reflection.

My fingers brush against the clothes, hung randomly, recalling the party or holiday or daytrip each item reminds me of. I'm not prepared for the avalanche of emotion—or perhaps lack of it—provoked by being back. I grip the wardrobe door to stop myself fleeing again.

The floorboard outside my bedroom squeaks, and Dad's there. "Your mum made pasties for lunch, are you coming down?"

I can't face her again. I'm overwhelmed with fatigue. I try to count the hours I've been awake, more than twenty-four, I think. "Do you mind if I stay up here? I might lie down for a bit."

He pauses, then nods. "Sleep well. It's good to have you home."

5.

It's four o'clock when Ren cries out into the darkness. I reach for her makeshift drawer-bed on the floor to tuck the blankets around her, but she's not there. The drawer's not there. Just an empty space.

"Ren!"

I leap from the bed.

"Ren!"

Dad stands at my door, yawning. "Grace, calm down. It's just a dream."

"Ren? Sarah?" I correct myself. "Where is she?"

I should have asked sooner. First. As soon as I walked through the back door.

It's not four in the morning; it's barely midnight. We sit at the table, drinking tea. Mum's asleep, or at least pretending to be to avoid me.

"Do you know where…? I mean, have you…?"

"She's fine. She's good. She's beautiful and adorable, and so much like you at that age."

"What age? Now? Have you seen her?"

"Ah." His eyes dart around the room and he sips his drink. He inhales slowly and circles his hand over his bald spot. "Yes. We have."

This is a good thing.

It's a bad thing.

A complicated thing.

They know where she is, and how she is. They're her grandparents and they *should* know. So this is good.

I don't know any of it. I don't even know what she looks like and I haven't held her in my arms for so long. For parts of the last few months, I haven't even thought about her. I've been childless—*Charis* was child-less. Whole weeks passed when I didn't feel the pain of not being with my baby, when her name didn't flutter into my mind and smear sadness across me. This is very bad. I abandoned her with a horrible man who barely even acknowledged her when I was living with him, who probably couldn't even tell me when her birthday is.

"Gracie, you have to understand—"

"When?"

"Sorry?"

"When did you see her?"

"Umm…" His shoulders slump. "From time to time… every couple of weeks… or so."

More than once. More than just bumping into her by accident. More than creeping over to the house and spying on them from a distance. More than me.

"Does she know who you are?"

"Yes."

I jerk backwards. I guessed that would be the reply, but I wasn't ready for it. I lift the mug to my lips with both hands and watch the steam rise as I drink.

"She knows you're her grandparents? She—"

She hugs you when she sees you and offers kisses and runs to you when she's scraped her knee and calls you Granddad and Nana?

He doesn't answer. I want him to hold me and tell me everything's going to be okay, but the table is between us and neither of us moves.

"What about me? Does she know about me?"

"She's a baby, Gracie, she can't understand people who aren't there."

He states it matter-of-factly, without blaming me, or rebuking me. Just explaining. But *people who aren't there* turns into *you weren't here.* And in turn, that's my reprimand.

"She sees your photo," he adds in consolation.

He nods toward the corkboard where Mum pins our family photos. I gaze wistfully at the overlapping Polaroids and aging Kodaks and printed-out snaps, so familiar I could describe each of them without looking. Darren and me on the beach building sandcastles and eating candy floss at the circus. Darren proudly showing off his Under 11s football trophy. Me and my friends dressed as gray-faced zombies for Halloween.

And, among them all, Ren.

6.

Ren stares at me from several of the photos on Mum's board. She's mixed in with the older, faded ones of me and Darren. Am I imagining it, or confusing her with myself? She's the spitting image of me in some; in others, she has Neil's intimidating scowl and dark enigmatic eyes.

Behind me, Dad sits with his hand across his mouth, as if to prevent blurting out anything else. I glance back at him, then return to the photos, my finger tracing the soft chubby cheeks and dimples.

She's got honey-colored ringlets now, long enough to tie into little bunches on the top of her head. Her cherry-red mouth either smiles broadly or pouts.

She's at the beach, and the park, and standing on top of a rocky tor on Dartmoor with her arms stretched out. She's eating ice cream, a chocolate ring around her mouth. She's beside the monkey enclosure at the zoo while chimps swing from branches behind her; she's leaning across a jigsaw puzzle with complete concentration; she's holding Dad's hand on a wide path.

This isn't *my* daughter, not the baby in my dreams. She's happy, content, clean, thriving. How can she be any of those things with Neil as a father? How can they let her be happy with him? He's cruel, evil. He broke me. Why haven't they taken her away from him?

Why is he better than me?

I draw back and wordlessly beseech my father for clarification, the man who raised me and promised to always stand by me. I don't understand.

"Gracie…"

I hold my hands up to repel him. "She sees my photo. That's what you said, isn't it? She comes *here* and sits in this room, without me."

"Gracie, it's late. I have to go to bed—I'm working in the morning."

I wave him away. "Go, then." And he does, because there's nothing more for him to say.

I pull a chair from the table and sit in front of the wall of pictures. After a while, they all swim into one another and I can't tell the difference between me and Ren, between Ren and Darren. In one photo—facing the camera and holding a toy rabbit by the neck with a shifty smile—Ren looks so much like Neil I slide it beneath another with a shudder of recollection.

It's six when Dad comes back down, already dressed in his work clothes. He boils the kettle for his flask, and then again to make us both a mug of tea. He puts mine on the table and leaves the house without a word.

"Tell me about her," I say when Mum comes down.

"I didn't want you to find out like this." She sighs and leans over my shoulder to kiss my cheek. I shrug her away. "I should have taken her photos down, shouldn't I?"

The tea Dad made me is untouched, gray and unappealing. She pours it away and flicks the switch to boil the kettle again.

"She looks so different."

"I've been lying in bed wondering how to explain."

"You make a happy family," I continue, having my own conversation while she has hers.

"Gracie…"

"I'm glad." My eyes glaze over, losing focus so the photos merge into one large brown jumble—like when you're a kid and you're convinced you'll make an amazing, brand new color by combining the paints, but it always turns out mud brown. All these memories are muddy.

"We did it for you—"

"When I left, we had no contact. How do you go from nothing to having them over for fucking tea?" I stab one of the photos with my finger: Mum, Neil, and Ren at *this* table. Dad must have taken the photo—he wouldn't have thought about turning the image to include himself.

"It wasn't that simple. She was all we had left; we couldn't let her vanish. We thought if you came back, you'd—"

"I left her with a monster, and suddenly he's the world's greatest father? He stole my baby. He *attacked* me."

Mum frowns and tilts her head a little. "You know that's not what happened, don't you? You'd been drinking."

I throw my head back and laugh with frustration. "You still don't have it right. I wasn't drunk, nowhere near it. Neil lied, and you believed him. That's why I left. You were on his side from the start. You didn't even ask me."

She holds her hand up to stop me talking. It worked when I was little; it works now. "You lashed out at him, and he restrained you. Yes, he hurt you, but not on purpose."

"He hit me, he always hit me. Don't you remember the bruises? Don't you remember all the times you asked if everything was okay, and how relieved you were when I left him? My back... You saw the marks on my back. The scars haven't faded."

"Grace. Stop."

I slump back into the chair. There's a photo of me and Ren together. I'm lying on the grass, and she's using me to steady herself as she stands. Just after this, she fell and lay fully across me. I feel the weight of her pressing against me and her arms stretching around my torso to cuddle into me.

Mum won't look me in the eye. Ren screams. Neil hauls me over his shoulder and trudges up the stairs. I didn't protect her. I couldn't save her.

7.

The house swallows me up. I squeeze myself from its walls and gulp the fresh air outside. I stumble into the road as though it will offer salvation. A car skids behind me, and the driver beeps the horn aggressively. I wave my apology, but she speeds off.

I walk. The streets have a between-Christmas-and-New-Year inertia, a sense of new starts and hope and promise hangs in the air. I'm almost caught up in it myself. When I reach the dual carriageway that interlaces the city, I have a choice. North or South.

South takes me to the Hoe, back to my arches. It would be easy to disappear again, to run, to hide. I could ditch Grace and be Charis forever, or someone else—anyone else. I'd have to go home to pack up my things. I'd have to walk past Mum and Dad, aware I was hurting them all over again. I'm furious with them, but I still love them.

Running away won't solve anything. Because of what they've done, I still have a link with Ren, there's a chance I'll get her back, that'll I'll be a real mother again.

I look left and right, north and south. I can't go home yet, but I will. We'll sit together as the year flips over to the next; we'll watch the Hootenanny as we always do and listen to Big Ben chime out twelve times and stand at the window to see people's fireworks being set off.

And tomorrow we'll remember.

I'm idling toward Neil's house, because how could I not be drawn toward my daughter? The journey is longer than I remember, or perhaps I'm slowing down. The familiar route has small changes—a particular house has been painted, another's gate has been replaced. The foliage is winter-sparse, and mulchy leaves coat the pavement.

Eventually, I cross the main road and walk between the garages and I'm opposite Neil's house. My stomach tightens and convulses. A thousand images of my life here converge, flooding my head with terror and grief. I hunker down, convinced Neil will rampage from the house and drag me inside as though I've never been away.

I edge closer, skulking behind a tall leylandii hedge. My heart stops when I see Neil at the front room window. He's gazing down at the floor, sipping from a mug, animated as though talking to someone. He laughs and points at something in the room.

Laughing? Neil? I don't recall ever seeing him laugh, not properly.

He ducks out of sight, then... *then*... he stands, and Ren is in his arms.

And oh, she's beautiful. More adorable than the pictures on Mum's wall, even more than I remember. I'm as awestruck as the moment she was handed to me in the hospital, captivated and in love. She snuggles into his neck, wraps her arms around him, and gives him a sloppy kiss. A moment later, she's crying. I start forward, leaping to her rescue.

No, not crying. Laughing. Hysterically. He's tickling her, and she's curled into him with delight. She throws herself backwards—I gasp— and he catches her, swinging her back onto his shoulder and hugging her tightly.

She points to the floor, and Neil bobs down. He hands her a teddy—the teddy I gave her for her first Christmas. She still has it. He kept it. I don't mean to cry.

Jacob slips his hand into mine without a word. We watch intently.

8.

Mum has always cooked something special for New Year's Eve. When Darren and I were little, we ate in the evening, allowed to stay up until midnight, so the meal would have several courses which would be produced over several hours. I'm not sure we ever made it to midnight, but Dad always said we did, and that was good enough for us.

As we got older and wanted to be out with our mates, Mum cooked lunch, still stretching across the afternoon, but always finished in time to get ready and go. Sometimes they'd invite friends for the evening or go to a neighbor's house. They were always in bed by the time we scuttled home in the early hours.

"I haven't planned anything. I didn't see the point, for just the two of us," she says.

"No, of course not."

"Would you like a piece of Christmas cake? I'm just going to get myself some."

"No, thanks."

We've forgotten how to talk to each other, dancing around the politeness. Something else that's my fault, I suppose.

"I found something I thought you might like," she says, beckoning me into the kitchen. She waves her hand at a shoebox on the table. "Just a few things."

Inside, there's a pair of pink shoes, a newborn Babygro, a metal daisy hairclip, a crayon scribble on the back of an envelope which Mum's dated: *Sarah's 'goggie,' 17 Nov, aged 18 months.* And my scan photo; Ren before she was Ren, before everything went wrong.

"I can't believe she was ever that small." I hold the sleepsuit and imagine her in my arms. I inhale the scent, but it doesn't smell of her anymore—it holds the aroma of washing powder and cardboard. I drop it back into the box. She's huge in comparison, now. Not my baby.

"It was hard for us too, you know," Mum says eventually.

I bow my head.

"I remember walking into your room the day you left. You hadn't taken much, but I knew straight away—we'd lost both our beautiful girls."

She waits. For what, an apology?

"So, Dad went to see Neil, and they talked. A little about you, mostly about Sarah, about what would be best for her."

I don't want to hear this. I shake my head and grimace.

"He was struggling, I don't deny that. But he was trying. Some of the neighbors were helping out, his mum too of course."

"She hates me," I say with venom. I shudder at the idea of her even holding Ren for one second.

Mum purses her lips. "But it wasn't enough. He was juggling work and Sarah—"

"And the pub. Don't forget the pub."

"Grace," Dad says, appearing at the door and dropping his bag to the floor. He walks to Mum and kisses her cheek, as he always does when he comes in from work. He squeezes her shoulder, and she smiles tightly.

"Dad told him we wanted to be involved—that we loved Sarah and wanted to help."

"Help?" I scoff and cross my arms against my body.

"She could have ended up in foster care," Dad says, and I jolt with the shock of it. "We needed to stay close to her, so she'd still be here when you came home."

"You were so certain I'd be back?"

Pause. "No."

Too many emotions swarm around, bottlenecking in my stomach. Shame and guilt and rage. I'm pulled in multiple directions, fighting them. I choose to be furious; I choose to let my rage bubble over. Showing weakness can be fatal.

"So he brings Ren here? He comes into *this* house where he left me unconscious, and you welcome him! How can any of you bear it? Is he sorry for what he did—have you asked?" I jab my finger toward the living room, my gaze lingering on the stairs. "Does he look at that spot on the living room floor and feel regret?"

"You were both far too young. A lot has changed. We try not to dwell on the past."

"How convenient. Just ignore me entirely. Great." I throw myself around the room like a petulant teenager. I see myself doing it and cringe.

"Is it ideal? No, of course it fucking isn't." Mum pounds her fist on the table. "We had no choice. *You* left us no choice."

I recoil as if she's slapped me. Mum never swears. It cuts into the space between us.

"It wasn't my fault," I whisper. "None of it was my fault."

9.

When the bells ring out and the fireworks are let off around the neighborhood, I'm in my pajamas, watching from my bedroom window. The sky lights up with orange and green and blue explosions which sparkle and crackle, and the whole town feels united. I wonder if Sandra and the others watch with awe, or if it's just another night for them. I wonder what Marco's doing.

On my desk is a plate of sandwiches and a mug of cold tea Mum brought up for me while I was pretending to be asleep. She whispered my name, then covered me with my duvet and crept from the room.

It's a brand new year.

A year without Marco in it, but also without Ren. Without violence and shivering in damp corners of the squat and sleeping with strangers, but with memories of it all. In the security of my childhood bedroom, those dark thoughts still drive into me.

I don't sleep. I lie in bed and grip the mattress as the past few years nudge against me and goad me. As the pre-dawn sky lightens, I stand in the garden and listen to the sporadic traffic. It's not cold. There's no breeze. There are no stars. The world is empty and dreamlike. I close my eyes and let the soft mizzle rest on my face.

Mum comes out and stands beside me. "Thought you might like a cuppa."

"It's peaceful." I take the mug from her.

"You used to sleepwalk. We used to find you out here like this all the time."

"I'm awake."

She points toward the small lavender bush by the fence. "Sarah helped me plant that. We found your old spade."

"Oh."

"Do you want me to leave you alone?"

"Yes. No." I take a deep breath. "I'm still angry."

"I know."

We raise our mugs in unison.

"Tell me about Ren."

She beams with love and pride. "She's such a wonderful girl—happy and clever and kind. She scrunches her nose, like you did, when she's concentrating. She loves jigsaw puzzles and helping me bake little buns." She pauses to gauge my reaction.

The words are floating high above me, and I try to grab them and understand them. The baby I left had no idea what a jigsaw was—her favorite thing was banging wooden blocks together.

"She has your eyes, and your pout when she's cross. And your stubbornness."

I smile sadly, unable to picture any of this. It's so alien.

"Why do you call her Ren?"

And I tell her the story, the real story of Neil at the hospital causing that horrific scene and me not standing up to him.

"Oh, Gracie, even then?" she says after a moment of contemplation. "I wish it could have been different for you."

I shrug. "Sometimes people get what they deserve."

"No. No one deserves that."

I watch two bees hovering around Ren's lavender. They bicker and fight before buzzing into next door's garden.

"Serenity's a lovely name."

It cheers me to hear Mum saying it out loud. "I found it hard to bond with her. She always seemed to fight against me. I'd imagined her as Serenity for so long, she was a different child when she was born." I shake my head. "Stupid. Doesn't make sense."

"I don't think it's stupid."

We lift our mugs and drink lukewarm tea.

6:23 A.M.

"Hello," says my darling Jacob, sitting cross-legged at the foot of my bed again. "You're back?"

It's the exhaustion, I suppose—my mind playing tricks, my remorse reflected back at me.

"You're sad, so I'm here."

I wonder what he'd have become, if he'd been born—if he'd have been this sweet and compassionate in real life. "It's nice you look after me, thank you."

He grins. "It's what little boys do for their mummies."

"Do you think of me as your mummy, then?"

"Of course." He doesn't give me time to react. He grabs my arm and squeezes. "Look at the clock. Look at the time!"

All I see are the hours unslept. "Why?"

"It's almost time." He bounces on his knees on the bed and looks so excited.

I'm about to protest, to say yet again I don't understand what he means. But I sigh and leave it unsaid. There's little point in arguing with your own psyche is there? Insanity would be an indisputable way to lose Ren for good.

I prop my pillows against the headboard and lean back. Jacob curls into me, fidgeting to get comfy, spreading warmth through me like those nights under the arches, so long ago.

"Do you want me to sing you a lullaby?" he asks.

"That sounds lovely."

He sings *Twinkle, Twinkle Little Star*, and when he's finished, he reaches up to kiss my cheek. I feel his hand press against my stomach, his lips on my skin. He's too real, and I'm troubled. What's wrong with me? Does everyone see ghosts? Are we all walking around with these beautiful reminders of what might have been?

"It won't be long, I promise." And he's gone.

"I wish you wouldn't do that," I mutter into the vacant room.

The Mummy Doll

1.

Rain hits the window in dense rivulets. It's been torrential for three days, causing flash flooding around town. The street is deserted as the water pummels the tarmac.

A long time ago, in another lifetime, rain just like this pounded against the concrete and rocks of the Hoe while I sheltered beneath my arches. These spotted memories don't feel real. Perhaps they're a dream and I'm actually lying on the settee in the living room on that first day, with the searing pain of the rake gashes across my back and drained from the emotional reality of leaving Neil. Perhaps the house is so quiet because Mum's taken Ren to the park, and they'll come home with cake to cheer me up.

I doze with these images in my head, and when I wake, I'm despondent and hollow. It's still raining. I drag myself around the house, rinsing my breakfast dishes so Mum won't have to do them later and sweeping the tiled kitchen floor. I wander aimlessly and stand outside Darren's old bedroom, the room which should have been Ren's but never was.

My hand rests on the handle. I haven't been in here yet. It's a junk room again, I imagine, a place where things are thrown because there's nowhere else to put them. But I have to see it, to put ghosts to rest.

I open the door and gasp.

It's pink and has the mural and Ren-sized four-poster bed Mum promised. It's just like we planned. There are framed photos of Ren on the wall opposite the bed, blown to A4 proportions and positioned in a mosaic fashion.

My doll's house is in the corner, liberated from the loft. My grandfather built it for my fourth birthday. He painted the roof tiles individually and carpeted each room with off-cuts. Nanny Joan made curtains. The furniture was all handmade too and gifted over the course of several birthdays and Christmases. The dolls are seated at the dining table: Daddy, Granny, the baby doll in his highchair, the little Gracie doll.

Wait, where's the mummy doll? There used to be a mummy—she wore an apron and had long brown hair. I scan around, but I can't find her. I pat my hands across the carpet and peer under the bed.

Several stuffed animals are wedged against the footboard. TuTu, my first teddy, is tucked among them—threadbare in places, matted in others. I curl onto the unicorn duvet cover, with TuTu folded into my arms the way I used to hold Ren.

My head won't quieten, circling the same thoughts and ideas. I'm beyond anger now; I'm serene and quiet and remote, gazing at my life from a vast distance, watching it play out on a big screen while the audience munches popcorn and laughs in all the wrong places.

Mum knocks gently on the open door. "I'm home."

"You finished the room." A redundant comment.

"Yes."

"It smells of her."

"She stays over sometimes."

I could have been here; I should have been. Playing with the doll's house, tucking her in and reading stories at bedtime, leaving the little nightlight on and telling her I'll be right next door.

"I'm making curry for dinner—do you want to help?"

"I'm not hungry."

She sits on the bed beside me. "Don't do this."

"What?"

"Fall backwards. You spent four months living God knows where, surviving whatever it was you're not telling us about. Don't give up on Ren." She squeezes my arm.

"Does Neil know I'm home?"

"Yes."

"Could you... talk to him for me? Ask him if I can see my baby?"

Mum smiles sadly. "That's something you need to do yourself."

But I don't.

I don't contact Neil. I don't let myself imagine what it would be like to see her again. The impetus subsides. I grind to a halt and disappear. The hours move into days.

2.

It's Friday when I open my eyes. A dream haunts me—I'm fifty years old, and I've spent my entire life as a recluse. I live in this house with my elderly and cantankerous parents and will live in it long after they're gone. I never remarry, never have more kids, never see Ren again, never make new friends, and lose contact with the few I do have. I glide around this house filled with cobwebs and malevolent shadows, like something out of a black-and-white Hammer horror film.

In the kitchen, Mum's left a list of chores. I push it under the toaster. I'll get around to it. I fill the kettle and pour milk over my Shreddies, prodding them with my spoon until they're a thick, soggy mulch. I watch the kettle, waiting for it to boil, picturing it covered with cobwebs.

After breakfast, I walk to the village, convinced I'll be sucked into the walls for eternity if I remain inside any longer.

It was a Saturday morning treat, running to the village to buy sweets. It was an old-fashioned shop, with huge jars lined up on tall shelves behind the counter. Darren liked cola bottles and long strawberry belts, and I'd get a quarter of Jelly Babies, biting their heads off and putting them back in the bag to prevent Darren stealing them once his were gone. Mine always lasted longer.

Before that, when I still had to hold Mum's hand to cross the roads and wasn't allowed to carry my own pocket money in case I lost it, this street was enormous. Mum knew everyone, and we always had to stop and wait patiently while she chatted.

"Hello, stranger," says a familiar voice.

Kirsty. I almost collided with her. She's holding Charlotte's hand—so big now, walking and talking—and pushing a sleeping newborn with the other.

"It's been so long," she continues while I desperately try to think of something to say. I'm not used to talking to people anymore. "How are you? And... Sarah, wasn't it?"

"I'm fine, thanks. Sarah's... living with her dad now."

Her face falls. "Oh, I'm sorry. I haven't put my foot in it, have I?"

"No, it's fine—a long story. Still ongoing really," I add, surprising myself. I force a smile and turn to the pram. "So, who's this little guy?"

"Liam. Four weeks."

"He's gorgeous."

I avert my gaze—I can't look at him without seeing Ren's scrunched up face as she slept and her tiny fingers reacting to the dreams she was having. I can't look at Charlotte without seeing the photos on Mum's wall and imagining what Ren's voice sounds like and how many words she can say. Charlotte, a few months older, produces complete sentences.

"Are you free for a coffee? I've got some time, I'd love to catch up."

Taken off-guard because I was expecting a quick getaway, I scramble for an excuse—an appointment, a prior commitment—but there isn't one.

"Great," I hear myself saying, with a wide, forced smile and we wander toward the bakery mid-way along the street, chatting about the weather and Christmas and how long it's been since we last saw each other. I remember the day Jacob played with Charlotte, while I hid, and wonder if she remembers too. She eyes me warily, and Kirsty laughs.

"She's going through a shy phase," she says, and ruffles the girl's hair.

When we're settled at a table in the café, Kirsty says, "I'm sorry to hear about Sarah. Do you see her often?"

I consider how much to share with this relative stranger. "It's more complicated than that. Long story short, I..."—exhale, long, slow, controlled—"left my husband a few months ago, and I've been sleeping rough. I've just gone home to my parents."

Her eyes widen. "Wow. I don't know what to say." She fidgets in her chair, and fusses with her mug. "On the streets, with all those... What was it like? Oh, God, I'm sorry—don't answer that." She blushes and squirms.

I gaze at the table, at the chip on the rim of my mug. I pick it up and put it back down again.

"I'm sorry," I say at last. "I shouldn't have said anything. I'm kind of learning how to fit in again." I sip my coffee. "Look, I'm not the person you met in the summer. It would have been nice to be friends and have our kids grow up together, but things changed. I understand if you want to go."

"No, it's fine," she murmurs, but I sense her pulling back. She cuts the corner off her Danish pastry and gives it to Charlotte, watching her much longer than necessary. She sits back, leans forward, opens her mouth to speak but nothing comes out. The baby murmurs and fidgets but his eyes remain closed.

The atmosphere is excruciating. If she doesn't leave soon, I will.

"I've got all these questions, but they seem so rude." She giggles self-consciously. "I do want to be friends. I like you. These... setbacks can happen to anyone."

Not the way I've done it. Marco and Dominic and all the other men battle for their share of my memories. I wrap my arms around myself, feeling hollow and naked.

"Have you seen Sarah since you've been back?"

I shake my head.

"Don't you want to?" She pats Liam's blanket and gazes tenderly at Charlotte.

I wonder how hard it is for her to ask that question, to even think it—a contented, devoted mother like her, unable to imagine being parted from her kids.

"I do. But..."

"You're worried about facing her?"

"I'm scared she'll hate me."

Kirsty lays her hand on mine. "Of course she won't."

Charlotte starts to get fractious, pushing her coloring book aside and almost spilling her juice.

"I'm so sorry, I thought I'd be able to keep her occupied longer." She starts to gather her things, packing up the various toys Charlotte's been pulling from the bottom of the pram. "I promise I'm not running out on you, but..." She rolls her eyes as Charlotte drags her chair across the floor and leans to retrieve it. "We'll meet up without these guys and talk properly. You've still got my number?"

"I lost my phone."

She scribbles on an unused napkin and hands it to me. She hugs me as we say goodbye.

3.

I want to see Sarah. I want to see Sarah. I want to see my baby. If I say it enough times, it'll slip off my tongue.

I dial. I don't think. I just do it.

I hang up.

I dial again; hang up again.

I want to do this, I *have* to. I'm her mother. What kind of life will she have without me? She'll grow up hating someone she doesn't know, and this chasm inside me will increase and devour me.

I dial again and force myself to remain on the line, praying it'll go straight to voicemail. I need to do this, but…

"Hello?"

I freeze. Just the sound of his voice makes my heart thrash against my chest and vibrate into my skull. My hand shakes; I almost drop the phone.

"Hello?"

I open my mouth but all that comes out is a weak croak.

"Who is this?"

"Me," I whisper. I cough to clear my throat. "It's me… Grace."

Silence.

"Are you still there?" I ask.

"Yes."

And then we're both silent.

"I'm home. I want to see Sarah." I close my eyes, dreading his reply.

"Why? Why now?"

"Because I'm back."

"You've been back for days."

"Yes."

I wish I knew what he was thinking. I hope he's remembering the last time we saw each other with shame and remorse. But I doubt it. Part of me thinks he's beyond human emotion. His eyes were always so hollow when he was with me.

The seconds tick by. My clock flips to the next minute.

"I'll have to see you first."

"To check me out, you mean?" Irritation makes me bold. "To make sure I'm not rolling around drunk?"

"Yes."

"Oh."

What about you, I want to yell? What about all your late nights and hungover mornings, all the times I hoped you'd be home with us, but you were out instead? Why can't I examine your behavior?

But I bite my tongue, because he has Ren and I don't.

"She's my little girl," he says. "I have to protect her."

She was *my* little girl. I dig my nail into my arm to stop myself blurting out the truth.

I was my daddy's little girl. He didn't think about that when he was beating me, did he? My nail goes deeper, marking the skin.

"When?"

"Tomorrow, about four—I'll get off work a little bit early. Costa in the mall."

"Okay."

Okay, I say, like it's no big deal.

4.

Twenty-seven hours later, I have nineteen minutes to go. I'm distractedly browsing the makeup counters in Boots. I've got six shades of lipstick on the back of my hand, but I can't afford any of them. My money, left over from my last couple of clients for Marco, is dwindling. Mum's already started mentioning looking for a job.

I check my watch. Fifteen minutes. I gaze at the perfumes without trying any of them. I consider buying some tights. In the body lotion and bubble bath aisle, I open different bottles. A coconut one reminds me of Marco, and I return it hastily, feeling sick and agitated.

Nine minutes. Close enough. My breathing is shallow as I walk slowly toward Costa. It's full of schoolkids and flustered parents; a group of students from the art college poring over a portfolio of black-and-white photos; besuited office workers on their laptops.

Neil's already here, elbows on table, chin resting on his clasped hands. He doesn't move when he sees me but watches as I join the queue.

He hasn't changed—still striking, sexy, dangerous. He's unshaved, and his eyes are puffy and lackluster. But if this was the first time I saw him, I'd be interested. A couple of girls in school uniform are staring at him and giggling.

I order a cappuccino. I take the tray and turn. I want to run away, but I head toward him and sit opposite him without a word.

He leans back and crosses his arms, superior and severe. I revert to the fifteen-year-old who met a man at a party and thought herself in love. I revert to the child who'd do anything to make him love her, to the child who tried to grow up too quickly and failed.

The longer we don't talk, the harder it is to make any sound. I cough, and Neil starts. I fidget in my seat and he scowls. I wait expectantly.

"Your parents said you've been living with a friend or something?"

Maybe they have, but it's not what I've told them. I haven't told them anything. I smile but don't reply. He's trying to trick me. He's going to make this as hard as possible. He wants me to beg and squirm.

"You should have stayed away. No one needs you—Sarah doesn't."

"She's my daughter. You can't keep her away from me."

"From a mother who abandoned her and will mostly likely do it again, I think I can. Shall we ask a solicitor?"

My fists clench under the table. It felt safe to meet him in such a busy place, but now I resent the people who'd gawp in amusement if I shouted and screamed, if I *caused a scene*; the people who'd judge me and privately side with him. Tears of frustration scratch the back of my eyes.

"So, that's it? You dragged me all the way here to say no?"

"And to see your face when I said it." He smirks, and I flinch as though he's hit me, conjuring all those weeks and months before I was strong enough to leave.

I was kidding myself anything could be agreed. He's enjoying watching me suffer. He hasn't changed; he's still the man I married.

"I've got the scars," I say in a voice as deep and compelling as Charis's. "You remember, don't you—the scars on my back?"

His eyes narrow.

"Oh, that's right, you never saw them. I left you the next day." My voice quivers. "They won't fade—they'll be deep and raised across my body forever, like hideous tattoos. My memento of you."

His hand rests on his mug, but he doesn't drink; he's a statue.

"Mum remembers them. She cleaned them up and bandaged them. You should ask her about them. I think she took photos…" I linger on that thought, that pure invention.

His face is white, drained.

I like the way he wriggles in his chair. I like the way his eyes don't meet mine anymore. I like his hands pressed against the table as if he's ready to scarper.

"You're threatening me?"

I lean forward, encroaching onto the small table, pushing myself into his space. "How does it feel?"

He stirs his coffee, sips it, uses his napkin to mop up a few drips. Stares across to the counter and toward the window and scans the other tables. It's emptying out now—the conversations around us echo up into the high ceiling. He picks up his used sugar sachet and taps it against his cup.

"We should never have got married. I didn't love you. It was a mistake."

All my hate, all my recent history is bundled into a knot in my stomach, expanding and filling me up until I might burst. I can't even begin to respond.

"So," he says, drawing it into a long sigh which fades into the air above us. "I'm sorry."

Sorry. As though one word will atone for all he did, all he put me through, all the things which have happened since. For the scars lacing my back and the worthlessness he left me with. One word so easy to say yet means nothing.

And still he won't look at me.

"I'll bring her over on Saturday," he says finally.

Once he's gone, I sip tepid cappuccino and listen to the bubbles of conversation floating around the room, the comfortable chatter and laughter of friends. I remain there long after my cup is empty, as customers leave, and the mall shops begin to close.

5.

I fret. I worry. I teeter between elation and terror. My clothes are strewn across the bed and the floor. I need to look responsible yet friendly, mature but fun. Don't I? Does it really matter? Not to a baby, of course. But to Neil, under his scrutiny—I remember his sneer if my skirt was too short or my midriff showed as I reached into a cupboard, his taunts about my stretchmarks and chubby thighs.

None of my clothes feel right—they belong to a different person, a different time. I change several times—each outfit clinging and hanging and fighting against me.

Neil should be nervous too, after lying to my parents for months—fudging the truth, dismissing and excusing his abuse—because I wasn't here to contradict him. Calling it love, when I now know that was the biggest lie of all.

He's recast himself as the hero who swept in to take over in lieu of his absent wife. He did the best he could—that dear baby's lucky to have one loving parent, at least. How can I argue against that?

I sit in Ren's room and push a lorry around the floor, imagining Ren doing the same. A lot of these toys were mine or Darren's, stored in the loft for this very circumstance. Not quite so soon, I suppose. They probably thought they had years before grandchildren appeared. I move the Daddy and Gracie dolls around, acting out a little scene where Gracie is cross because Daddy's locked Mummy in the cellar and won't let her out. I crawl around the room looking for the Mummy doll. It might have got left in the loft—I ought to ask Dad to look for it. The house is wrong without her.

Mum's baking a cherry cake—she says Ren likes picking out the cherries just like I used to. I watch her and remember my failure at making Ren's birthday cake. She asks me to stir the batter, but I'm concerned I'll get it wrong.

"You can't go wrong with sponge cake," Mum scoffs, but stops when I don't laugh with her. She pours the mix into the tin and puts it in the oven. "It's going to be okay."

I duck down to look through the little window in the oven door. "I know."

"Not the cake. Everything. Ren."

I dip my head and set the bowl aside. It'll never be the way it should have been. Those vile months can't be recovered. Ren will be Sarah; I'll be a stranger.

Dad potters in his greenhouse, as though this is any other Saturday morning. He moves plant pots around and waters his tomatoes. I'm not a gardener—we agreed this long ago when I pulled up some prized flowers I mistook for weeds. I watch from the window, hoping his composure will transfer to me.

"He won't change his mind, will he?"

"She'll be here."

"It's just, he might change his mind."

"You need to relax."

But I can't. I fidget, I bite my nails, I tap my fingers against the mug until Mum restrains them and removes the mug from me. I pull at my shapeless sack of a dress and ask Mum if I look okay.

The cake is golden brown on top and slightly crispy around the edges when Mum takes it from the oven and says it's just the way it should be.

When the doorbell rings, my heart misses a beat, I hold my breath, my stomach spasms. I stand at the kitchen door on shaky legs.

Dad answers it. I listen to the cheery greetings and feel sick.

"Ganda," Ren calls before I see her, and he sweeps her up into his arms and squeezes until she squeals with joy. Plump arms wrap around his neck. Her arms. She's here. So close.

She's startled when she sees me. She clings to Dad and hides her face in his neck, peering through his hair with bashfulness and inquisitiveness.

She slides from Dad's arms and rushes to Neil. She's steadier on her feet than the baby I left. Her bunches jiggle as she moves. Her fingers weave themselves into Neil's hand and she leans to suck the thumb of the same hand, forcing herself as close to his legs as possible. Her other hand scrunches up the tulle skirt of her party dress.

"I told her we were meeting a new friend and she wanted to wear her special dress," Neil explains quietly.

New friend. Not Mummy. As though I'm just anybody. Not Mummy, as though I don't matter. I stare at Neil until he looks away in embarrassment.

"Oh how lovely," Mum replies. "What a thoughtful little girl you are." She kisses Ren's cheek. "Do you want to say hello?"

We're in limbo. I'm not sure if I should go to her or wait. I should be eager to hold her and squash her against me, impatient to have her with me again, and bury my face in her hair and kiss her chubby cheeks.

But I'm not. I think I'd be happy if we remained like this, seized in the moment. The maternal ties have loosened and stretched, held together now by a few fibers. I'm removed, displaced—the memories and thoughts and yearning I've tormented myself with over these last few months have been myths, fairy tales.

Ren is no more real than Jacob. The Ren I knew vanished the moment she was ripped from my arms. They're both just sparks of my imagination.

"Sarah, shall we go and say hello together?" Mum crouches, and Ren clutches her hand. "I'll come with you."

She considers for a moment then steps forward and Dad follows. Her steps falter and she lifts herself onto tiptoes.

I don't know if I'm supposed to hug her, shake her hand, or ruffle her hair. I wait for the penny to drop, for her to remember me, to hug me tightly because it's been so very long. In the end, I do none of them. I say, "Hello Sarah," in a voice almost smaller than hers.

6.

Sarah kneels on the floor piecing a wooden train track together with such concentration. It's not finished before she's choo-chooing the little green train along it. Dad completes the circle, so the train won't crash into the abyss of carpet.

"I've made a cherry cake, Sarah," Mum says once it's clear no adult conversation is likely to break out. "Would you like to help me get it?"

She jumps up eagerly, then glances at me and scuffs her feet into the carpet to follow Mum.

Dad stands and stretches his legs. Neil is twitchy, leaning forward and resting his elbows on his knees one moment, sitting back and stretching his arm across the back of the settee the next. Their clipped, monotone conversation lapses and we listen to the happy chatter from the kitchen.

I watch my parents embracing the role of grandparents and in-laws; Neil is polite and amenable in return. I recall the times he'd spit their names at me as though they were dirt. The past, it appears, is conveniently rewritten. Perhaps it wouldn't have happened like this with me around; I'd have been a reminder of Neil's brutality.

But now I'm back it *should* be remembered. I want to roll up my sleeves and expose the silver strands, to lift my dress to reveal the deep, red scars. I want to whisk Sarah to a place where she's Ren again.

They have shared memories now, inside jokes. Mum refers to *the picnic*, Neil mentions a specific toy Sarah always insists upon playing with. Then they remember I'm in the room and their words dwindle. I'm intruding, forcing myself into a space I have no right to be.

And yet, Neil does? Neil, who was so wrathful and malicious, but who's been here day in, day out, taking care of my daughter. I need someone to explain it to me. It's a game to him. I see past his façade of contrived conformity. I see the way it wriggles through him, the way his expression falters when my parents turn from him. He's waiting to punish them. He claims to love his daughter, but it's a trick.

Sarah's cake lies half-eaten and mangled while she sneaks toward Granddad and teases him with her sticky hands, a glint of mischief in her eye. They giggle as he wrestles her arms away and pretends to eat her hands.

"Yummy, yummy, more cake for me!" he says in a big scary-monster voice, and Sarah squeals.

"Doll house, Ganny?" Sarah asks. "Careful?" She wags her finger, the way Mum does, and I imagine it's a conversation they've had many times when they played with the house together. Mum may have explained it's very old and she needs to be very careful with it.

"We need to wash your hands first." And they leave the room.

It should be me, washing her hands and cutting her cake and wiping her mouth.

"Can I go and watch her play?" I ask no one in particular.

Neil is rigid, intent on the wall opposite. It's satisfying to wrong-foot him.

"Of course you can, Gracie," Dad says, while Neil scowls.

And then, here she is, here I am. In her room, the way it should always have been. Mum pats the floor and I sit down just behind them. Sarah looks at me, then returns to her dolls. She babbles their conversations and sits them at the table.

"What are they having for tea, Sarah?" Mum asks.

She considers for a second, her brow furrowing, her finger to her lip. "Milk and cheese."

"Yummy," I say with a shaky voice. "That sounds nice."

Mum nods her encouragement, but I've run out of things to say.

"Do your dollies have names?"

"Daddy. Sarah. Ganny." She holds them up, one at a time, and places them back with precision—they haven't, it seems, finished their tea yet.

"Wasn't there a mummy doll?" I ask Mum, lowering my voice, practically mouthing the word *mummy*.

"Um, maybe." She flusters and puffs out her cheeks. She scans the floor. "I'm sure there were a couple more, once. They might have got misplaced when we brought it down. In the loft, still?"

There were no others. I remember them clearly; each had their own place at the table, and now there's one seat spare.

"Oh," says Mum with a shrug, "I don't know then."

It seems such a mundane thing to lie about, but she is. Her voice always goes just a little higher, a little thinner. We turn our attention back to the doll's house and I point at the crib.

"Does the baby have a name, Sarah?"

"He Jacob."

I feel a cold chill spread across my body. Jacob—that's what she said, crystal clear, with no mumbling and fudging of the syllables, like with her other words.

"Jacob? How funny, she's never told me a name before—he's always just been Baby. It must be a friend from nursery."

Or she's met my darling invisible boy too, the child who doesn't exist. I don't probe further; I don't want to confirm or refute Mum's theory—I'm petrified of the answer.

"Ganny go shop," Sarah says, handing me the appropriate doll. "O'there." She points into the corner.

I don't move, overcome by my inclusion in the game, and when she notices she pouts and repeats her instruction. Mum's right, she does look like me sometimes.

"Sarah." Neil is at the bedroom door. I stiffen at the sound of him and drop the doll to the floor. "It's time to go."

Sarah continues to play. She takes the Granny doll and brushes her hair. Her eyes dart around; she knows she's being naughty. She grins to herself and looks like Neil.

"Sarah," he repeats. "Shall we put your shoes on?"

Mum helps her tidy the toys away. They walk down the stairs hand-in-hand. Neil and I follow. On the stairs together just like we were months ago when he was hauling me in the other direction. I wonder if he remembers, if he's picturing it. I grab the banister, and watch my knuckles whitening. With a simple flick of my foot, I could have him tumbling down and sprawling to the floor. I pause to leave an extra step between us.

Sarah sits on the bottom step while Neil puts her shoes on. He holds her coat and she slides her arms into the sleeves. I sit half-way down and hug my knees to my chest. Sarah kisses Granny and Granddad, but eyes me warily once more.

I wave as they leave. Sarah raises her hand in response, and Neil ignores me entirely.

I've misplaced a limb; it's bounced down the road and driven away. I may never see it again. The road is forlorn, the houses are morose. The trees bow with respect. The gates lament my loss.

7.

I kneel on the floor in Sarah's room and place the Sarah doll in the kitchen with the Granny doll so they can bake fairy cakes together. It's what they did the day we left Neil—they baked while I slept. The baby's in his crib. I discard the daddy on the floor behind me.

Jacob watches me from Sarah's bed, lying flat on his stomach and peering over the edge.

"It's not a good time. I don't want to talk right now."

"We don't have to talk. I'll just be here with you."

"Why would you want to be anywhere near me? I'm a bad person, a terrible mother. I…" I shake my head and let the sentence float away.

"Because you're important."

"You said that before, I don't think I am. I'm not important to Sarah. She wants her daddy—she doesn't need me."

"She will."

"You always talk about the future like you know what's going to happen."

He shrugs and smiles in his sweet, infuriating way. "You called her Sarah. Isn't she Ren anymore?"

"No, I don't think she is."

He slips head-first off the bed, and lands beside me. He circles both arms around me and nuzzles into my shoulder. "I can feel your heart beating. She's still Ren inside you."

I push him away. "Why are you here? What do you want?"

"I want to make you happy. It won't be long now, I promise."

"How can you possibly help me? You're not real!"

I throw the Sarah doll at him; he fragments and vanishes. His voice is already a whisper. I reach out to the spot he was sitting, and it's cold, of course.

"I'm sorry," I say, looking toward the ceiling. Because that's where he comes from, isn't it, *up there*, a little angel sent to watch over me?

Without looking, I grope across the duvet for the doll, to place her back in the house, and my fingers touch something else. I hold it up—the Mummy doll, right where Jacob was lying. I search around, for something it might have fallen from, despite the fact I searched on top of everything and under everything days ago. And yet, here she is. Her hair's shorter than I remember, chopped raggedly—something either I or Darren must have done—and her apron is missing. Her dress is yellow, A-line, and her feet are on tiptoes as though she should be wearing high heels. I wipe a smudge from her cheek and place her at the head of the table.

8:3Ø A.M.

I missed the dawn, finally dozing off just as Dad was leaving for work. There's no sun, just a gray vagueness to the morning.

Downstairs, the landline rings, seeping into my dream before rousing me. It's a peculiar sound, these days—we all use our mobiles. Only cold callers and my grandmother use the landline number. If it wasn't for her, we'd never answer it—but you never know when she'll have fallen and be lying on her kitchen floor, or locked out of her house, or wandering along the road in her nightie and slippers.

I strain to listen to the conversation, to Mum's voice gradually becoming more fraught.

The conversation is long. Not a cold caller, who would have had a firm *No thank you*. Not my grandmother either, who would have deserved a much jollier response. I can't hear what she's saying, just murmuring rising through the floorboards.

Mum climbs the stairs and knocks on my door. Inexplicably, I shut my eyes and pretend to be asleep.

She enters. "Gracie?" She shakes me by the shoulder. "Gracie."

I open my eyes. She's pale and serious, her hand to her mouth, her eyes welling with tears.

"What's up?"

"Gracie, something terrible's happened."

"Ren?" I'm bolt upright.

"No, Neil. He's been stabbed. He's in hospital."

It takes me a moment. I let the words seep into my head and shake themselves up. "Is he okay?"

"He's in surgery."

The room spins for a second. "Will he be all right?"

Her gravity remains. "They didn't say."

"Oh." I'm disorientated. In equal measure I see Neil towering over me, fist raised, and lying unresponsive in a hospital bed. "Who phoned?"

"The police. A neighbor was looking after Ren while he went out last night. They're bringing her here."

"She's coming here?" I'm going to see Ren again! I smile but rein myself in when Mum frowns in reproach.

"Dad's going to come home." She moves away and looks back. "Are you okay?"

"I'm fine. Why?"

"He's still your husband. I imagine it must be a shock."

"I just want Ren to be okay."

My husband. I haven't thought of him as that since he attacked me with the rake. Before then, he seemed salvageable. I could help him, mold him into someone better.

Such a long time ago. Only months, but it feels like years. The scars itch at night, to remind me they're there. I stand in front of the mirror and twist so I can see them, taunting myself with their presence. I suppose I could be proud of them, see them as a symbol of my survival. Yet I still think of them with shame and regret.

I peer from the window when the police car pulls up. I clutch the windowsill when the officer helps Ren from the car seat in the back and carries her to the house. She's still in her pajamas and socked feet.

Just as she was carried away from me in the summer, she's being carried toward me now. Tonight I'll help bathe her and read her a bedtime story, and stroke her cheek as she falls asleep, and creep from the room leaving a soft nightlight to diffuse her fear. I'll do all the things I'm supposed to. Because I'm her mother and, for now, nothing else matters.

Just Grace

1.

The second Ren was born, I was lost, bereft. I'd spent nine months closer to this little human than I'd ever been to anyone else, and now she was gone. She wasn't mine anymore. She was her own unique person—other people could interact with her, hold her, love her. I had to share her, and I didn't want to.

I wanted her back. But it was too late.

She was Serenity; I was just Grace again.

I'm just Grace now, lying on Sarah's bed, vaguely aware of the room darkening. Just Grace when they walked to the car earlier, and I witnessed the hug she gave Neil before clambering into her seat.

Just Grace when I asked, "Is it always this quiet when she leaves?" and Mum had no answer for me.

I drift around the house like a ghost, disappearing and re-emerging. I search for Jacob, but he's not here. It's just me.

Neil did this.

He made me a shadow of myself. I don't fit here, or anywhere. Again, still. I've left pieces of myself all over Plymouth, and I can't reassemble them—I'll remain fragmented and damaged.

Dad's awake early. The smell of Sunday-morning bacon sizzling pervades the house. I haven't slept much. It's hard to fall asleep, hard to remain there. My head churns with terrible thoughts I can't banish.

I drink black coffee while Mum and Dad tuck into their breakfasts.

"You should eat something," Mum says.

"Not hungry."

"I think it went well, yesterday. Don't you?" She nudges Dad's hand for agreement.

"Uh, oh yes," he mumbles with a mouthful of mushroom.

"It'll be easier next time, and the time after that." Her smile is excessively cheerful.

The coffee is too bitter—I take a mouthful and force myself to swallow. "I'm going for a walk."

I leave before they object, slouching from the kitchen and ignoring whatever secret eye contact they're exchanging.

It's cold outside; sleet falls in thick dollops but doesn't settle. I take a roundabout route to nowhere, trudging familiar roads, taking sleepy backstreets, trying to get lost. Impossible, of course—I grew up here, each street and tiny passage and little shortcut through a hedge is imprinted on me.

I used to walk with Ren, on mornings like this. I'd bundle her up in her pram when her cries were too much to bear and we'd walk. It would settle her. I'd walk until she fell asleep, walk while she stayed asleep. The moment I stopped, or returned home, her eyes would be wide with complaint.

Does Neil take her out on adventures like I did? Does he hold her hand while she toddles beside him? Do they wake early and huddle on the settee to watch Cbeebies in their pajamas? Or is she hungry, while Neil grumbles through a hangover? Is he sleeping while she cries in her cot? It's easy to put on an act in front of people, in front of in-laws who apparently are more than willing to believe you're a changed man.

Mum calls me, the abrasive ringtone cuts into the air. I know it's her before I swipe the phone from my pocket because she's the only person who's got my new number. Her number was already listed in the contacts when she gave it to me. It might remain like that, a rudimentary phone given to a child too young to be trusted, able to phone home and nothing more.

She'll be checking where I am, if I'll be home soon. She'll claim she wants to make a start on dinner, and do I want two potatoes or three.

Ahead of me, suddenly, Neil and Ren are walking together. They're a hundred yards away, or more, dawdling, splashing in the sleety puddles. I freeze in the middle of the pavement. Should I stop? Turn around and take a different route? Continue…? I meander a few steps, then bravado takes over and I speed up. I'll catch up to them in a couple of minutes, I'll smile and say hello and tell Ren how much I like her yellow Wellies. I'll match my pace with theirs for a little bit, making Neil uncomfortable because he won't want to raise his voice in front of her. I'll smile sweetly as I wish him a nice day and walk on.

Closer, closer. I'm almost level when I realize it's not them after all. A different man with a different daughter, singing nursery rhymes about the rain. I smile and say, "Good morning," as I pass them and hurry away.

2.

Kirsty takes me out for dinner. She doesn't take no for an answer, practically dragging me from the house, and linking my arm as we walk as though I'm going to wriggle free.

She talks a lot—on our way to the pub, as we order food, as we sip our drinks and wait for it to be served. She meanders smoothly from one subject to another, gently prodding me for a response and happy with a smile or an affirmation.

"How have you been?" she asks as we settle to eat.

"I saw Sarah. My ex brought her over."

"Oh, I'm so glad. How is she? As bright and bubbly as ever?"

"Yeah. Yeah, she…" I rest my fork on the side of the plate. "She doesn't remember me."

Her smile fades. "Oh Grace, I'm sorry."

"I probably shouldn't have expected anything else."

"She's very young. I don't think Charlotte would have recognized me at that age. A week is a lifetime for them."

"Aren't babies supposed to know their mothers, by their scent or something?"

She laughs. "I think that's puppies."

"I didn't even get a hug. I didn't touch her." I sniff back my tears. "I don't think I could bear it again."

"It'll be different next time. She'll remember you from this visit, she'll start to feel more comfortable with you."

"Neil won't let her. He hated having to bring her."

"It's not his choice."

"What can I do about it? I've made a mess of things. I've done—" I stop abruptly. She's not a close friend, I can't tell her everything. I can't tell *anyone* everything.

"You've done what?"

I shake my head. "It doesn't matter. But the point is, Neil can probably do anything he likes, and I won't be able to stop him. I wish…" I drain my glass.

What do I wish? That I'd never met Neil, that I'd stayed at home and let Janie go to the party by herself. She'd have fallen in with the cool crowd and our friendship would have disintegrated. But I'd have passed my A-levels, gone to uni, found new friends, met someone my own age. I wouldn't have Ren, of course. But—

I stand abruptly. "Another one?" I offer, before my thoughts wander too far down that dark, disturbing path.

The weekday atmosphere isn't as raucous as the weekend, but the music still gets cranked up, and only strangling diners remain at their tables while a swathe of drinkers push back from the bar. Kirsty checks her watch and says she has to go. We grab our coats and head outside.

"Thanks for this evening. I really needed it."

"Me too. I don't get to do this often. It's nice to have a break from… Well." She dips her head, bashfully.

We head in different directions—Kirsty with purposeful strides and me at an amble. I pull my bobble hat further down my forehead and thrust my hands into my pockets. It's slippery underfoot; the dampness of today's heavy drizzle has frozen. I wander up the street. The moon's shining brightly, casting silvery light across the rooftops. I allow my gaze to drift.

A couple of flats above the shops have *TO LET* signs in their windows. I imagine living in one of them—of opening my own front door, putting my coat on the hook, paying the babysitter and peeking in at Ren sleeping peacefully in her room. I could get a job in the Co-op or one of the other shops—something I once sneered at but would suit me perfectly now. Living and working in the same street. Small and contained and protected.

Music from the pub infiltrates the still night air. I dance a little as I walk, shimmying my shoulders, swinging my hips.

A figure steps from the shadows of one of the doorways, blocking my path.

Neil.

"By all accounts," he says in a smooth, slimy voice, "you should be dead in a gutter."

3.

"I'd like to get past, please."

I stare at the pavement, at our shoes almost toe to toe. Despite it only being ten o'clock, the street is quiet. The Co-op staff are locking up; a lone car races to the top of the road.

"I'd like to get past, please," Neil parrots back.

This is where I should be safe, in my own neighborhood, with friends and family close by. I don't feel safe at this moment.

"What do you want?" I ask. "Are you following me?"

He hasn't moved, hasn't said anything. Like a schoolyard bully, just there, malicious and intimidating.

"Don't be like this. We should be friends." He runs a finger down my cheek, the tip of his nail catching my skin.

I brush his hand away and take a step back. With speed, I could dodge past him. Or turn and run back to the pub. I'm too slow. I've had a couple of drinks. In these shoes, I'd stumble on a crack in the pavement and go flying.

"Where's Sarah?"

"I've got a neighbor watching her. No one you know."

"Perhaps you should go home to her." I move sideways and he stretches his arm to the wall to prevent me passing.

"I've been thinking about access, you and Sarah. I've been wondering what I get in return."

"Nothing. You get nothing in return." Up close, his breath is a mix of lager and cigarettes. "You've been drinking. We'll talk about this tomorrow. Call me."

"No." His movement is too quick. I slam into the wall, caught off-guard. My shoulder cracks against the edge of the shop window. "You shouldn't have come back. You should have stayed in whatever hovel you were hiding in."

"I just want my daughter. We can work something out, share custody."

"Why would I do that? I won. You left."

"You… you…" How do I verbalize his abuse? Why do I have to? He knows what he did; he must remember. And yet he's standing in front of me, revising history. "Do you hurt Sarah the way you hurt me?"

He snarls like a dog and grabs my arm and drags me around the corner. I wriggle, but he's too strong, and I'm afraid of what he'll do. We're on the edge of the dimly-lit carpark behind the shops, deserted save for a few cars parked for the night. We're alone apart from the flats which overlook it. I prepare to scream. He presses his hand against my mouth, grinding my lips against my teeth.

Where's Charis when I need her bravery? Where's Jacob to protect me? Where's the passerby, ready to intervene?

If I scuffle enough, I might unbalance him and we'll crash into the dustbins to make a noise, attract attention. Lights in the flats might switch on, windows may open.

"I know where you've been," he whispers, pressing his nose against my cheek. "I know what you've been doing. Naughty girl. Do you think your parents would like to know? Doesn't make you a very ideal mother, does it?" He pushes my arm behind me, up my back. I'm immobile.

"Ren belongs with me."

He frowns with exaggerated confusion. "Ren?"

"Serenity," I say robustly.

Since the day in the hospital, I haven't said her name in front of him. I've cowered and retreated. No more. I won't do that anymore.

He's blank. He doesn't even remember giving her a name I didn't choose.

"You think you can just come back and ruin everything with your lies? You're nothing. You're… you're…" He sneers with disgust. He can't even bring himself to say what I am.

And still, apart from existing, I don't know what I've done wrong. His fury expands disproportionately; erupting, bubbling over, because of all the things I've done or not done.

His hand is around my throat, squeezing me. Just the one, as if I don't deserve the effort of both. We're back where it started, Neil pushing me to the floor, keeping me down. I twist and writhe from his grip as my wooziness increases, as the oxygen depletes.

Puddles of icy rainwater seep through my jeans and coat; the ragged edge of a pothole sticks into my shoulder. Two handed now, he presses my skull into the tarmac and crushes my windpipe. I clutch his wrists, no longer trying to pull him off, but pleading with him. His face clouded by fury and wrath, more extreme and unbridled than anything I've seen. Beyond sense and morality. Unleashed, full of vengeance.

"Help." Barely a sound. Lights flicker. Images flash in front of me. Delusions, memories.

"Use the knife," Jacob urges, jostling beside me, his angelic face contorted with alarm.

What knife? I grapple frantically against Neil's weight bearing down. Has he got a knife?

No, I remember suddenly.

I have.

Sandra's knife with its *DAVID*-engraved handle. Still in my inside pocket, untouched from when she gave it to me on the Barbican.

I can't fight him off and reach it at the same time. I brace myself and let go of his hand to unzip my jacket and fumble inside. Immediately his fists tighten around me and he laughs. So pleased with himself, so gratified.

My fingers curl around the knife, and I fumble to flick it open. The blade springs out. It's too dark to see properly. Neil hasn't noticed it at all. I hold it between us, close to both our faces, and it glints in the lamplight.

His hand falls from my neck. He stands and backs away. I choke and cough, gasping for air.

"Oh, hard now, are we? Gonna use it, or are you chicken?" His voice quivers.

"You were going to kill me."

I'm still on the ground, an untenable position. Exposed and vulnerable. Jacob holds his arm out to help me to my feet. My beautiful baby. He's solemn and petrified.

For him. After everything he's done for me, I have to do this for him.

I flourish the knife to prevent Neil coming closer. Admiring the weight of it, the smooth curve of the handle, the cold, steel blade.

"Do it," he says with derision, catching my hesitation. He holds his arms out, giving me a clear target. "Pathetic."

He lunges and grasps my wrist, coercing my fingers open. I'm losing my grip, losing my advantage. He levers it back and forth until the blade is inches from my chest, curling my arm until he has complete control. I try to gain the momentum to throw it to the ground, to give myself a few seconds to regroup.

Jacob's hand circles mine; his small fingers cool on my skin. The pressure he exerts is enough. Two against one. He cements my hold on the handle.

"Jacob! No!"

"Who the fuck is—"

Jacob pushes my hand forward, thrusting the knife into Neil. I feel resistance. And then the ease with which it glides into his torso.

Neil emits the smallest of groans, a tiny breath of air.

We stare at my hand. We watch blood spread across his jumper. I withdraw the knife and blood oozes from the wound.

He reaches out for me, for help, shocked and confused.

He slumps to his knees. Falls to the ground with unblinking eyes.

A pool of blood seeps around him, spreading and dribbling across the tarmac.

"Help!" I yell without thinking. "Help!"

"Run," Jacob pleads. "Run."

At the sound of footsteps coming toward us, and the sharp glare of light from the flats above, and the bulk of Neil's body at my feet, and the blood so dark and immense, I run.

4.

The living room lights are on; the TV's blaring out some comedy or another.

"I'm home," I call out, my voice shaky and thin. I rush upstairs and lock myself in the bathroom. I press myself against the door.

I can't breathe. My heart races, beating loudly and filling the room. My hands are covered with Neil's blood. I turn them over, marveling at how much there is. It was such a tiny cut. How is there so much? His blood is streaked across my face from when I covered my eyes. There are splashes of it on my coat.

Think. Think.

I've still got the knife in my fist. My fingers unfurl it into the sink with a metallic clatter. I fumble with the tap. The blood is congealing into the lines on my palm. My heart line. My life line.

Oh my God, what have I done?

What have we done?

The water runs red. I wash the knife, cutting myself in my haste. My blood mingles with Neil's. The cut stings.

I wash myself and stare at my mascara-smeared face in the mirror. Behind me, so silent and still, Jacob watches. A ghost now, standing there with no expression, no understanding. His body's transparent, fading away. Despite my coat, I shiver.

In my room, I hide the knife in the pile of jumpers and bags I've discarded at the bottom of the wardrobe. It's where it should always have been. Why the hell do I still have it? I should have got rid of it weeks ago.

I drop my coat to the floor and roll it inside out; I take off my jeans, covered with dark stains.

What have I done? I should go back. I should get help. I should... I should...

I drop to my knees in the middle of the room. I lean forward and rest my forehead on the carpet and reach my hand out as though Neil's lying beside me. Imagining his motionless body at my fingertips. Was he breathing when I left him? I never checked. I just ran.

Downstairs, my parents are moving around—TV off, mugs gathered and taken into the kitchen. Dad locking the front door. The same reassuring routine every night. Blissful in their ignorance. I can't tell them. But I'll have to.

Oh God.

I hear a siren. The siren. The ambulance someone must have called for Neil. Someone who unsuspectingly walked across a murder scene, walked through his blood and realized he wasn't just a drunk, passed out. *They'll* have checked his pulse, perhaps. *They'll* have looked after him.

He would have killed me. I still have the pressure around my neck; there'll be a bruise soon, Neil's fingers replicated in broken capillaries. It was self-defense. Him or me. It had to be him. It was always going to be him.

What have I done? What did these hands do?

For a second the only sound is my ragged breathing, as though the world outside has vanished. A silent, empty world without death and pain and violence.

Then another siren breaks into the darkness. Not Neil's—a different one, conveying the next in line to be saved. Because nothing stops. Day after day, we just get on with it.

I glance at the clock—11:55 p.m. Soon it will be tomorrow. I think of the crashing waves across my concrete beach, and the rattle of trolley wheels on cobbles, and early mornings at the park when Ren wouldn't sleep, and the rake that scarred me, and the hands that held it.

And I think of living in a new flat, and Ren sleeping in her cot in her own room while I sit in silence with a mug of tea, and the job I'll get to provide for us, and the brand new life I can give her now.

It's 11:59 p.m., and I'm wide awake.

ACKNOWLEDGEMENTS

A huge thank you to Elizabeth Seckman, Ruth Schiffmann, and Kyra Lennon who read a very early version of this novel. Although many aspects of the story have changed, a lot of their suggestions remain intact. I appreciate their time and enjoyed the discussions we had.

I'd also like to thank Jessica Bell who gave poor Grace a second chance, and Amie McCracken for helping me breathe fresh life into her. And Jane Pierce, for her expertise.

Thank you to Luisa, Vikki, Helen, and Shelagh who bought me coffee when my eyes turned screen shaped; to the people at the gym where I work who ask after my 'other life'; and to everyone who's been confronted with the question, "If you were_____, how would you___?" and not quickly run in the opposite direction.

And finally, to my family—my parents, who never had to deal with me running away; my sister for being calm and grounding; my sons for being amazing; and especially my husband Peter, for being with me every step of the way.

VINE LEAVES PRESS

Enjoyed this book?
Go to *vineleavespress.com* to find more.